Synopsis

Tig Monahan, radio therapist, finds out the hard way that nothing is fair in love and war . . . or family.

Everything is falling apart in psychologist Tig Monahan's life. Her mother's dementia is wearing her out, her boyfriend takes off for Hawaii without her, and her sister inexplicably disappears leaving her newborn behind.

When a therapy session goes horribly wrong, Tig finds herself unemployed and part of the sandwich generation trying to take care of everyone and failing miserably. Just when she thinks she can redefine herself on the radio, as an arbiter of fairness, she discovers a family secret that nobody saw coming.

It will take everything plus a sense of humor to see her way clear to a better life, but none of that will happen if she can't let go of her past.

I Like You Just Fine When You're Not Around

ANN GARVIN

TYRUS
BOOKS

Published by
TYRUS BOOKS
an imprint of F+W Media, Inc.
10151 Carver Road, Suite 200
Blue Ash, OH 45242. U.S.A.
www.tyrusbooks.com

ISBN 10: 1-4405-9545-3
ISBN 13: 978-1-4405-9545-5
eISBN 10: 1-4405-9546-1
eISBN 13: 978-1-4405-9546-2

Printed in the United States of America.

10 9 8 7 6 5 4 3 2 1

Library of Congress Cataloging-in-Publication Data
Garvin, Ann, author.
I like you just fine when you're not around / Ann Garvin.
Blue Ash, OH: Tyrus Books, [2016]
LCCN 2015043827 | ISBN 9781440595455 (pb) | ISBN
1440595453 (pb) | ISBN 9781440595462 (ebook) | ISBN
1440595461 (ebook)
LCSH: Domestic fiction. | BISAC: FICTION / Contemporary Women. |
FICTION / Family Life.
LCC PS3607.A78289 I3 2016 | DDC 813/.6--dc23
LC record available at *http://lccn.loc.gov/2015043827*

This is a work of fiction. Names, characters, corporations, institutions, organizations, events,
or locales in this novel are either the product of the author's imagination or, if real, used
fictitiously. The resemblance of any character to actual persons (living or dead) is entirely
coincidental.

Many of the designations used by manufacturers and sellers to distinguish their products are
claimed as trademarks. Where those designations appear in this book and F+W Media, Inc. was
aware of a trademark claim, the designations have been printed with initial capital letters.

Cover design by Sylvia McArdle.
Cover images © iStockphoto.com/korinoxe; retrorocket; BlackStork; GoMixer.

This book is available at quantity discounts for bulk purchases.
For information, please call 1-800-289-0963.

Dedication

To my mom and dad,
who figured out love some sixty years ago.

Chapter One
Horn Broken, Look for Finger

Tig Monahan tried to imagine what it would be like to lose her mind. Was it like a quick, fully aware, terror-filled slip on an icy sidewalk, or slower, where a tiny skidding sensation goes unnoticed until suddenly you realize all four limbs are in the air and your face is in a ditch. With her mother, Hallie, it was hard to tell what she'd been aware of, or how the knotted neurons in her brain foretold her foggy future. Either way, her mother's mind was not her own, her secrets were locked inside, and Tig was left to ponder the icy aftermath.

It was almost six P.M. and Hallie's nightly agitation was right on time; actually, a half-hour ahead of schedule, due to the recent relocation from Tig's home to Hope House.

"Where is he?" her mother said, her voice flapping like a bird startled from its roost. "Is your father here?" Hallie worked the worn platinum wedding band, loose beneath her knuckle, around and around. "He said I should wait." She shoved the bedside stand out of the way and stood, the evening version of her dementia giving her a kind of agility that her laid-back daytime confusion seemed to eschew.

"It's okay, Mom. I'm here. I've got you."

Her mother emptied her purse onto the bed. "Wendy, get your father."

"It's Tig, Mom," Tig, the forgotten daughter and sister to Wendy-the-absent-Monahan, said. "What are you looking for?"

Hallie stopped in her frantic search through her purse and snapped, "What do you think I'm searching for? It's always right here, in this pocket." Her piercing blue eyes were clearly seeing one daughter where the other one stood, reminding Tig of how sure her mother had always been. Sure and blunt and lovely. Her signature soft, sun-blond hair now frayed and wild, white; her once full lips turned inward with the sourness of age.

"*N'est-ce pas?*" her mother said, changing from agitation to despondency, to French, a language she loved and remembered better than her family. She snatched Tig's hand in her pale fist.

Tig worked to keep her own anxiety locked inside, knowing that when she cried, it only upset her mother. "We can't all cry," her mother used to say when Tig and Wendy were girls. "Someone has to man the battle stations." Tig struggled against her grief, her lips twitching in effort.

A nurse swept into the room, responding to the call bell Tig had silently rung for assistance. Over her mother's head, Tig said, "I thought maybe tonight she wouldn't need a sedative. I thought if I spent the whole day with her it might help."

The nurse drew a line with her lips and looked sympathetically at Tig, as if to say, *Here's another one who just doesn't get it yet. Another relative really low on the learning curve.* "Alzheimer's softens for no man, no how, no way. It's been one week. She was at your home for much longer than that. She needs time to acclimate." To Tig's mother she said, "Hallie, let's get you settled for the night."

Hallie Monahan ignored the nurse and began tearing at her sheets. Tig said, "My mom ran her own business. She was a vet, and a single parent. You have no idea how much she would hate being seen like this. Hate being here."

The nurse spoke to Hallie in a tone that made Tig want to curl up on the wrinkled bedding for a nap. "Hallie, love. I have your medication here. Try some orange juice. Here you go." Inexplicably, Hallie turned, flipped the small pill into her mouth and slammed back her orange juice like a drunk in a biker bar.

She returned to her sheets and buried her arm up to her elbow into the pillowcase and searched. "If I could tell you," her mother said.

Behind her, Tig said, "Mom, let's sit down." When her mother didn't budge, Tig said to the nurse, "She had an almost photographic memory. *Photographic.*" The emphatic way she said "photographic" got her mother's attention, and for just a moment she gazed at Tig with what almost seemed like clarity. But, just as quickly, her mother's face fell and she returned to yanking at her ring.

"I shouldn't have moved her out of my house."

Her mother upended her now-empty purse for the tenth time, muttering, "It's here. It's always here."

"You did the right thing. Just let this medicine take effect. You should go home and get some rest. Don't you work in the morning?" The nurse gently massaged her mother's back. Tig pulled the bed sheets tight, arranged the waterproof pad, and retrieved a rolled-up nylon from the floor.

"Yes, but I'll just stay until she falls asleep."

Tig placed her arm around her suddenly-still mother. "I've got you, Mom," she said, and guided her to the edge of the bed.

Hallie sighed and said, "I just can't keep it secret anymore."

"What, Mom? What secret? What are you looking for?"

Her mother sighed and said, "You're nice," as if Tig were a sweet stranger who just didn't understand, and her mother couldn't be bothered to explain.

● ● ●

A dull ache in Tig's neck woke her from a surprisingly sound sleep. She'd fallen asleep holding her mother's hand at an angle that made her arm tingle. Not wanting to let her mother go, she switched hands with her and tried to wriggle blood flow back into her cold fingers.

As if disgusted by Tig's pathetic display of affection, Hallie snorted in her sleep and pulled her hand free. Seeing her mother asleep in a standard hospital bed seemed to lift the curtain of denial from Tig's vision. Her mother had always had colorful red lips, blue eyes, and yellow hair, but here in this parched place, she was monochromatic: an even palette of sand after an era of drought.

Tig resisted putting a dab of lip balm onto her mother's pale lips. Her mother hated to be fussed with. When Tig had complained as a teen about getting ready for prom, saying that all her friends had appointments for updos, her mother had said, "What a colossal waste of time and money. I hope you know by now that beauty is about a little lip gloss and *joie de vivre*."

Tig believed that lesson, alone, had probably paid for her graduate school, since she'd avoided mani-pedis, complicated hair dyes, and spa visits. It was also a lesson in self-esteem, that self-worth cannot be bought and applied from a bottle. The unfairness that this woman from Tig's memory, so ripe with life and possibility, could have been transformed into this husk of a woman made Tig feel dry by proxy.

A nurse she didn't recognize pushed a wheeled medicine cart past her mother's room and glanced inside without expression. Tig stood, stretched her back, and rocked her head side to side. Her phone lay where she'd left it on top of a comforter she'd brought from home. She'd planned to call Pete, her boyfriend, but had fallen asleep instead. Tig hit the power button; the phone lit up and displayed the time: 6:30.

As she leisurely compared it to the wall clock with the huge numbers, Tig whispered, "Six-thirty? Oh my God." She grabbed her bag and race-walked out the door and down the hall. Before life had become impossible, she had begun her therapy hours at seven A.M. so that people could get a little therapy high-five and then go to their day jobs. Every night that she spent with her mother, seven

A.M. came sooner and sooner, and the past week it had become a habit to skid into her office while calling her dog sitter and trying to brush her hair out with dry shampoo.

After a quick gargle in the clinic's bathroom, Tig drove to her office and sat behind her desk. She took a sip of coffee from a cup with *Go On, I'm Listening* printed on the side, because that's what she did as a relationship therapist: she listened.

After a busy morning of one-on-one visits, Tig was determined to finish her last day of work, shower, walk Thatcher, and take a nap before heading back to her mother's room. She would wrangle her silent and invisible sister home, empty her trash, and work to get her boyfriend to understand she needed more time before following him to Hawaii for his sabbatical.

Today, the only thing that sat between Tig and the rest of her life was the fighting Harmeyers. Jean and Newman Harmeyer, the counseling world's most insufferable couple. Not the couple, really. It was the husband who was insufferable . . . unbearable . . . repugnant.

"She knew exactly who I was when she married me." Newman Harmeyer cast scathing looks at Tig and his wife Jean, the soft flesh at his jaw jiggling.

Tig assessed the couple seated across from each other in her office, more sparring partners than teammates. She opened her mouth to speak, but Newman interrupted her. "She's the one who's changed, nagging me about work all the time. So what if I go golfing and buy a few rounds afterward? I always come home."

"Eventually," said Jean, and she lifted her chin.

"It's not like I'm fooling around."

"You could be. I'd never know. I don't know what you're doing most of the time. We never make love." To Tig, she said, "I tried to get him in for a checkup."

"I'm tired, Jean. I don't need to go to the doctor. I don't need therapy. I just need a wife who gets it."

"Oh, I get it, all right."

Tig scrubbed her eyes under her glasses and shot a quick look at the clock on the table between her and the angry couple on the couch across from her. Ten more minutes, and she could say goodbye to Newman Harmeyer.

"Did you just check the time?" Newman Harmeyer fairly spit the words at Tig.

Startled, Tig rolled her chair back a guilty inch.

"What?" he demanded. "Are we not interesting enough for you? Is that it? For Christ's sake, Jean. Why are you wasting my time?"

Tig blinked hard, but, as irritated as she was, she glanced at Jean Harmeyer's tasteful, pained expression and opened her mouth to apologize.

Newman took advantage of Tig's hesitation, and launched into his next tirade. "You'd rather go home, would you? Get on with your day?" With a disgusted shake of his head, he said, "Ridiculous."

The sneer in his voice sliced though Tig's veneer, rattling the thinning tolerance that caged her fury. She heard her mother's voice from her youth, "Girls, I am on my last nerve."

Tig slid her gaze away from Jean Harmeyer's stiff face, turned her attention to Newman Harmeyer, then narrowed her eyes. "I apologize to both of you for my inattention. I have had a difficult week. My mother has been very ill. That said, I think we should call it quits before either of us says something we might regret," she said in her most precise psychologist's distinction.

Newman Harmeyer had the bearing of the playground bully, cocky with a history of successful intimidation in his portfolio. "I'm paying you to listen to me, not whine about your mother. You got something to say to me? Because now's the time. We won't be back to this dump." He gestured dismissively around her small windowed office with the overly sympathetic spider plant and silent, easy-to-spill-your-guts-on couch.

In that moment, Tig thought about her lovely, kind, mother who was now anxious and confused in a nursing home, while this man was free to berate and abuse as he saw fit. As if from above, Tig saw herself, sitting in her own office, being treated like a naughty child by this vile man. In that second, a second she would regret later, she felt the sleep deprivation clear and the blanket of fatigue that shrouded her courage lift. She felt sure the universe was giving her permission to take a good healthy swing.

Tig pivoted in her padded office chair to squarely face Newman Harmeyer. She saw he had the childlike glee of a boxer briefly free of the ropes, just before the knockout punch.

"Seriously, Mr. Harmeyer, your problems couldn't keep an insomniac awake." She paused and watched as the dimmer switch behind his eyes ratcheted up a few degrees. "I didn't need the last six months to get the picture. I get it. Your wife gets it. Every clichéd, old, desperate man in the universe gets it. Your wife is more competent than you, more attractive than you, and makes more money than you, so you're having a midlife tantrum. But you won't admit that. Instead, you take it out on her by drinking, detaching from the family, and denigrating your marriage. You are doing everything but actually having an affair, which would allow Jean to divorce you without guilt."

With a shaky hand, Tig stood and smoothed her black trousers, tucked the yellow legal pad under her arm, and put herself between her desk and the stunned couple. *Shut up, Tig. Shut up*, she thought, but she couldn't stop. It was as if she was defending her mother, her client, and herself when she added, "And you're a prick." Tig met Newman Harmeyer's shocked look without flinching, despite being aware of the heat creeping into her cheeks.

Newman said, "*What?*" and hauled himself to his full height.

Tig squared her shoulders. "Here's a piece of advice for free. Why don't you join the Peace Corps and spend some time with people who have real problems? While you're at it, get down on your knees and thank the Lord that this amazing woman over here hasn't divorced your sloppy, reptilian self."

Newman Harmeyer clenched his right fist and took a step closer. Tig. She noticed the vein at his temple and reflexively took a step back, glanced at her desk telephone, and gauged the distance.

Surprising Tig, he turned on his heel, took the two steps to the office door, wrenched it open, and let it swing wide and crash against the wall.

"Come on, Jean."

As if she were slowly waking up, Jean Harmeyer stood and followed her husband, nearly colliding with him as he stopped to say with a gritty grin, "You just lost your job, missy." With his eyes on Tig he walked through the door, catching his cell phone secured on his hip, and it bounced back into the room. The couple stopped and stared at the disobedient device, seeming to balance its electronic value in their lives against the value of the perfect, righteously indignant exit. It was a neck-and-neck competition.

Finally, with a slight tilt to her lips, Jean Harmeyer disappeared through the doorway while her husband bent and reached for his phone. After missing with the first pass, he tucked his tie beneath his belly and made another swipe. Phone in hand, he gestured with significant force and spittle, saying, "You're going to need a lawyer."

Tig grasped her desk and dropped her head. The abrupt quiet in the room was interrupted by the incessant beep of a delivery truck backing up outside the coffee shop next door. Tig pulled her dark hair up and away from her face and neck and held it briefly before letting it swing down and brush her cheeks. Tig read the simple reminder taped to her desk.

1. You count, too.

She peeled the note from her desk, carefully placed it in her large leather bag, and watched her shaking hand as she pushed the zero button on the phone to connect to the receptionist. "Macie? Have the Harmeyers left?"

Macie's pixie voice popped through the speaker. "Oh, I heard them. He bitched all the way out the door. I don't know what you said, but he is *pissed*." Macie extended the word *pissed* for emphasis.

Tig rested her head in her hand. "I doubt they'll need a referral to another therapist. They won't be back."

"Don't count Mrs. Harmeyer out. She had a killer look on her face and she rescheduled for herself."

"She did? Wow, good. Maybe she'll stand up to him after all." Tig paused and then said, "Give me a few minutes to get myself together, and then can you dial the business office at my mother's nursing home?"

"Sure Dr. Monahan, take as long as you need."

"By the way, where can I get that bumper sticker your brother has?"

"Mean People Suck?"

"No, the other one: Horn Broken, Look for Finger. I think that might be my new motto."

Chapter Two
Lipstick and Cigarettes

With an unsteady hand, Tig pulled her smartphone from her purse, obsessively checking her messages. Nothing. If only Wendy would call. If her older sister would come help with their mother, Tig could go with Pete on his sabbatical, guilt free. Tig whispered, "Frickin' Wendy."

Wendy defied birth-order personality predictors of the firstborn child. She was supposed to be what Tig was: dependable, conscientious, cautious. The leader of the pack. Instead, Wendy acted like the littlest chimp, equally likely to swing from a chandelier, buy a convertible, or finagle a free cruise from a handsome millionaire. She was not the girl to count on when papers needed sorting, furniture had to be moved from a childhood home, or mothers relocated.

Somehow, Tig managed to get a dose of both first and second child. She was structured and responsible, a caretaker but also a people-pleaser, while Wendy swanned around, all show-off energy and big ideas. Tig needed some of that indomitable energy now, because as it stood, Tig couldn't even go to work without guilt and then losing her shit.

The desk phone rang and Tig picked it up. Macie's voice said, "I have Hope House's business office on the line."

Tig cleared her throat, calling forth her professional, no-nonsense voice. "This is Tig Monahan. I'm trying to understand why I have not yet received any bills for my mother, Hallie Monahan?

"Yes, Dr. Monahan. As you know, we cannot release information about your mother's trust and the specifics of her care here unless I have permission from your mother."

"My mother isn't capable of that. I'm her daughter and her power of attorney. I need to know the financial details in case I'm required to make decisions in the future."

Unruffled, the woman on the phone said, "I assure you that her bills are taken care of, and will be in the future as well. Rest easy."

"Forgive me if your assurance isn't enough for me." She checked herself and said, "I'm sorry. I'm just tired." The line was quiet and Tig waited for a softening. When none came, she said, "I'll stop in. Thank you."

Tig hung up, pulled a cardboard box from beneath her desk, and rearranged the diploma and cactus inside to make room for her empty coffee cup, a glass jar of almonds, an Oh Henry! bar, and a stick of melon-flavored lip balm. She had agreed to go with Pete. She had committed to accompanying him on his sabbatical, and at least packing up her office was a step closer to honoring that wobbly commitment.

She laid the photograph of Pete on top of a stack of Hawaii brochures. Pete gazed up at her with his perfect teeth displayed in his it-never-rains-in-California grin. Tig closed her eyes and ran her thumb across Pete's smile.

Macie poked her head into Tig's office. "Mrs. Biddle is here."

"No way. I thought we had closure last week."

"You did. She just showed up wearing that T-shirt that says My Other Shirt Is In the Laundry. Says she just needs a few minutes. I could suggest she take those minutes to actually do the laundry."

Tig considered this and said, "Maybe if I don't berate Mrs. Biddle, I won't feel so terrible about everything else in my life." Macie started to speak, but Tig said, "Send her in. I need to redeem myself. Maybe when the Harmeyers' lawyers come and try to take my license away, she'll speak up for me."

• • •

Forty minutes into the appointment with Mrs. Biddle, Tig realized that, instead of making her feel better, Mrs. Biddle was making her feel anxious and, frankly, hopeless. Mrs. Biddle undid the blue plastic child's barrette that held her dyed jet-black hair in place on the left side of her head. She had an identical yellow barrette holding her hair behind her right ear. She pulled her hair tight and re-clipped it, forcing her bangs to poof forward and create a kingfisher-like headpiece. There was no way this woman was going to save Tig today or when the lawyers came.

Mrs. Biddle clasped her hands. "I can't believe she's gone." She was only sixty-five, but with the facial puckering of a career smoker, Mrs. Biddle looked seventy-five. There was no doubt in Tig's mind that the strongest muscles in Mrs. Biddle's body were around her lips. The rest of her muscle tone had gone out of her like the flame of a candle, the conquering breath being the death of her daughter. Tig suspected the older woman lived on lipstick and cigarettes.

She touched Mrs. Biddle's arm. "Go home tonight and have a good meal," she urged. "Remember how important creating unusual meals was to Francine? She'd want you to thaw out one of those dinners she left behind for you, maybe call a friend over."

Mrs. Biddle looked into Tig's eyes. "Would that help you, if you'd killed your only child?"

Tig shook her head. "You didn't kill Francine. People get cancer for lots of reasons. She hadn't been around your smoking for years and years. I thought we'd moved beyond that kind of thinking." Tig examined the lines surrounding Mrs. Biddle's tired eyes. "I'm so sorry, but we're out of time for today. I want you to think about the meal you will choose to eat in honor of your daughter tonight. Call a friend, and consider bringing home that puggle at the Humane Society you talked about."

Mrs. Biddle took a breath and moved through the office door. With surprising speed and strength, she reached back and briefly gripped Tig's hand, looked her in the eye and said, "Why are you leaving? You know you don't want to."

Tig opened her mouth to protest, but Mrs. Biddle released her hand and stepped away before Tig could utter a word.

• • •

With her coat slung over her arm and her bag dangling from one shoulder, Tig walked to the front desk where Macie sat, fringed black bangs in her eyes, clicking through computer screens. "Well, I did it. I finished my last day, ruined my career, and made myself miserable."

"You'll forget all this in Hawaii, Dr. M."

"I'm not sure I'm going right away," Tig said. "I think I'm going to tie some things up at home first, get my mom settled."

Macie tugged the gauge in her ear lobe. "Oh. Is that okay?"

"How long before the Harmeyers call Julie and ask her to fire me?"

"He already called."

"It's good it's my last day." Tig stared at the floor.

"How's your mom?"

"Not so good. That's why this decision to wait to go to Hawaii feels right. You know, aside from calling Newman Harmeyer a prick, I don't feel too terrible. I really should feel worse."

"Oh, yeah, calling someone a prick is totally therapeutic." Macie fiddled with her gauge again. "There's research."

Chapter Three
Runners Run

As Tig Monahan turned onto the highway, a cavalry of sunshine raced through the windshield as if it might save the day from the disaster to come. She switched on the radio, opened the sunroof, and accelerated. Between the music, the breeze, and the feelings of guilty freedom swirling around her, Tig—fixer of the troubled mind, daughter of the year—forgot, for just a moment, the cost of liberty: the psychological fee associated with breaking all promises and putting your confused mother into memory care when it's the last thing you want to do.

With practiced automation, she signaled and turned onto her street. The speed radar trailer at the entry of her neighborhood blinked the Too Fast warning in red and blue. Tig braked hard and watched her purse tumble upside down onto the floor. If she were superstitious, she might have crossed herself and said a quick prayer. Instead, Tig tried to retrieve her phone and wallet while swerving at the last minute and bumping into her driveway.

She shoved the door of her Subaru open, and rushed to her front stoop. The purse slid off her shoulder as she pulled the screen open, sending her keys clattering to her feet. She said to no one, "Today, I don't even effing care."

Tig dumped her bag onto the hardwood floor. Her black labradoodle, Margaret Thatcher, looked up from the black leather couch and banged a friendly Morse code with her tail. With great dignity, the curly-haired dog stood, dropped her front paws to the floor, and executed a flawless downward dog.

"Hi, girl. Did you have a nice day with Stacy?" Stacy was Tig's next-door neighbor, a single thirty-something graphic designer who worked from home. She was Tig's unofficial dog sitter and was always available to rescue Thatcher from whatever scheduling conflicts Tig got herself into. She scratched Thatcher's back, and said, "I made a big decision today. Is Pete here? Where's Pete?" Tig straightened and quickly peeled a note off the front door. *This Is Home.* She folded it carefully, the tape crinkled and stuck together in her hand while she snatched another note off the hall closet: *Coats and Shoes.*

"Pete?" In the kitchen, yellow Post-its fluttered like leaves on the light oak cupboards and stainless appliances, remnants of her mother's confusion and evidence of Tig's exhausting life as a caregiver. One by one, she ripped each note free from its place.

Hot.
Forks.
Cups.
Turn Off!
Towels.
Dishwasher.
Stove.
Tig Cell Phone.
Help: 911.

With one hand clutching imperatives, she yanked the empty suitcase from her bed onto the floor and kicked it under the bed. At the sound of the front door opening, she shoved the Post-it notes into the garbage next to her bed, and covered them with tissues.

As Tig rounded the corner, Pete strode into the living room, wiping his face and smearing his sweaty palms across his Runner's Run T-shirt. The Runner's Run was a twenty-four-hour running match where sleep was profane and mileage was the Holy Grail. The goal: to rack up as many miles as possible in a twenty-four-hour period by both pacing and killing yourself. It was neither fun nor just a run, in Tig's opinion. Her only role in her boyfriend's athletic endeavors was to hold the Gatorade and the Go Pete! sign.

"You're home," he said. The late afternoon sun sat loyally on his shoulders and the scent of the final moments of a successful summer day wafted into the room. Margaret Thatcher licked the salt from Pete's fingers, bumping her tail against the wall.

Tig pulled another Post-it from the thermostat that read *Don't Touch* and stuck it into her back pocket. Pete didn't seem to notice. Tig followed his eyes to the spare room off the living room, where several pieces of luggage-sized duffel bags sat clustered in the doorway.

"I thought you'd be later," he said. "You know, tying up stuff at the office."

Tig stepped closer to him. "I know you think I haven't been getting ready for the trip, but I have. I've been cleaning out files all month. So, I came home to talk about the trip."

She stretched to kiss him, but he stepped back, saying, "I'm sweaty."

Tig glanced at his packed bags and said, "Looks like you made a lot of progress today." When he didn't respond, she said, "Since I'm home early, let's go get something to eat and celebrate. Maybe we could stop in to see my mom later."

"I," he started, then said, "I think we should talk about something."

"Yes! Good. I want to talk about something, too."

Pete touched the scar behind his ear, an early sign of nerves to those who knew him. A tiny poker tell to loved ones wanting a read.

Tig said, "Should we talk at dinner?" She noticed Pete's hesitation, and said, "Or here. Here's good. What's up? Is something wrong?"

"I don't think this is something to really worry about, but it's been on my mind lately. I think I should talk about it. In fairness."

Tig frowned and said, "Okay. I feel like I should sit down. Should I sit down?"

Pete grabbed the bottom of his T-shirt, exposing his tight abdominal muscles, and wiped his face. "I don't know why this is, but I'm just not that excited about you, lately." He squeezed his eyes shut and tried again. "I mean, I'm not excited about anything right now. This sabbatical. Going to Hawaii. That's why it's not about you."

A cold frost gripped Tig's neck and shoulders. "You're not that excited about me?"

"That came out wrong. What I mean is, this whole trip. I don't know why I'm not more excited about going." He wiped his face with his T-shirt again and added, "With you."

Pete paced away from her and turned. "This isn't coming out right at all. Something isn't right with me."

"Something isn't right with you," Tig repeated.

"I should be more excited."

"I think you need to stop saying that." Her counselor self kicked in and she said, "Are you saying that you don't know how you feel about this trip?" Her non-counselor self said, "Since when? Since yesterday? Since last week?" Margaret Thatcher seemed to follow the conversation and, as if taking sides, the dog walked over to Tig and leaned against her leg. Tig absently touched the top of her silky head, extracting a tiny measure of quiet comfort from the dog's solidarity.

Pete stared at her. Then, with resolution, he grabbed a duffel. "I've just been thinking. Maybe I should go to Hawaii, alone. At least at first."

"What are you saying? Am I disinvited?" Tig couldn't decide how she felt about this. The tables were turning in both the best and absolutely worst ways. She'd come home to tell Pete to go and she would follow. However, now that he was suggesting this very thing on his own, and with this new lack of excitement, Tig shivered.

"No, not forever." He pushed the screen open and swung the luggage out the door. It landed in a thud on the front stoop. "Though I'm not sure you ever really wanted to go."

"Wait a minute. That's not what we're talking about." Tig watched Pete grab another duffel bag. She wrung her hands, and looked around for support: a wall, a chair. Something to stand on that wasn't sinking. "You invited me. You said I could stay six months or the full year, so I said yes. I didn't ask to come with you."

"I know, and I still want you to come. Maybe just not right away."

All of a sudden, Tig felt defensive and confused. "What are you saying? I left my job."

As if Tig had opened a door labeled the Bright Side, Pete moved to her. "This will give you the time you wanted to get your mom settled. Pack up the house more. Maybe find renters like you wanted. I'll get set up in Hawaii and then you can come."

"You are doing this for me?" She stalled. In that second, Tig recognized what she was doing: she was trying to help Pete get through the conversation and save face for herself. She was getting what she wanted, but in the midst of this, she found she only wanted it if he loved her. She needed to know but was too afraid of the answer. With her emotions zigzagging, she tried to recover a little self-esteem. Tig said, "You don't want me. That's what you're saying."

"No," he said, "you're taking this wrong."

"How should I take it? No woman ever wants to hear that the person she," and she hesitated here, meaning to say *loves*, but instead said, "made plans with, is not that *excited* about them." Tig moved around the room as if tiny fires had broken out, overwhelming her with heat. "I don't want to hear that from my mailman, let alone my boyfriend," she muttered. She watched Pete toss the last bag out the front door and said, "Could you just stop? Did I do something wrong?"

"That's just it. No. I didn't think it was fair to go to Hawaii without talking about this." Pete moved and Tig put her hand up to stop him. He tried again. "This will give you more time to get everything in order, like you wanted to before this sabbatical came up."

Tig opened her mouth to speak. She wanted to say, *But I want to say that!* Instead, she clamped her mouth shut. *Dignity*, is what she thought. Her mother used to say, "Be pleased, not eager."

"It's true, Pete. At first, I couldn't imagine leaving my mom in the nursing home alone while I snorkeled with you. Then she hurt herself and I did the thing I don't ever do. I let go, for a change." She thought of her stately and completely confused mother sitting in her unfamiliar room at Hope House, and added with a spark of resentment, "We talked about getting married! How dare you attach the word 'fairness' to this?" For the second time in twenty-four hours she saw that she did not know what she wanted, and she could not shut her mouth.

Pete's lined face lost its boyishness. The scar on the side of his head pulsed with the clench of his jaw. "I knew you were going to say that."

"This is all so out of the blue. You made a decision before we'd discussed anything."

"I'm trying to discuss this right now. And I'm not leaving you."

Tig straightened her shoulders and said, "I don't know what you are doing here, Pete." She looked him directly in the eyes. "Hawaii and us, that was your idea. It took me a while to get on board, but . . . ." She frowned. "Call this what you want, but don't call it *fair*."

He opened his mouth to say more, looked down at his triathlon watch and then his shoes and said, "I just thought . . . ."

She saw in that moment how uncomfortable he was, and in a flash she felt sorry for him. It was what made her an effective counselor, an oft-requested caregiver, this overriding feeling of empathy that flooded her emotions and sank her defenses. She thought maybe if she didn't make a fuss, if she did what she always tried to do with people, to *be no trouble to anyone* . . . . She said, "Okay. I have to do some thinking. You should go." And then she did something she wanted to slap herself for later. She hugged him, and kissed his soft, salty lips, effectively and completely letting him off the hook.

Tig stared at his back as he walked away, and as the screen door slammed shut, she rushed to it. With the last bit of courage her ego could manage, she said, "Don't call me! Don't." She started to turn away and raised her voice. "Period." She knew in that instant that he wouldn't. She knew there would be no tearful *I'm sorry*s or long explaining conversations. That wasn't Pete. That wasn't either of them. Then her strength seemed to ebb away, and Tig felt herself dissolve like a sandcastle in a hard wind. She wiped her eyes with a brutal tenting of her thumb and forefinger.

She sank to the couch and reached for her phone. But who could she call? Her mother, whose memory had been erased as effectively as chalk on the sidewalk after a summer shower? Her self-obsessed sister Wendy, who only answered her phone one in ten times? There were other people. Friends. But most of her friends had warned her about Pete, calling him the "boy-man of Madison, Wisconsin." Friends who, one by one, disappeared under the scheduling nightmare that exists when you move your mother into your house and become her caregiver before you become a mother yourself.

She took a tortured breath and rubbed her chest, remembering her mother's soft hands on her sternum after a bad dream, how her mother's touch used to calm her childish concerns. Sometimes Hallie was quiet during those times. Other times, she'd distract Tig by telling her about the animals in the clinic.

"The Great Dane walked right in like he owned the place," she might begin a story. "His name was Bo, Boregard Halsey. He was a crabby old dog with a heart murmur. He'd get excited and pass out, which made him look like he had roller blades on. He'd go over and his legs would stick out like an old wooden stool." Her stories could make Tig laugh, or could help her fall back asleep. The magic lay in her mother's talk about the continuation of life, the business as usual goings-on that confirmed the world had not ended. This was her mother in a nutshell.

These memories did nothing for Tig now other than make her feel a profound sense of loss. She put her head in her hand. Thatcher moved again to Tig's side. "C'mere girl," Tig said, stroking the dog around the soft folds of her neck. "I don't know what just happened." As the dog clambered up onto the couch beside her, Tig sighed and said, "We got a runner, girl, and runners run. That's what they do."

Chapter Four
An Inconvenient Truth

Tig lay with Thatcher on the couch as the sunlight faded, her cell phone still in her hand. The sun moved, time passed, and Tig snuggled closer to her best friend as the temperature dipped in the room and the shadows circled. She heard the sound of someone approaching the front door, which she noticed only now was still open, and she and the dog scrambled to a sitting position. "Pete?"

"Hey, Dr. M, it's me." The high-pitched voice of her former assistant, Macie, warbled through the screen. She carried the cardboard box Tig had packed earlier. "You were so ready to leave us behind and party on with your new life, you left this on the front desk. I thought I'd just drop it by." Macie opened the door with her free hand, and poked her head into the foyer. Tig braced herself against Margaret Thatcher and stood. "You look kind of disorganized, Doc."

"I'm not going to Hawaii, and I think Pete left me."

"What?"

"He left. I'm not going." Tig brushed her hands together. "So there you have it." She took the box from Macie and dropped it on a dying philodendron on the coffee table.

Macie pulled the box off the struggling plant and followed Tig into the kitchen. "What the heck happened?"

"I'm not sure, but whatever it was, it happened really fast." Tig looked around at nothing. "I'm giving myself permission to act very non-counselor-like for the next twenty-four hours. Right now, I'm going to send him a text." Tig said *text* like she meant *bomb*.

"I'll write, 'Your loss bucko.' I'll put an exclamation point on it." Tig pressed the buttons on her phone, saying, "Why does it keep changing 'bucko' to 'cuckoo'? Wait, maybe I'll leave it 'cuckoo.'"

"That'll show him," Macie said.

Tig glanced at Macie. "What, not strong enough? How about, 'Don't call me when you're lonely, pal'? Can you italicize text?" She dropped her hands and said, "Wait, what if I want him to call me when he's lonely?" Macie pulled a piece of lint off Tig's shoulder as Tig said, "No, I don't! I know. I'm going to send him the very succinct and always appropriate, 'You suck,' no exclamation point needed."

"Rule number one of texting, Dr. M: never text when drunk or angry." Macie eased the phone from Tig's grasp, then guided her over to the kitchen table.

"Right. That's very wise, Macie. Okay, then."

"Doctor M, let's get you a glass of water. Then you can fill me in."

Tig eased herself onto the solid wooden chair next to her beloved farm table. She and Pete had bought the table together at an estate sale. She closed her eyes, remembering. They'd driven back from the sale and were eating at No Hablo Inglés, their favorite Mexican restaurant, where red, green, and white crêpe paper piñatas mocked their serious conversation. After the bike accident that had left a dramatic scar on his head, Pete also lost his sense of smell and could only taste hot, spicy foods. She'd said, "You have to wash your running clothes more, honey. You smell terrible."

"It's my 'go green' solution to global warming."

"I think even Al Gore would agree that washing a T-shirt occasionally is not an excessive use of resources. The inconvenient truth here, sweetie, is that you stink like chicken soup and mildew. Why not stop buying new running shoes made by small children in Malaysia, if you really want to help the universe?"

"You're such an eco-bully, Tig. Are you coming to Hawaii with me?"

No hablo happy, she'd thought. The constant push, push, push that went with Pete's enthusiasm and decision making made her feel anxious, not loved. She hadn't made her decision and she didn't like being pressured. The slightly soapy rim of the amber-colored water glass, the nubby texture of the lightweight plastic against her fingers, felt stingy and cheap. "It's not what I want or don't want," she'd said. "I have responsibilities, Pete."

"People do what they want to do. You and I both know that."

Pete's eager persistence had won her over. He was a charismatic man and she loved him. Her counselor brain wasn't much of a match for those two facts. Quieting her noisy memories, she focused on Pete's partner resume. The top criteria were all represented: Funny. Check. Smart. Check. Kind. Integrity. Sexy. Check. Check. Check. The second tier was also well represented: Fit. Employed. Kid Friendly. And finally, the tier that should not be named, the tier that was important but shallow and only whispered about with best friends: Nice lips, toenails clipped, and adequate penis size; not huge, not miniscule, just adequate.

On paper, Pete looked perfect and he felt pretty perfect, too. So she had committed to at least six months in Hawaii, thinking, *Finally, an uncomplicated, nice, normal guy.* Finally, someone who seemed to fit her. And so what if he was more impulsive than she. So what if he exercised like he was running from a swarm of locusts. So what if there were times when she relished the quiet of his long runs and multi-day bike rides. So what.

The real truth was that she needed a break. She'd agreed to accompany him to Hawaii in a wild moment of anger at her sister, Wendy, an inability to continue to come up with excuses for Pete, and pure exhaustion brought on by being her mother's sole caretaker. The last one simply broke Tig's heart. Every time she entered her front door now that her mother was gone, she felt loss, guilt, and grief. It didn't matter that her mother had become unsafe in Tig's home, or that her urinary tract infections seemed to sprout out of nowhere. Tig missed her. The best thing for her would be to get out of this house for a while.

Now, however, all of her reasoning, plans, and ideals had been shoved aside like a dusty curtain, and she had no idea what to do. She turned to Macie and said, "When you say 'I love you,' do you mean it like a promise, or do you mean it like, 'I feel this right now, but things might change tomorrow'?"

Macie blinked. "Who, me?"

Tig shook her head. "Never mind. Sit with me. We'll make a new plan."

"We? You want me to help you plan?" Macie smiled and sat at the kitchen table. Tig yanked a yellow legal pad from under a stack of unopened mail, and a wrinkled page of doodles flopped into view. Tig scrawled *Options* at the top of a fresh sheet of paper.

"What are my options?" Tig wrote *#1*, circled it, then wrote, *Get job back.*

Macie smoothed the crinkled paper and examined one of Tig's doodles. Sketched in blue ink were a palm tree, a cruise ship, and a hula dancer. "You're a good drawer, Dr. M."

Tig grabbed the page from Macie's hands, strode to the sink, shoved it down the garbage disposal, and flipped the switch. The disposal made the sickening sound of something shoved beyond its limits. "What else can I put on the list? Help me brainstorm."

Macie widened her eyes and said, "Not to be, you know, negative, but you can't get your job back."

Tig said, "C'mon, what else?"

"You could go to Hawaii. It's not just his Hawaii, you know. You don't have to stay here."

Tig scowled. "Don't be ridiculous. That idea has 'pathetic' written all over it. 'Pathetic' and 'stalker.'"

"When my cousin got dumped, she took a pole dancing class. It's all about empowerment. Building strength."

Tig frowned. "I don't want a fad. I want a future. Besides, stripper classes are the scrapbooking of the new millennium. It's just a Band-Aid."

"Only with better abs. Dr. M, you've got a lot of mascara on your face."

"Stay focused! We only have one thing on the list." Tig looked at the ceiling, then wrote, *#2: Get a different job.* "What other job could I do?" As Macie wet a paper towel, took Tig by the chin, and wiped at her cheeks, Tig said, "I hear Starbucks has great bennies." She pushed Macie's hands away and wrote *a. Starbucks, b. Pottery Barn,* and *c. Ann Taylor* under the *#2.*

"I'm not a therapist, like you, Dr. M, but I think maybe you should take a break from work."

"That would kill me. All I would do is think about Pete and my mother."

"Well, that might be okay. Don't you tell people to reflect a little to get better?"

"I don't need to get better. Better than what? I'm good. Pete's the one who needs to get better. What kind of person does this?" Tig gestured around the room as if displaying the obvious. As if the broken pieces of their relationship could be seen scattered around the room.

"So what exactly happened? I thought you didn't want to go with him, but now you do?"

"I wanted to tell him that I needed more time but then *he* told *me* I needed more time and that he . . . ." Tig paused, because really this was the hardest thing to stomach and the thing that was clearly at the root of her emotions. "He wasn't that excited about me."

"Oh," Macie said, like the "Oh" had been caught in her throat and she'd been slapped on the back.

Tig wrote on her list, *#3: Quilt.*

"Do you quilt, Dr. M?"

"No, but I could. I'm artistic, deliberate."

Macie nodded. "On my days off, I like to stare at the ceiling. You can't believe the great ideas I come up with. I designed this tattoo during one of those sessions." Macie rolled up her sleeve and showed Tig a string of ivy with the word *love* written in every leaf.

Tig added a *#4* to her list, then froze; her body sagged, and a heavy tear dropped onto *Ann Taylor*, smearing the *lor*. Macie put her arm around Tig's shoulders, and Thatcher trotted over and put her head in Tig's lap.

"I didn't know Pete was capable of this. We talked about getting married in Hawaii."

"You were engaged?"

"Sort of. I mean, I agreed with Pete when he talked about a beach wedding. Puka shell rings. I chalk it up to last-ditch spontaneity, magical thinking, and reality television."

Macie sat back, bit a dark purple nail.

Tig took a deep raking breath as if inhaling over an old-time washboard. "I'm sorry, Macie. I bet you never knew I was such a mess."

"Um. I just didn't know very much about you, I guess." She gave her head a little shake and said, "It doesn't matter. You're not a mess, Dr. M. Why not just rest? You don't need a plan."

"I've been getting up for school or work or both for the last twenty years. Lying in bed without a plan is as luxurious to me as sitting in quicksand." She looked down at the palm of her hand, and saw nothing but an open schedule and a long lifeline.

Macie let her cry and then said, "Okay, Dr. M. Let's drink this water and put you to bed."

"No, I have to go in and see my mom."

"Not tonight, Dr. M." Macie steered her into the bedroom by one arm, where she dragged a folder off the bed and knocked a faded blue shoebox onto the floor. The loose top fell open and yellowed envelopes spilled onto the carpet. Tig scooped up the letters and box and sat on top of the gray quilted bedspread. She fingered the corner of an envelope, releasing a faint odor of dust into the air. "These letters are my mom's. I've been going through her things, I suppose as a way to keep her close. My dad died before I was born, you know."

"I don't think I've ever heard you talk about either of your parents until just recently."

"I don't know very much about him, really. I didn't think I was interested. I've always been so fierce about my mom being enough. *She* wanted so much to be enough. But now, I find that I am very interested, now that she wouldn't know I'm asking."

Macie eased the letters from Tig's hands. Tig started to resist, then relented and let Macie help her into bed. "I'm sorry you have to see me like this."

"I'm honored, Dr. M. You help a lot of people every day."

Tig sighed. "In these letters, apparently my mom used to call my dad 'the Goat.' Weird nickname, huh? I think it's because he was a hard worker."

Macie smiled. "Your mother was quite the romantic."

The sound of her neighbor dragging a rolling garbage pail to the street seemed to return Tig to the room. "Maybe Pete is right that something wasn't right between us. He's always had strong intuition."

"Dr. M, excuse me for saying so, but leaving didn't take much strength."

"Maybe Pete should take the pole dancing class." Thatcher jumped onto the bed and happily took the spot where Pete used to lie. Tig turned away from Macie and put her arm around the dog. She spoke into the black dog's hair, "I'm about to ask something totally unprofessional, but could you stay for a little longer?"

Macie nodded, and when Tig's breathing relaxed she took Tig's phone and typed. Later, when Tig woke, she would see that Macie had found Pete's number and typed a quick text: *You suck*. No exclamation point.

• • •

The next morning, Tig woke on her stomach, feeling the press and warmth of the body next to her. It was a full minute before she realized the body was her dog's, not her boyfriend's. She let her mind drift to the month before, when she watched Pete through her lashes as he combed his hair to cover the scythe-shaped scar near his right temple, a macabre cowlick in his short hair. She watched as he worked his lean shoulders into his favorite bright red shirt—a purchase from one of his exercise-adventure outings to Peru or Colombia—ignoring the mirror. She remembered his bemused expression when she'd joked upon seeing this particular shirt for the first time, "How many bandanas had to die to make that shirt?"

He'd moved carefully that morning, so many weeks before— trying to find matching socks, stepping into an old pair of running shoes. Out of view, he clipped his best friend, his sport watch, to his wrist. He reappeared in her line of sight with just the breath of time she needed to close her eyes; he'd bent and kissed her forehead.

She smiled and rolled onto her side and put her arm around the sleeping body of Thatcher. The more recent memory of the night before returned with the feeling of dense fur on her cheek. Thatcher, eager for breakfast, slapped her tail as Tig pushed to a seated position. She stepped out of bed, silently following her memory of Pete out of their room. Listening to their conversation again now from the vantage point of loss, Tig tried to figure out where her relationship GPS had led her astray. Had she expected too much, or had there been a kind of bait and switch? Had there been signs at the beginning of the relationship that read both *Scenic Road* and *Dead End*? Had she turned toward one and ignored the other?

At the sink, she filled her coffee carafe with water and her thoughts floated to another memory, when Pete had said, "Did you see Hope House called? That private room you were waiting for opened up."

"Stop pushing! I know she has to go." She had felt immediately sorry, and said, "Do you think my mom hurt herself on purpose? Do you think on some level she was trying to orchestrate her own death?"

"She cut herself trying to peel an apple. If she wanted to die, I doubt she would try to sever her thumb." He paused and softened. "If anything subconscious was going on, it was that she didn't want to be a burden. She knew you would never put her in a nursing home unless she hurt herself."

Tig had snapped her head up. "She'd be right! And, if I had been around during *your* accident, I wouldn't have put you in one, either."

"Thank God you weren't around. You would have been fired for unethical caregiver infringements." He raised his eyebrows suggestively and leaned in to her, his private chemistry of odors mingled with her coffee as he drew her in for a kiss. She lingered over the softness of his lips and the contrasting stubble at his chin, her irritation dissipating.

He pulled away and said, "I better go, or I'll write a completely different plan for our day. Go see what your mom wants for breakfast. Which, by the way, I know you are thinking about even as we kiss."

"How is it that you know me so well after just one year?"

"You're not exactly full of quiet mystery." He strolled to the door, and without turning his head, said, "I'm making our arrangements for Hawaii. Keep that rolling around your pretty little head."

Now, as she sipped her coffee alone, it was all she could think of.

Chapter Five
Pain for Your Troubles

Tig walked past flowering lavender, red-hot geraniums, and newly planted rose impatiens lining the brick walkway of Hope House Long-Term Care and Treatment Center. She had originally reserved today for packing for Hawaii. Now she couldn't bear to be home. Tig had arrived at Hope House in time for breakfast, head still wet from a quick shower. Now she glanced at her reflection in the tall mirrored doors of the memory care unit and saw that her eyes were already tired from a restless night, as she approached what promised to be a long day of trying to decipher her mother's confused threads of conversation.

The electric doors parted as if to say, *Let's get it over with.* Just inside the front doors, against the western wall of the foyer, stood a tall glass-covered bird sanctuary. Tig counted eight birds grooming and flitting with indecision around the enclosure.

"Poor bastards," said a voice near her.

Tig gave a sidelong glance to the older man just inside the door. With his crisp white shirt and blue sports coat, Tig assumed he was a husband or older friend visiting a loved one. "Oh, I don't know," she said. "They look happy."

"Sure they are," he said, making a clicking noise with his tongue, the kind Tig used when she was disgusted with her hair.

Tig smiled politely and watched him walk down the long hallway. Beneath his pinstriped sports coat he wore crumpled blue-and-white striped pajama bottoms that stopped above his bony, hairless ankles and mismatched, ill-fitting slippers. A nurse popped out of a room and guided him down the hall saying, "There you are, Mr. Stanson. Are you sure you don't want to put pants on today?" Tig reconfigured the man in her mind from visitor to inmate, and for just a moment rested her head on the cool glass of the aviary.

Behind the central nursing station sat a blond woman with a telephone resting on her shoulder, a chart opened on the desk. She wore a uniform top patterned with patchwork bears with stethoscopes and wide smiles examining each other for pathogens. Tig hurried and counted twenty-two steps past the main desk to her mother's door. A dark-haired man in street clothes exited the room next to her mother's, holding a plastic water pitcher. Tig eyed him for signs of non-patient status: matching street shoes, unstained khaki pants, shirt buttoned correctly, knowing grin.

"I'm visiting my mother," he said, a dimple punctuating his smile.

"Can't be too careful," Tig said, embarrassed to have been caught in her shoe-to-collarbone assessment.

"It's true," he said, "I noticed right away you weren't wearing white Velcro shoes and an elastic waistband."

Tig glanced at her own mother's room and said, "You know you're a regular here when you can engage in nursing home banter."

The man smiled and looked like he might say more. She had an impulse to touch his arm, to sit and leave her lipstick on the edge of a Styrofoam coffee cup while telling him her troubles. It should have been awkward, this pause, but instead it felt like a breath. A moment untouched by the trudging march of time. Tig touched her hair and said, "Ah, well."

He smiled again. "Yes."

On the door, just under her mother's room number (twelve), hung a framed biography of the resident within and a photograph from her past. The picture was the same one that Tig had kept on her desk: her youngish mother with her daughters and Tubby, the family's beloved, fat black Labrador. Tig had written her mother's story carefully so the nurses and therapists would have some idea of the fullness of the life beyond the heavy door.

Hallie Monahan worked for 35 years as a veterinarian in the clinic that she opened in 1971. She was known for her good sense, compassion, and humor where people's pets were concerned, and she made home visits long after medical doctors stopped making them. She was married to Daniel Monahan for eighteen years until his untimely death at 43. Consequently, it was she who taught her two daughters how to throw a baseball, to make killer seafood paella, and to take the fishhook out of a Saint Bernard's nose. While she preferred the chaos and expense of several animals in her home, her girls always came first. Her eyes have always been robin's-egg blue, her left incisor always a little cockeyed, and her singing voice more than a little flat. She went to Paris once and forever after peppered her conversation with French, just for fun. Hallie was never dull, scattered, or priority-confused. She was and always will be a force of nature—so enter with a smile and leave your old-lady expectations at the door. Welcome.

Now Tig thought it seemed obituary-like, and wanted to take the red pen from her purse and edit it where it hung. She glanced down the hall and saw the dark-haired man at the nurses' station looking in her direction. She waved and pushed into the room, and there she stayed until she decided that maybe her presence was causing more harm than good.

Around four-thirty P.M., her mother began her transition from sweet-natured and pleasantly confused to irritated and aphasic. At six P.M. she was angry and insistent that she wanted to go home. Beseeching looks accompanied her plaintive requests.

"I want to go home," was really all that was left of the evening. Tig tried distracting her with photo albums of dogs, took her for a walk in the greenhouse, and even plied her with leftover pie from her dinner.

And between mouthfuls Tig would become hopeful, then disappointed, when she realized that what she thought was a conversation was really just a broken record of the same request.

"I want."

"I know. You love pie."

"When?"

"Always, you've always loved pie."

"Can I."

"You can always have pie, Mom."

"Go home?"

"You are home, Mom."

Her mother, entirely disgusted, came out with the very clear, "You eat it," shoving the wheeled hospital table away with the half-eaten slice of pie. Tig put her fork down and swallowed the mouthful of overly sugary pie filling that left a slick residue on her tongue. When the nursing assistant came in to help her mother to the bathroom, Tig said, in almost as wretched a whisper as her mother, "I want to go home." And she did.

• • •

Outside, the temperature felt a simpatico seventy degrees, there was nary a breeze, and she caught sight of a handful of lightning bugs hovering a foot above the ground. This was a night for lovers. In her car, she closed her eyes, feeling the eyelid grit of the chronically sleep-deprived, then after a few minutes opened them again and drove the already too-familiar route from Hope House to her own home. Once in her driveway, the thought of moving from the seat of her car up the steps and through her door felt impossible and without reward. It was as if she were at the starting line of an obstacle course where the grand prize was entry into another obstacle course, this one called "Pain for Your Troubles."

Finally she shoved out of her Subaru and hauled herself into her house. Tig remembered the last time she had come home late from a night at Hope House. Just as she had put her hand on the cool, brass knob it had been whisked from her with a rush of air. Pete had been in front of her, his hair wet from a shower, his handsome face washed clean. Without a word, she had placed her head on his chest, both of her arms hanging straight at her sides.

He had said, "Another tough night, I take it." Without removing her head from the center of his sternum, Tig nodded and took in the distinct smell of Pete. She always said, after a shower, that if Pete could bottle his own particular mix of boy and man-earth-scent, they could market it together as a kind of couple's therapy. One whiff and you were sure you were home. The trick to maintaining that pheromone bliss, Tig knew, was that both people involved must not speak—a bargain Tig could never keep.

She'd said, "I don't want to leave her."

Pete, having heard this many days and nights and mornings, picked up an army-green book bag and an old canvas mail bag filled with running clothes and said, "The truck is coming in a week. All the moving boxes, tape, and bubble wrap are in the garage." With hands as dry as an old Western saddle, nails shortened to the quick, he briefly touched her cheek and said, "This is a good thing."

Only now did she remember what she'd mumbled just loud enough for him to hear: "For who?"

Now that Tig knew what was coming, that he'd leave without her, she wished that she'd stuck to her guns, that she'd said, "I need another month." She had wanted to stay and help her mother, to pack up their family memories slowly, maybe even alone without the over-motivated audience that was Pete. But she had not asked for more time. She had not. She had been game. And this is what she had gotten for being game. She got to be alone.

Inside the house, she turned and watched the ghost of Pete slouch through the front door and sling his bags over his shoulder. In her mind he mounted his bike with a graceful kick over the seat. Pete, whose exuberance she both loved and chafed against, because of his healthy no-holds-barred way of thinking. The kind of thinking he inherited from his almost bionically healthy parents and shared with his Olympic-swimmer sister, the people in his life who never, ever false-started or asked for a sag wagon of support like Tig had. She pushed through the screen, and called to this Pete apparition, "I get it, Pete. I was difficult. I didn't want to go. But you loved me, I know you did."

Ghost Pete said, "Call Wendy," over his shoulder, and it was this innocent, imagined phrase that seemed to begin her final unraveling.

Chapter Six
No Such Thing As Fair

It was early-afternoon at Hope House. Tig could tell the time not by a clock, but by the post-meal anxiety that was just beginning to ramp up. Nobody had lost their speech yet, but there were a lot of complaints about the food.

She'd spent a fairly calm day with her mother doing three things: thinking about Pete while walking her mother, replaying their relationship for signs of dissatisfaction while walking her mother, and attempting to use her counseling techniques to clear her mind while walking her mother.

During bathroom breaks, she looked at her smartphone's priority number directory, and looked for clues to Pete's insistence that something wasn't right between them. It didn't take long to see what Pete might have characterized as "unexciting": her cell favorites listed the number one position as her sister Wendy, then Hope House, Tig's job, and Corner Pizza sequentially down the list, all occupying the premier real estate positions in her phone. Wasn't this proof of disorganization and a busy life, though, not a prioritization of importance?

She ached to talk to Pete, to deliver the speeches she had prepared last night while tossing between sleep, outrage, and grief. She wanted to shout, "How could you?" sometimes with fierce anger, other times with a sad emphasis on her feelings of rejection.

A female voice asked from behind the privacy curtain, "How do you wear your hair, Mrs. Monahan?"

"That's nice of you to ask. I like it pulled back. A ponytail is fine. It keeps it out of my eyes when I'm working with the animals."

Tig gently moved the ceiling-to-floor drapery to the side. A tall nurse with high braids was deftly arranging her mother's gray hair. Both women looked at Tig without recognition.

"I'm Mrs. Monahan's daughter. My name is Tig."

"I'm Serena," the woman said to Tig. Then, to her mother, "Look, Mrs. Monahan. Your daughter's here."

Hallie's face widened with pleasure and lost some of the grayish lines around her eyes.

"Wonderful. I've missed her. It's been weeks. Where is she?"

Tig rushed the three steps to her mother's side and caught the edge of a commode chair with her purse. She untangled the strap from the portable toilet and bent in front of her mother.

"Hey, Mom. Good to see you. How's the hand?"

"*Bien.*" Her mother held her hands up in front of her face and turned them palms out as evidence. She didn't seem to see the bulky bandage covering the soft flesh of skin between her thumb and forefinger. The white gauze looked ungainly on the petite, soft, strangely unlined hands of the seventy-six-year-old woman. "I love it when someone brushes my hair. Your dad does it for me all the time."

Tig said, "What?"

Serena finished the ponytail and squeezed Hallie's shoulders. "I'm going to let you two catch up." She maneuvered herself around the side rail, wheelchair, and rolling bedside table.

Tig whispered as the woman passed her, "I was here just yesterday. It hasn't been weeks."

"I know. They told me in the report." With a warm touch, she added, "Have a good visit; she has her occupational therapy in thirty minutes. I'll bring her meds before then."

"I know. I know her schedule." Tig tore her gaze from the nurse's beautiful skin and calming countenance and took in her mother's sky-blue blank expression.

"Mom?" Tig waited for her mother's attention to light upon the cell phone Tig held out. "I have this for you in case you need me. For anything, anytime. Every button is programmed to call me."

Her mother took the device, regarding it mistrustfully.

"Go ahead, push any number and hold it down."

Tig positioned the phone clear of Hallie's bandage, pressed the keypad, and they waited. Moments later, Tig's own phone rang to the tune of "I'm Bringing Sexy Back."

Startled, her mother glanced around.

"It's here, Mom. You just called me. You can call me anytime you need to, day or night. We'll put it right on your table so you don't miss it."

Her mother watched as Tig placed the phone next to the sweaty, flesh-colored water pitcher and requisite smashed-at-the-corner tissue box. Hallie said, "Well," as if meaning to continue with "done" or "thank you" or "what a wonder," but managing only the telltale half-thought that was so very Alzheimer's-like. Then she pushed back in her armchair and gestured to her rumpled hospital bed. "Sit," her mother said. "I just ate breakfast and I have a little time before my first case comes in."

There was a light-blue-and-white waterproof Chux pad, creased and disheveled, in the center of the bed. On the white sheets Tig could see the branding of the MUHL laundry service at the loose tail that dragged on the floor. She shoved the Chux pad aside, sat, and picked up her mother's hand. "What animals are coming in today?"

"Oh, Callie has the appointments; I haven't any idea. Probably a neutering, and maybe a dental."

Her mother retrieved her hand and clasped her fingers in her lap. She looked around the room with interest, paused at a vase of daisies, and smiled.

Tig followed her gaze.

"Where'd the flowers come from, Mom?"

"Dad, of course, who else?"

"But Dad," Tig started to say, then thought better of it and let her voice trail off.

"Dad should be home soon. We'll all have dinner." Hallie pushed a missed strand of hair away from her face and turned. "Won't that be nice for us?"

"Pete and I broke up, Mom. Remember Pete? He helped you get some exercise." Her mother patted her knee and followed the sound of a buzzing fly to the corner of her picture window. "I was going to Hawaii with him, for work." Her mother turned and looked into her daughter's eyes. Tig touched a lock of her mother's hair. "How are you doing, Mom?"

A troubled expression settled into the space between Hallie's eyes, the place all of her worries lived. "When my daughter comes, could you ask her about my keys with the French spoon key ring? I've been looking everywhere for them."

"What keys are you talking about, Mom? I don't remember seeing any spoons or keys when we were moving you."

Disappointment flooded her mother's face. "Of all the people I know, I wouldn't think you would take my keys. The clinic key and car keys are on that ring, the French spoon key ring I got in Paris."

"Mom, I don't know what you're talking about. What keys?"

Hallie put her face in her hands, the bandage awkwardly pushing her cheek up. "I just can't believe this. You're just like your father."

"Do you know who I am, Mom?"

Searching her daughter's face with the frantic energy of someone who knows the answer but can't trip the memory, Hallie's eyes filled with tears. "Where are my keys?"

Just then Serena swept into the room with a small cup of pills. Tig looked helplessly at the nurse. "I've upset her. She lost some keys?"

"Hallie, my gosh, where did those lovely daisies come from?" Serena lifted the water pitcher, filled a matching plastic cup, and handed Tig's mother her pills. Automatically, Hallie took the cup and gazed into the nurse's face.

"*Fleurs.*"

"Yes. Now drink up; take these pills, and let's get on with our lives."

"Sounds good. I'm forgetting something, though."

"You have therapy in just a minute."

"Ah yes, that's it, of course. Send in the next patient."

"Will do." Serena tugged Tig's arm and led her smoothly out the door and gazed at her. "She'll get a little better for awhile, but you know this disease is progressive. It's a train without brakes."

"I was hoping for a plateau of some kind, a little respite, a chance to say goodbye."

"She's a little better when Dr. Jenson comes. He should be here soon, if he isn't held up at the hospital."

"Really? Maybe I'll go to therapy with my mom, see if I can catch him today."

"Tell me something," Serena said, looking closely at Tig. "Is Tig a nickname?"

"Yes and no. Tig is a nickname all right." Tig smiled. "My real name is Tiger Lily, after Tiger Lily from *Peter Pan*. My older sister's name is Wendy. They didn't expect there would be another child and, when there was, my mom thought Tiger Lily was the perfect name. She was a trip, my mom."

"Yes, you can still see that in her. So it's Dr. Tiger Lily, is it?"

"Yes, but Tig is better than Tiger Lily."

"Oh, I don't know. Tiger Lily has a terribly sweet quality to it that might be something to aspire to," Serena said, winking as she turned away.

• • •

Tig walked her mother to the physical therapy room where a nursing assistant took over at the door. Stepping back into the hall, Tig dialed her sister's phone. "Dammit, Wendy, I wish you'd pick up once in a while. I just left our mother in the hands of a man with a tattoo of Jesus on his neck and the Ten Commandments printed alphabetically up his forearm."

She moved down the hall, and dodged a tiny woman wearing spotless navy blue tennis shoes in a wheelchair. "I'm sick of cold toast for breakfast!" the woman shouted over and over as she propelled herself furiously across the carpeted floor.

Undaunted, Tig said, still on the phone, "This man asked our mother which was more fun—physical therapy or occupational therapy? I'm thinking, since our mother can't come up with her own last name, that 'fun' may not be part of her current cognitive capacities. At least he's trying. But you wouldn't know anything about this." She paused and took a breath. "When are you going to help in some way? She's your mother, too!"

As Tig slammed though the exit, an alarm sounded. She stopped, held the heavy door, and glanced back into Hope House. A nurse peeked her head out of one of the patient's rooms and said, "That's the WanderGuard alarm. Mr. Heartly is too close to the door with his sensor bracelet." The nursing assistant jogged in her white Crocs to Mr. Heartly's elbow. Holding his ropy arm, she steered him away. "C'mere, Mr. Heartly, hon. Let's get you away from that door. How about we take a walk to the craft room?"

"This is so unfair," Tig said to her mother's memory, and she stuffed her phone into her purse. As if the voice of her mother lived forever in her ears, she heard her often-repeated lesson about fairness: "No such thing as fair, Tig. Don't expect fair. Expect unfair and be prepared for possibility. While there is rarely fair, there is always possibility." She felt the pinpricks of tears and her throat filled.

In the full sun of a beautiful day, Tig hovered her finger over Pete's number. He had been her sounding board and, unlike most men, didn't try and fix every problem she had. He would listen when she talked obliquely about a problem client or her errant sister. Granted, sometimes he would go off on a tangent about human nature in general, but she didn't mind that.

She dropped her head back to feel the warm sun on her face. Feeling eyes on her, she looked up into the nearby face of a young, tanned groundskeeper. She saw him try to identify her role. Family? Nurse? Confused resident? "Don't worry," Tig called to him, "I'm not resident-confused, just plain old pedestrian-confused," and showed him her clean, unadorned wrists. "Just having one of those days."

He nodded and bent over the flowering perennials that, Tig noticed, just happened to be bleeding hearts.

Chapter Seven
Beautiful Euthanasic Precision

Tig pushed into the Frank Lloyd Wright-ish Prairie-style building that just a week before had been her place of work. She had often reflected on the irony of this new, clean, uncomplicated structure entertaining the knotty feelings of so many people searching for solace. The incongruous meeting of architecture and purpose, Tig always thought, invalidated the feelings of those who entered, as if the building were saying, "Everything's fine," when, of course, to the clients passing through these doors, so little was fine.

The carpet hushed her steps as Tig approached the reception desk. Macie, her copilot-like telephone headset askew, battled with a series of worried expressions as Tig neared, mouthing a quick and silent, "Are you okay? Where have you been?"

Macie placed her hand on the earpiece of her headset and glanced at her desk phone as if she could see the person who was on the other side of the connection. With her voice directed to the microphone she said, "That's right; Tuesday at two P.M. is our soonest appointment." She held up a finger to Tig and continued, "Well, you get back to me. I've got an emergency on line two. I have to go now." She punched the disconnect button, and said, "You look tired, Dr. M. You doing okay?"

"I don't know what to do with myself. I went to see my mom and then I made a lot of appointments for things I haven't had much chance to get to. You know, dentist, hair removal of all forms, a personal trainer session, a mammogram. I tried to get a colonoscopy, too, but I'm too young, apparently. I'm sure I'll cancel most of them. Self-care is not my forte."

"Wow. So, that's a lot of stuff."

"I need to keep busy."

Macie lowered her voice and said, "Have you heard from Pete?"

"No." Tig touched her sternum for comfort and, finding none, said, "I'm really sad."

Macie said, "If it helps, it's only been a week and it sucks around here. I realized something. You're the only therapist we had that used mascara and didn't wear Birkenstocks."

"That's not true. Chris doesn't wear Birkenstocks."

"Tevas. Same difference. Worse, actually, because he wears them with obviously ironed blue jeans." Macie rolled her eyes as if this were the ultimate fashion infraction.

"A therapist is only as good as the earthy, earnest clothes she or he wears."

"I disagree, Dr. M. Coolness factor is a must. Therapists are in dire need of street cred." Macie flipped her tongue stud against the roof of her mouth.

"Maybe that can change today. I'm going to talk Julie into getting my job back."

Macie looked at her computer screen. "Did you call first?"

"I didn't want to give her time to think of a reason to say no."

Macie, with a hesitant look on her face, called Julie Purves, the clinic's director, and waved Tig into the last office in the suite. Tig rehearsed her speech one last time as she approached the closed door. *I'm sorry about the Harmeyers. I'll apologize and work overflow, and with only new clients unless my old clients ask for me, until a permanent position opens. I'll take call every weekend and not accrue vacation or sick leave.*

Just as she was about to knock she heard, "Come on in, Tig."

The director's suite was similar to Tig's old office, with eggshell-white walls, plum upholstery, and requisite bookshelves holding addiction books.

"As I'm sure Macie told you, the prodigal therapist has returned."

Julie leaned forward and said, "Did you forget something?"

"I forgot I want my job."

Julie's gaze did not waver and her expression remained calm. After twenty years in practice, it took a lot for Julie to break from her serene demeanor. "We've been through this, Tig."

"I had a whole speech prepared, but the fact is, Hawaii's out." Tig felt her shoulders slump an inch and knew her eye concealer couldn't disguise the shadow of recent losses under her eyes. "Honestly, it's just as well. I can't leave my mom. Besides, who would see Mrs. Biddle?"

"Mrs. Biddle is not your personal responsibility."

"Did you know, that woman hasn't eaten a green vegetable since the seventies, and she can name every last birthday snack she made for her daughter from kindergarten on?" Tig walked to the window and slid off one of her leather ballet flats. She stretched and hit a fly with beautiful, euthanasic precision. "My mom, on the other hand, followed all the health rules . . . all of them. And on a really good day, she can maybe come up with my sister's first name, the one that never visits." Tig turned and dropped her shoe. "I never should have quit, Julie. I never should have trusted . . . ." Her thoughts trailed off as she considered who she shouldn't have trusted. Herself? Pete? The universe?

"I'm sorry to hear about Hawaii. But, as I remember, the reasons you wanted to leave were not just about following a man around. I remember a discussion about burnout and the grief of watching your mother deteriorate. I heard you say you needed time for yourself."

"Well, it seems that it was all about following a man around." Tig shook her head with disgust. "I've lost track. Was I justifying following a man around with higher thoughts of caring for myself, or did I really believe them, and have only now lost my compass?"

Julie walked around her desk and slid an armchair forward. She removed a pile of manila folders from the seat and placed them carefully on her desk. "You're thinner and paler than I've ever seen. We've known each other for ten years, and you look even worse than after Wendy took off the first time."

"Don't sugarcoat it, Julie. Let me have it."

"I'm not letting you have it. I'm speaking as your friend. Hawaii or no, since you have the time off, you should take it. Moving an ill parent to a nursing home can't be done without a little respite."

"Is that how the more evolved people do it, Julie? Take time and orchestrate rather than react and fill in holes?"

"Isn't that how you counsel people, the Harmeyers notwithstanding?"

"Oh, shit, Julie. I'm so sorry about the Harmeyers. That was totally unprofessional of me."

Julie Purves was the kind of counselor who knew the value of silence.

Tig answered that silence by saying, "You and I both know that nine out of ten therapists need their own therapists. I can get therapy without giving up my job as a therapist."

"You need some time off to understand what part you played in not going to Hawaii."

"The part I played?"

Julie gave Tig's leg a brief, motherly squeeze and stood. "Why didn't you let us throw you a going-away party?"

"I didn't want a big deal made of my leaving."

"Maybe you knew you weren't going to go."

"No! I was one hundred percent committed. But, if I was making a mistake, then I didn't want a brass band. Turns out, I did make a mistake. I trusted Pete." Tig inhaled and visualized each tiny alveolus, every last air sac, in her lungs expanding, then collapsing when she exhaled. "Maybe you're right."

"I don't want to be right, Tig. But, consider this. Maybe not trusting yourself was the only mistake you made here."

Tig said, "I should look at this like I dodged a bullet . . . like I could have ended up married. Now I'm free to do anything I want."

"What do you want to do, Tig?"

"Right now, I'm trying to see this as a beginning. As a celebration and chance to look forward into the future."

"So you're going to celebrate then. You're happy; that's why you came back?"

"If you gave me my job, that would make me happy."

"I couldn't even if I wanted to, Tig. Your replacement is coming from the West Side clinic tomorrow. It's all set."

Tig sighed. "It was worth a try."

"Tig? Don't go get another job right away. Do what you tell your clients to do. Reflect. Take a minute. Figure out what you want to do with the rest of your life now that so many variables have changed."

As if hearing only a part of that lesson, Tig said, "No job?"

"Not right away, no."

"I was thinking of taking my mother back home. She's just so miserable."

"And you, Tig? Are you miserable, too?"

Tig gave Julie a little nod and said, "Totally."

"I will tell you this: misery loves company like self-absorption loves wallowing. Your mother doesn't need your misery. She needs support and love and therapy. She needs safety, routine, and care. Your mother is a full-time job."

"No job for Tig."

"Nope. No job for Tig."

• • •

Back in reception, Macie said, "No go?"

Tig shook her head, leaned on the counter, and closed her eyes.

Macie said, "What am I going to do if you're not here? I'll have to get another piercing."

"Don't do that. I don't see how you can drink any liquid without leaking as it is. Seriously, this is a disaster. I could kill Pete," she said without any real heart behind it.

Macie's eyes darted over Tig's shoulder and froze before the telephone console lit up with a call. With a pointed look at Tig, she whispered, "Incoming," and answered the phone.

Jean Harmeyer approached the reception desk.

Tall, thin, and dressed in an elegant wrap dress the perfect color-match to her chic brown hair, she looked as striking as she did rich. Dark sunglasses covered Jean's eyes, but she'd clearly spotted Tig.

Tig said, "Mrs. Harmeyer, I am so sorry." She took a step forward. "I just put my mother into the nursing home. I've been distracted. Exhausted. That's no excuse. I want you to know I'm taking a leave."

"So you're not working? Good." Jean set her jaw, an expression Tig had become familiar with over the past months in therapy.

"Please accept my sincere apologies."

"You mean for calling my husband a—let's see, how did you so delicately put it? An 'impotent prick'?"

Tig dropped her hands to her sides and turned her palms out.

The cool feeling of feminine fingers touched Tig's wrist and an unmistakably throaty laughter broke the tension.

"You misunderstand me, Dr. Monahan. I haven't had that much joy shoved into a minute since the birth of my twin girls. The fact is, my husband is a gigantic asshat." Her laughter echoed in the high-ceilinged room. Jean glanced at Macie. The receptionist's wide-eyed attempt at a noncommittal stare was almost as funny as Jean's outburst. Jean pointed at Macie's face. "You know exactly what I'm talking about; he made some of the appointments. Wasn't he a dickhead?"

Jean turned to face Tig and said, "Turns out he was screwing one of his interns at the office. She's twenty-two. How clichéd is that? He told me about her after leaving your office. He wanted to prove to me that he wasn't impotent. Don't you love it?" She took a step closer to Tig. "I left him! I've wanted to for at least two years, but you know, the kids. And, seriously, who has time for that much drama?" She paused and said, "But you gave me permission. You said out loud exactly what I've been thinking. No therapist had the courage to do that before."

Jean traded looks with Macie, whose expression of disbelief matched what Tig was feeling in every way, including the open O of their lips. "Every counselor is all about—" Jean lifted her hands for air-hung quotation marks. "—*How does that make you feel?* and *Let's explore these emotions.* Fuck that. Explore this, Newman!" Jean Harmeyer flipped the best French-manicured bird Tig had ever seen. "God, I feel great."

Tig smiled in spite of herself and said, "I'm not sure how I feel about this. I don't think I can take positive credit for acting so ethically wrong."

"Hey, no offense, Dr. Monahan, but I don't really care how you feel about it, because I feel amazing."

"How are the kids through all of this?"

"They're in their own worlds, all they care about is that their world goes unaffected. Newman was never around before and he's not around now. As long as I'm around making lunches they'll be fine. But listen, Tig, now's not the time to get wimpy on me. We've got work to do."

"Work?"

"First of all, Newman's scrambling. I locked his golf clubs, shoes, and every last stitch of his clothing into a storage closet over on the Beltline Highway and changed the locks to the house an hour ago. I've got a meeting with a lawyer scheduled at two-thirty. He's going to go ballistic when he realizes I left him first."

"Mrs. Harmeyer, have you thought this through? Your husband is a big, angry guy. Are you sure you want to provoke him?"

Jean gave a quick, convincing nod. "He is a scary little prick, but you should see the photo I have of him. Totally nude except for a pink Donna Karan push-up bra. It's an oldie, from when he still had his girlish figure, but it's clearly him." She added with a hint of wistfulness, "He used to be kind of fun." Shaking her head, she said, "I can handle him."

Tig laughed and Macie, wide-eyed, looked between the two women.

All business now, Jean said, "Now we have to act fast. One of the first things he's going to do is sue you and this clinic as a contributing factor to our divorce, but I'm going to deny everything. That's one of the reasons I'm here." Jean grinned. "He won't have a case without my testimony, and there's no other record if you don't write it down. No harm, no foul."

"Is that legal?" Macie fiddled with her eyebrow ring.

"Hell, I don't know. That's why I'm seeing a lawyer tonight, but I wanted to cover my bases with you." She took in a deep breath and exhaled. "God, I feel like I've been asleep for years. You know how it is. You're busy with kids, with brushing your teeth and buying more plastic lunch bags. I have a full-time job. I haven't had the time to hold my husband's nuts accountable. I've just been dealing. That's what women do."

Tig knew this was true. She had counseled scores of married couples that had put up with dismissive, even abusive, behavior from their spouses. Since the idea of "happy" hadn't been on the horizon for a long time, just plain managing was a large enough goal to strive for. Tig knew a thing or two about managing.

Jean focused on Tig's face. "Now listen. Here's the other reason I'm here. I produce a radio program for WXRT. Last week, my expert on women's health decided to—get this—have a sex change." She raised her eyes to the rafters. "No kidding. The world is coming undone. She told me that she believed it was a conflict of interest to continue being the resident expert on women's health, considering she didn't want to be a woman anymore. She's given me a two-week notice. That leaves me with a huge hole in my programming."

Tig said, "I've listened to that show. Don't you take questions from callers?"

Jean smiled. "That's the one, *Health and Humor with Hannah*. Only we'd have to change it to 'Harold' after the hormones kick in, and I'm not sure our listeners will stick with that programming. So, the show runs twice a week on Tuesdays and Thursdays, just after lunch from one-thirty to three o'clock."

Tig nodded her head.

"I'm thinking you should fill that spot."

"Me?"

"Absolutely. Your brand of counseling is just what the world needs. Straight talking, tell-it-like-it-is therapy."

"No, no way. I wasn't counseling you. I was shooting off my mouth. That wasn't ethical, and I wouldn't do it again."

"No, I know," Jean said, shaking her head with enthusiasm. "Of course not. You can't say 'douchebag' on the air." She held up a finger. "Wait, no, sure you can. Anyway, hear me out. This is something better than traditional therapy, better than shock-jock crap. We're going to bring the talk shows to our doorstep. You'll see."

"Jean, you know what kind of counselor I am. I try hard to stay kind, just, and sane. I just slipped up."

"And look at the great results! You're supposed to be good at not making judgments too quickly. Look, Newman wasn't always an ass. He started by testing the waters, like a little kid does. A toe over the line here, a missed dinner there. Then came drinks several nights a week after work, weekend golf junkets with the boys. Sure, I complained, but what kind of leverage do I have—or credibility, for that matter?" Jean looked over to Macie for support.

Macie raised her eyebrows expectantly, urging Jean on.

"That's the trouble, really," Jean continued. "What was I realistically going to do? I had colicky twins and a gluten allergy. I was killing myself trying to find spelt and pump breastmilk for when my maternity leave ended. Next thing you know, I look up from my double-mammary yeast infection and I'm married to a good ol' boy and he's calling me the ball 'n' chain." Jean's face registered disbelief and outrage. Exactly the look you'd see on a person who thought her destination was Bali but exited in Cleveland instead. "You know how it is, Tig; it's easier to get people to a proctologist than to a relationship counselor. I only got Newman here after seriously threatening divorce. If there had been someone to hold him accountable years ago, maybe we wouldn't be where we are today."

"Jean, I just screwed up my own relationship. I don't think I'm the expert you need."

Jean Harmeyer's dark eyes sparked and she licked her lips, working the pitch out in her mind. "See, the flaw in marriage is that there's no accountability before taking it to the divorce courts." She waved a hand in the air, like brushing away an annoying fly, and added, "I know, theoretically people are supposed to be generous and loving enough to see past their immediate needs and think of their partners first. I suppose this is exactly what would happen if Audrey Hepburn and Gandhi had married, but I married effin' Newman. You think he ever thought to himself, 'Gee, I wonder if Jean might like to sleep for four hours in a row'?" Jean punctuated her sentence loudly with a "Ha!" and pointed at Macie, who appeared to be quietly absorbing every word. "He didn't give a crap, and the only one complaining was me. What are a few complaints, when you're hardly home to hear them? But, you air those complaints on the radio, a relationship expert weighs in, and you get some influence. You might even get some change."

Macie chimed in, "I totally get what you're saying, Mrs. Harmeyer." She stood up behind her desk. "There's no small claims court for marriage. No place to tattle. No place to get a reality check and pass around time-outs."

"That's it!" shouted Jean. "We'll call it *It Ain't Business, It's Personal*, with Dr. Tig Monahan."

"Or call it *Is That Fair?*" Macie clapped her hands.

Tig scowled, putting her fingers to her lips to shush them. "Why would anyone care what I have to say? I'm not a lawyer, and I hate those sanctimonious television judges."

"You're still thinking inside the box," Jean said. "This isn't court. It's radio. You'll have the power of the airwaves behind you. The world needs a hand when a couple is stuck between 'Hey, this isn't fair' and 'I want a divorce.' Right now, that place is more mythical than the G spot." Jean looked at Macie and said, "The real G spot is defining what's fair play in marriage and accountability. Now that would feel amazing."

Macie grinned and said, "My G spot is at the intersection of 'up yours' and 'kiss my ass.'" Then, with a little less conviction she added, "But that's probably why I'm not in a relationship."

Unconvinced, Tig said, "Don't you want a lawyer; a moderator? Someone who does this for a living? One of those collaborative divorce people, maybe?"

"God, no, I don't want a legal authority on my show. That's up to our listeners. We'll have all the appropriate disclaimers, 'These are not the opinions of the radio station' . . . blah, blah blah. We'll say this isn't counseling or should not be substituted as counseling, and that you're not to be held responsible." Jean walked over to Tig. "Look, I knew this was going to set off all your moral bells and whistles because, the other day aside, I know that you're a caring, careful therapist. I didn't come to you because you're a loose cannon. I want a balanced opinion of fairness. You will get to say fair or not fair. You will be supporting people, validating what they already know is true."

Tig raised her hand. "I have no interest in being the resident Kevorkian on marriage. I hate divorce and what it does to people."

"That's fine," said Jean with conviction, "then never suggest it. We will put that into the disclaimers, your position on divorce . . . that you know that it is necessary in some situations where either psychological or physical abuse is present, but should not be the first level of remedy or something like that. Our lawyers will write all that stuff. You can oversee that."

Tig considered this. "I would listen to people's stories and give them a kind of reality check? Like: 'No you're not crazy; making you wear a fireman's hat to bed every night is definitely one-sided.'"

"Exactly. In the beginning, before people call, you could talk about some of your counseling experiences, give stories of couples. You know, changing the names to protect the guilty and all."

"No way, Jean. Look. This is not what a counselor does. We don't tell tales; we don't judge and punish."

Jean's iPhone buzzed. "It's my assistant." She narrowed her eyes and said, "Dr. Monahan, you're going to need an assistant. Macie, are you interested?"

Macie blinked and answered without hesitation. "I'm totally in, Dr. M, let's do it."

Jean continued to smile. "Dr. M, yeah, I like that. Okay, now I have to go. I'm having a Bite Me cake from that dog bakery in town, Baking No Bones About It, be delivered to Newman just before he leaves the office today. Don't you love it? It was my assistant's idea. A copy of the bra photo is going to be stuck on the top."

Jean winked at Macie and trained her eyes on Tig. "Think about it; let's at least try a pilot." She handed Tig her card. "You can come to the studio, meet our lawyers, and tailor this to your specifications. You'll see. This is going to be great. What else have you got going on?" Waving over her shoulder, she strode out through the parted glass doors.

Tig put her hands on the reception desk's cool marble surface. "What just happened?"

"I'm not sure, because I haven't actually seen it happen before at this job, but I think you just moved on."

Already deep in thought by the time she reached the double doors, Tig almost didn't hear Macie call out.

"Dr. M?"

Tig turned, an expectant look on her face.

"I almost forgot to tell you. A nurse from Hope House called." Macie read from the telephone pad in her hand. "Your mother wants her keys back."

• • •

Tig drove home, her mind filled with conflicting thoughts about advice-giving, fairness, and whether she should even work or not. "To job or not to job, that is the question," she said aloud. It was a relief to quiet her heavy thoughts about Pete and her family momentarily. She unlocked her front door and stepped inside. Thatcher, having been returned from the neighbor's house, sat curled on the couch under the bay window.

"Glad to see you had your usual afternoon, soaking in the rays. I hope you got my taxes done between naps. Scooch over; you're taking up the whole seat." She inched the large dog over and sat, running her fingers through the surprisingly soft, wavy hair.

"Do you miss Grandma? I bet you do. I bet you're lonely when you're here by yourself." Tig lifted her face to the late afternoon sun and closed her eyes. When she opened them, she noticed the dust and dying plants on the bay windowsill. She broke a dead leaf off of a philodendron and the entire plant came up, the roots dry and brown.

"Did you know, Thatcher, that some plants have green leaves and sometimes actually bloom?"

A pile of mail lay scattered on the coffee table, including her cell phone and mortgage bill. An empty coffee cup ringed with a dark stain sat next to a crumpled napkin and an uncanceled check made out to Hope House. *Disarray*, she thought. *Trepidation. Proliferation.*

In her mind's eye, she saw her young mother's handwriting on vocabulary lists attached to the refrigerator. Her mother's unlined, smiling face.

"You girls will thank me when you're eating with the president of the United States of America and he talks about the *proliferation* of wealth or some such thing. You will be one of the few at the table who will know what he is talking about. You'll not only know what he is talking about, but you'll also know which fork to use. He will comment on what remarkable young people you are. I hope I'm alive to receive your thank-you letters."

Tig turned her head. A note in Pete's handwriting still hung on the back of the door:

Hallie. You live here. Do not go outside. The address is 612 Buena Vista Way.

Tig buried her face in Thatcher's hair. The dog's soft ham-slice of a tongue brushed Tig's chin.

"I hope you know that you must live and proliferate good health way beyond your doggie years. You know, if I ever am crazy enough to get married, you have to be my maid of honor. Wendy will just have to deal with it." Tig sighed. "Speaking of Wendy, did my negligent sister call yet?"

Thatcher yawned her huge, exhausted, you're-keeping-me-awake-with-this-silly-talk yawn.

Tig looked at her phone and considered whom to call about the radio offer, then went to sleep.

She woke in the night, turned to spoon Thatcher, and tried to recapture a dream, the tail of which sifted through her mind and sailed out of her grasp. Instead, Tig thought of her mother. Her memory played back, always clearer just on the edges of sleep. She recalled herself as a little girl in her mother's wedding gown. She biked everywhere, her lean tanned legs pumping the pedals of her blue Schwinn two-speed, a long chestnut braid sailing like the tail of a kite straight out behind her, the knot of a shimmery yellow ribbon hanging on for dear life. She could almost feel the ivory satin of the dress flap like the incredible wings of an albino bat, just shy of the spokes and gears of the bicycle. Her bottom narrowly missed the boy-bar on every quick down stroke and jerky upswing.

She would push forward over the handlebars, reaching out to meet the wind, racing the boxelder bugs, dandelion wisps, and voices from last night. She hated when her mother and sister fought; hated the clenched teeth, scrambled faces, hissing snake-like sentences, and slamming doors.

Tig would hitch up the shoulder of the buttery gown of her mother's wedding dress and grab the greasy hem, tattered by rough patches in the road. She shoved it into the waistband of her red gym shorts. She had been a prototypical eight-year-old girl, dress-up gowns mixed with skinned knees and scabs still healing on the palms of her hands. She loved how nimble she felt when she jumped off and grabbed the dress without tripping and landing in the hedges. She skidded into Mrs. Shaft's driveway, shaving down the toe of her tennis shoe and slicing a marigold to the quick as she made the turnaround. She was a genius at dodging obstacles and keeping track of her extremities without insult; something her sister, even at her advanced age of thirteen, couldn't quite master.

She'd walk her bike around to the side of her next-door neighbor's yard, and pull herself into the tire swing. If Tig swung up just right she could fold herself into the center, unobserved, sway and think. She remembered to pull up the dress and tuck the train and tulle into the tire. She thought she looked like the chrysalis in her second-grade science room, a caterpillar wrapped in silk, deaf and protected.

"Tig!" she'd heard her mother's voice calling once. Shoving herself further down into the tire, she smelled rubber, musty leaves, and the mothballs that had previously kept her mother's dress pristine.

"Tiger Lily, where are you?" her mother had called impatiently, on her way to annoyed. Tig had about three minutes before her mother added her last name to the call. She wasn't really in trouble until then; three strikes you're out, and then came the wooden spoon. Her mother never hit her with it. It was like a wooden exclamation point she held in her hand for emphasis.

Let her wait, she remembered thinking, to show she could be independent. She would kick the inside of the tire hard, and flakes of black fluttered down from the sides. *Five, four, three, two, one.*

"Here I am, Mama. I'm coming." She would call this in just a minute, but first wanted to torture her mother a bit longer before she answered, make her wonder if she had run away or been eaten by Hothead, the neighbor's pit bull.

"Come on in here and get cleaned up. It's time to start thinking about dinner," her mother called. Softening, she added, "Grab your bike, Tig. We're having your favorite dessert later."

Tig had stepped through the door, looking up as her mother reached out and cupped her chin. She loved her mother's hands.

Tig, the child, loved these times with her mother. Hallie was always so busy taking care of animals or fighting with Wendy that these times stuck out in Tig's memory. She recalled looking up at her mother, moving only her eyes so as not to disturb her. The tiny lines at the corners of her mother's eyes made them look like the soft sympathetic eyes of a whale, small and wise. Once, curled in her mother's lap, she had commented on the wrinkles, meaning to say how beautiful they were. Her mother had not been pleased by the compliment and grumbled about getting older.

Tig gazed up at her mother, saw that her mother's eyes rested on the oak tree outside, but it was her mother's mind where Tig longed to go. Unfortunately, there was a sign on her mother's face that read *Keep Out.* Sitting with her this way was like riding in the passenger seat of a car and not being able to see over the dashboard. Finally, unable to remain quiet, Tig said, "Mama?"

"Yes, Tig?" her mother said, without looking down at her.

"Can you tell me about the day you first saw Daddy?"

Her mother took a long breath and washed her hand over her face, like a washcloth wiping away the dust on the memory. "Oh, sweetie, you've heard this story a hundred times. Can't I tell another?"

"Please, Mama, I just like to hear it." Tig put on her best pleading face as she gazed up.

Resigned, her mother said, "I was sitting in a huge class at the university, a chemistry class. He had on one blue sock and one white sweat sock and the nerdiest glasses I had ever seen, black frames with scratches all over them."

She didn't speak or move, thinking that if her mother forgot about her, she might go on to serve up another new piece of the pie.

"I noticed he had really short nails," her mother went on. "The kind you get from biting them right down to the nub. I kind of thought it made him look flawed and sensitive. I guess I was right about that." She sighed and then said, "He had on an old brown sweater with worn cuffs and a tiny hole where the neckband met the shoulder seam. I told him I could sew it for him."

Her mother paused again and said in a new voice, the one she reserved for when the delivery boy dropped the newspaper just short of the stoop, or when the garbage men tossed the cans around, "I don't mind telling you about your dad, but we should talk about who he really was, the real man behind the story. But, why? It's just the three of us now," she said with conviction.

Tig remembered her discomfort with her mother's change from reminiscent to practical. She remembered wriggling out of her mother's arms, sliding onto the floor like Robin down the Batpole, throwing her arms up and skimming out of the wedding gown all in one motion, leaving the gathered luxury in the lap of her mother.

"I can do a cartwheel. Do you want to see?" Tig had said as she pitched her body upside down just short of a plant resting on the windowsill. When her mother didn't even yell at her, Tig brought up Wendy.

"Wendy says you should get married again. She says boys are nice."

Her mother touched the small snags on the gown's bodice and said, "Wendy should know." She sighed. "I probably shouldn't have let you wear this thing to play in, but I just thought it was such a waste sitting up in my closet; what's the point?"

Her mother seemed to be talking to herself, and no amount of cartwheels was going to derail her. "You don't have to get married," she'd said, finally. "It's not lonely being alone. In fact, sometimes being married can be lonelier than being single."

"Mom," Tig sighed.

"It's okay. If you don't ever get married, I won't care," her mother had said.

Tig had placed her hands right on her mother's shoulders. They were eye to eye, looking at each other. "Mama, I'm eight!"

This stopped her mother, and Tig, eager to recreate a happy family scene, walked into the kitchen. She glanced at her mother holding her wedding gown and rubbing her fingers on the frayed hem, the yellowed lace, the torn tulle. She picked up the dress and pressed her face into the folds and said, "Tig, if it's okay with you, I think I'll just hang this back in the closet; maybe the memories have some life left in them."

As if the last line of the memory was a lullaby, Tig drifted off. The last thing she heard was Thatcher sigh.

Chapter Eight
Big Yellow Taxi

After two weeks of yoga, spa visits, Hope House, and talking herself out of calling Pete, Tig felt more groomed and sick of herself, her problems, and her own thoughts. She left the first of several meetings with Jean and executives at WXRT studios feeling ready to work. Anything to stop thinking about herself, her mother, or her stalled love life. Tig drove home through the University Heights residential area and admired, as she always did, the solid wood porches, dormers, and ruddy masonry decorating one historic home after another. She turned onto her street, marked by an ancient, all-knowing oak, and slowed. An unfamiliar silver car was parked in her driveway. A petite woman stood on Tig's front stoop, stretching, hands on the small of her back. She wore a tight white T-shirt with a pair of black yoga pants. Even from this distance, Tig could discern the protruding belly button of a woman near the end of her pregnancy.

As Tig approached, her sister Wendy turned and held her hand up in a halfhearted wave.

The slow rush of feelings from white hot anger to love, from irritation to envy, and back to anger again made Tig feel like she was taffy being pulled in every direction on a hot day. She gripped the steering wheel hard as she tried to reframe her anger into something positive like, *Wendy's here! Yay!* rather than, *Fucking Wendy.*

In her driveway, Tig rolled the window down. "Oh my God, look at you." Her voice didn't sound as kind as she'd hoped.

Wendy's belly was the size of a large Weber kettle grill. "Yup. Look at me."

Tig said, "You know that word for when you're hungry and angry?"

"Hangry, yeah."

"What's the word for angry and super angry?"

"I don't know. But I should, shouldn't I? I make everyone super angry. Isn't this baby going to be lucky?" There was self-awareness in that statement and something else Tig hadn't seen much in her sister. Humbleness? Neither sister spoke. A fat, lazy bee bumbled by Tig's ear.

"You're pregnant."

Wendy nodded.

Tig said, "Wow, Wen. I might have been a little nicer when I called, if I'd known."

"No, you wouldn't."

"No. I wouldn't have been. You are such a selfish little shit."

Wendy lifted her chin, "Wow, you must be an awesome counselor. Thanks."

Tig laughed bitterly. "In fact, I'm not awesome."

Wendy ignored this and leaned against the front door. "How's Mom?"

Tig gave her a look. Wendy said, "Look, I came as soon as I was able, Tig. I had to make arrangements."

"It's not that. I'm just processing this. You being here."

In school, when the instructors introduced therapeutic silence to the counselor toolbox, Tig had thought there was nothing more impossible in the world than shutting up when you wanted to grab a client by the shoulders and shake them. She'd had a professor, Dr. Day, who would sit with her like a sensei and verbally jab her just to shush her. He'd have been so disappointed with Tig during the Harmeyer melee, but maybe he'd feel hopeful today. It wasn't counselor training that held Tig's tongue, though: It was because she couldn't pin down her slippery emotions long enough to commit to one feeling, name it, and get the words out of her mouth.

Finally, she said, "You didn't have to come here. I just needed to talk to you when I called."

"That's not what you said on the phone." Wendy shifted her feet and said, "Well, I came instead. That should make up for a few missed calls." Wendy smiled a megawatt grin that didn't make it anywhere near her eyes.

Tig automatically reached her arms around Wendy's shoulders, and hugged Wendy with an awkward combination of affection and difficulty. She said again, "Look at you." She touched her own flat abdomen. "How are you feeling?"

"Good. I feel good, considering I'm ready to burst."

"You do look ready." Tig scrutinized her sister's face. "How is it that your doctor allowed you to travel? Aren't you too close to your due date?"

Wendy picked up a small duffel bag at her feet and said, "I'll get the rest of my stuff later. Let's go inside."

"Is Phil coming this weekend?"

Tig opened the door as Wendy cleared her throat. "No. He's not coming. He's not doing anything anymore. At least, not with me. He's, um, decided he doesn't want this." She gestured in the general area of her belly.

"What? What are you talking about? When did this happen?"

"About the same time Mom fell apart." She ignored Tig's surprise and said, "I told you I've been busy. I'm not evil, Tig. I just had other things to deal with. I knew you could handle Mom. I mean, God, you've been doing it for a long time."

Inside, Wendy eased herself into a chair next to the fireplace and looked around. "I love your place; it's so cozy."

She saw a *Hot* note taped onto the glass enclosure of the fireplace and met Tig's eyes, then quickly looked away.

Tig pulled the note free. "What do you mean he doesn't want you?"

"Phil's been twitchy ever since I got pregnant." Wendy shrugged. "He says he'll always help financially, but that's where it ends for him."

"I'm sorry, Wendy."

"He's a dick." With a resigned sigh, Wendy shrugged. "Wait, no. He's not really a dick. This baby was an accident. A happy one for me, but it's just the opposite for Phil. He always said, 'No children.'"

"You're more understanding than I would be," said Tig.

Wendy smoothed her T-shirt over her stomach, as if that went without saying between sisters with a long, muddy path of differing personalities and conflicting opinions. "You know what gets me?" she said. "I always judged unplanned pregnancies. Thought they were for Catholics and ridiculously naive or irresponsible high school kids. Remember Misty from my class?"

"Yeah, she had some crazy kind of name. What was it? Misty Lawn and Garden or something."

"No," Wendy laughed, "it was Misty Morning Meadow. We called her 3M, and once she had the baby we called her M&M. We weren't very funny."

"Didn't she get decrowned from Homecoming Queen?"

"Yeah. Those were the days. Now, I hear pregnancy in high school is a status thing."

The two sisters sat with their dissimilar memories of high school between them—Tig the serious, smart one, and Wendy the fearless butterfly. Tig said, "So, nine months and no word about this to your family?"

"I was worried you'd disapprove."

"I'm not so hard as all that, Wendy. That hurts."

"This would never have happened to you."

"That's the problem, isn't it?"

An elephant-like blast from the neighborhood trombone player cut through their conversation. Wendy fidgeted, putting a few more inches of distance between her and Tig. "I've always used the diaphragm and it's been a great goalie for me. I suppose after a while, you add common user error to Olympic-caliber sperm and you get a baby." Wendy touched her face. "I guess, like everything, it's a numbers game. You have sex a million times, and you'll eventually have to confront the purpose of that act in the first place. Forget all the positions and the oils, it is for baby-making, after all.

"You can't win if you don't play."

"Well, I won big time." Wendy's smile had a wryness to it. "You probably don't believe this, you being the rule follower."

"Maybe you could stop taking swipes at me and just tell the story, okay?"

Wendy closed her eyes. "The thing is, I feel like I did win. I mean sure, I lost Phil, but look what I'm gaining. A whole human being, all folded up in my own little cup holder, ready to unfold and go to college."

Tig lowered herself to sit on the floor and Thatcher came padding over, panting her winning smile. She scratched the black dog's ears. "You think you can manage this on your own?"

With a steely gaze, Wendy said, "Yeah, I think I can manage this. Maybe Mom didn't think I could manage her affairs when she gave you her power of attorney, little sister, but don't worry. I can manage this."

The old roles and unjustified labels sprang forward: good girl, wild child. Tig shook her head. "Come off it, Wendy. I have power of attorney because I live here. It wasn't a commentary on your abilities. You are the older sister. I concede." Tig busied herself with the leftover adhesive from the note on the fireplace, scraping off the stickiness with her fingernail. *Hot.* Thatcher exhaled a profound sigh as if even she was tired of this old game of king of the hill.

"That's all about to change." Wendy's voice wavered like the tiniest twig in a summer breeze. "I'm able to travel because I'm staying. It's not traveling. I'm moving. I'm moving here. I don't have any place to really go, just yet."

Tig looked at her sister, her beautiful skin, her long eyelashes, and saw in a flash her older sister again, holding her hand, helping her on the bus. In that second Wendy looked like the puzzle piece that could fit into the Pete-shaped hole in her life. Now that Wendy had her own Phil-shaped hole, it felt even to Tig. "Wendy that's wonderful. It's perfect timing. We'll have to clean Mom's room, carve out space for you. I've often dreamed of you living closer, being around more."

A mix of relief and embarrassment washed over Wendy's face. Then, in a rush, she said, "I actually thought Phil might change his mind. You know, love me so much that he wouldn't give us up. It was clear he was trying, but the bigger I got, the more he was obviously failing, so I just packed and came here." She absently scratched the lowest part of her belly. "It's ironic, isn't it? I get so mad at you for being the perfect, responsible sister, and at the first hint of trouble I do what everyone does, run to you."

Tig shook her head. "Not everyone runs to me. Pete and I are finished."

"Really? Huh. Well, you guys weren't that serious."

"What makes you say that? We were serious. I was going on sabbatical with him."

"It just never seemed like you felt all that strongly about him."

"I loved him!"

"Loved?"

"*Love* him." More quietly, Tig said, "I do love him. I just . . . ." Her voice trailed off. Starting again, she said, "I left my job for him."

"That's no big sacrifice, is it? You weren't that crazy about that job, either."

"Either? No, Wendy. I loved him and my job. It's just that sometimes the clients are so exhausting."

"Careful, Dr. Monahan, your judgment is showing."

"Look, some of the couples I see are really difficult."

"Bitches."

"You don't understand."

"Sounds like you needed a break."

"It appears you are not the only one who thinks so."

Silence sat between them, until finally Tig confessed, "I'm jealous of you being pregnant. Pete and I talked about marriage and kids. I mean, we did it in a fantasy way."

Wendy lifted her belly an inch and shifted in her chair.

Tig said, "I used to say I wanted our children to have his eyes, attitude, and legs, and he would laugh and say he hoped our girl would be as strong as me. It was a compliment. At least I thought it was. I guess strong is a synonym for boring." Wendy looked like she was going to say something, but Tig continued, "Do you know how long it's going to take me to find someone new and right? To even get to the place of having children? Let's talk about something else. What about your job?"

"Teeth are everywhere and good dental hygienists are not. I have connections and good references. No worries. But the really good news is that I have plenty of money." Wendy shrugged at Tig. "Phil's an amazing money manager. He invested my whole salary while we lived together and it's all mine now. Plus, he's loaded and feeling really guilty about this whole thing. I guess the lesson learned here is that if you're going to become an unwed mother at thirty-eight, at least choose someone with money skills to supply the sperm."

Tig said uncharitably, "Well, that's something."

"Say what you want about Phil. That's more than just something." Wendy headed straight into the fray. "So fill me in on everything. What's happening?"

"He came home suggesting that I take a little time before following him to Hawaii, and added that he wasn't that into me. I blew the hell up at a difficult patient, left my job, and can't seem to settle Mom in her new place. I may or may not have a new job, and I can't seem to get enough sleep. So, if you were thinking being with Tig is going to be awesome, think again. Nothing about me is awesome."

Wendy pushed back in her chair. "Is my being here too much? I can get my own place. I just thought . . . ."

Tig took in the hollowness under Wendy's eyes, the bruised look there. She stood up. "No, without a doubt we need each other, probably now more than ever. I'm really glad you're here."

Their conversation sputtered with the intimacy of the moment, and Tig found her footing with more comfortable geography. "Listen, you're going to have to brace yourself when we visit Mom."

Wendy snapped, "I know. I'm not that out of it."

"No, I mean it's weird to not see her in charge."

"Oh, yeah." Wendy frowned. "The only time I ever saw Mom really out of her element—you know, before she got old—was when Dad died." She closed her eyes. "I remember her sleeping and smoking a lot. She took long baths, her big belly, with you in it, breaking the water. I napped on the floor of the bathroom with her in the tub." Wendy shook her head. "I think she tried to make up for those weeks for the rest of her life. Then when you were born she snapped back into her usual take-charge gear."

"I never saw Mom as anything other than on her game," Tig said. "Mom always went that extra step. No store-bought cookies for Valentine's Day, no missing even the smallest event."

"Remember when she borrowed those three tiny ponies from one of her clients for my birthday party? She said we could have them at the party and name them for a day, but then we had to give them back. I named mine George Washington."

Tig said, "I called mine Hoogala."

"Terri Osgood named hers Terri Osgood. Then she called it T-bone all day. George Washington ate the cake and pooped in mom's hydrangea. Party over."

"The party's over, all right. Alzheimer's is eating Mom's cake now."

Wendy folded her hands. "After Dad died, she listened to a lot of Joni Mitchell. Every time I hear 'Big Yellow Taxi,' I feel like my middle is sinking. If I'm at the mall and I hear it, I leave." Wendy hummed the melody.

Tig joined in with the harmony, along with her own made-up lyrics, "A big yellow taxi, something, something, paradise, something my man away. I can't remember the words."

Wendy blinked. "For years, I thought God took people to heaven in a taxi. You know what Mom said to me? I walked in to ask if I could go to Debbie's, and she said—you know, in that brutal way she sometimes had—" Wendy squawked her mother's voice, "You know what, honey? No one gives a shit about paradise when it's around, but once it's gone, well, hell, people notice."

"Really? She said 'shit'?"

"Yeah," Wendy said. "Early on, Dad was Mom's spine until he wasn't anymore. Even though Mom stepped up like a fighter pilot, all I could picture was our lives tarred, flattened, and smashed for a long time after that."

Tig stared into the empty fireplace, visualizing her mother when she was younger. "Hey, Wen, you're not paying Mom's nursing home bills, are you?"

"I thought you had a handle on all that stuff. Isn't that why you're always bitching at me?"

Thatcher stretched in a slow downward dog position, yawned and walked away, leaving the two sisters bickering.

Chapter Nine
I Like You Just Fine

In the parking lot of Hope House, surrounded by aging maples and weeping willows, Tig said to her sister, "Don't be surprised if she doesn't recognize you. She only gets my name right about one in two hundred times." Tig unloaded the trunk of her car. "Here, take this pillow; I'll get the lamp out of the back seat."

"They don't have lighting in her room?" Wendy studied the façade of Hope House.

"Of course they do, but they encourage bringing in personal effects, you know, things from their past, to make them feel more comfortable with familiar things around them."

"I'd think that would be depressing. You know, reminding you what you left behind. We had to sell your house, Mom, but lucky you, you get to keep the lamp."

Tig shot a look at her sister, then pulled things out of the compact car like Mary Poppins. "Well, they seem to think it helps."

"I'd rather start fresh. Cut the cord. This is my life now, let's get on with it."

"Well, I don't think the gerontologists did research on Cut the Cord theory. I think they did the research on Making Easier Transitions."

Tig balanced a blooming azalea on her hip. "Would you just take this painting? She used to have it in her bathroom."

"I know where she had it. I grew up in that house, too. Do we have to bring all this shit in right now? Why didn't you bring all this stuff before?"

Tig bit her tongue and then said, "I've been meaning to. I always go after work. Let me just grab the quilt."

Wendy walked to the front doors with a red, fringed pillow and the painting of an old crabapple tree.

Tig hit the door locks and the car horn beeped twice. She tried to jog a little while carrying the quilt over her shoulder and with the plant and lamp in her hands, and she called to Wendy. "Just wait, will you?"

Wendy spoke over her shoulder. "It looks like a nursing home."

"It *is* a nursing home."

"No, I mean, more nursing than home. This sidewalk is, like, a mile wide. It makes it look . . . I don't know, institutional."

"It's for wheelchairs and those golf carts. There are fifty acres of walkway around the facility so residents can get outside. Get some sun."

"So Mom has a tan, huh? I should prepare myself for that? Does she have a respectable golf swing now, too?"

She caught up to her sister at the glass doors. Tig stepped in front of Wendy, setting off the sensors. The doors parted.

"What's your problem? You're being a huge bitch."

Wendy sighed. "I just think that now that I'm here we could manage her at home."

Tig caught Wendy's arm and said, "Seriously, Wen, you don't know what you're saying. She is a full-time job. Even in the night." Remembering the sadness of her first days—touring the grounds, the unfamiliar staff, hoping for a private room for her mother—Tig tried to smooth her raised hackles. "I know how it looks, but this is what Mom wanted. She had a brochure and notes in her things. Hope House knew she was coming. C'mon, it's better inside." Tig gestured to the aviary in the entryway. "The birds are a nice touch, don't you think?"

A woman snored in front of the large glass case, her head hanging to the right, her left foot free of the metal footrest of her wheelchair. The central nurses' desk was quiet. Not an employee in sight. The telephone rang, unanswered, and the familiar music of a morning news program drifted around the hallways. Tig could hear the voice of a woman repeatedly saying, "Hello," with the precision of a metronome. It had the meter of a rare bird with the gravelly tenor of a pack-a-day habit.

"God," Wendy breathed.

"Come on, Mom's got a nice room down this hall. Just remember that she might not know you right away."

Tig wanted to get Wendy into their mother's room where she might be able to minimize the whole institutionalized-care experience. As they approached the room, a tall older man in a white lab coat emerged, eyes focused on the carpet, lost in thought.

Tig frowned. "Hello?"

Startled, he glanced up and brushed his hands together as if removing crumbs. "Oh, hello. I was just checking on your mother."

With Wendy behind her, Tig said, "I'm sorry; have we met?"

With a professional air he offered his hand. "Yes, actually, but you two were little girls. I'm Dr. Jenson. I work in geriatrics at the hospital next door. I just stopped in to see how Hallie is today."

Wendy stepped up to shake his hand and said, "How is she?"

"Very well, I'm happy to report."

"She's quite different in the early part of the day," Tig said.

"Yes, she is. That's typical."

"She's anything but typical. How do you know my mother?"

The man smiled and scrutinized Tig before saying, "Wow, you are just like your mother, aren't you?" To Wendy he said, "And you're the wild and winsome Wendy. You look just like you did as a girl."

Wendy flushed and retreated behind her sister, hiding her "wild" belly.

"You seem to know a great deal about us. I'm sorry, but I don't remember you."

Dr. Jenson dropped his gaze and missed a beat. "I knew your parents years ago. My brother was your dad's best friend. I was just a kid to them, almost nine years their junior." He lifted his arm and scratched the top of his head, mussing a thick patch of gray and black hair.

Wendy grinned and leaned forward. "You knew us?"

"My brother more than I. I just admired you all from afar. After your father died, my wife and I sometimes asked you and your mother over for dinner. She was a very independent woman."

"You knew my dad?" Tig's pulse jumped. "When was this?" After so many years of tiptoeing around her mother's need to be enough as both parents, and squelching her natural curiosity about her dad, a multitude of questions stormed into her brain: *What were they like together? Was my dad nice? Were they totally in love?* But the funnel of her mouth was only able to form one question. "Why are you here, exactly?"

A muffled buzzing interrupted the conversation. Dr. Jenson touched his hip. "Sorry, I'm being summoned. But let's get coffee sometime. I'd love to talk about your parents." Then, as if retreating into the more comfortable territory of science-speak, he said, "I'd like to suggest, with your permission, a visit for your mother to our neuro-psych lab for memory work. There has been some progress using visual imagery and retrieval techniques in cases such as your mother's. I also do ongoing research that explores non-traditional ways to help people transition to long-term care. I'll give a report to Jean Timmons, her regular physician."

"So you know Dr. Timmons, too?" said Tig.

"Yes." Dr. Jenson's intense gaze seemed to deconstruct Tig as she stood. She touched her hair self-consciously, feeling more like a little girl under his gaze than a professional woman. He shook his head slightly and handed Tig his card. "It's so nice to see you again." Turning then, he rushed down the hall, his lab coat flapping goodbye.

Tig studied the card in her hand. *Dr. Jeffrey Jenson, MD/PhD Gerontology/Internal Medicine/Neuropsychology.*

Wendy said, "Weird, right? He knew us. Small world. He's handsome for an older man. In a Clint Eastwood kind of way."

Absently, Tig said, "I guess. Are you ready?" Without waiting for an answer, she pushed open the wide, heavy door and called out in a quiet voice, "Mom? I have a surprise for you."

Hallie Monahan sat in a large padded chair paging through a *National Geographic* magazine. Her hair had been brushed and pulled back with combs to frame her face. A trace of pink lipstick glossed her smile. She wore her new whiter-than-white walking shoes and blue jeans that had been purchased especially for the well-hidden elastic waistband. The rolling bedside table held a cup of coffee, a large bouquet of daisies, and the television remote. The nurse call button and hospital bed were the only telltale signs belying the ordinary setting. If not for these, Hallie could have been any elderly woman. No one would have guessed that she couldn't recall her address or find her way to the bathroom.

With the decorative pillow pressed to her chest, Wendy rested the painting against the wall and approached. "Hi, Mama. It's me. Wendy."

"For God's sake, honey, of course it's you. How are you, sweetie?"

Wendy stepped closer. Hallie opened her arms and Wendy bent forward into their mother's embrace. Her mother's brown spots, blue-green veins, and papery white skin would be frightening in a horror movie, Tig noted, put out by her mother's easy recognition of her sister.

Hallie grunted and released her daughter. "Well, you look just the same."

Clearly relieved, Wendy gestured to her belly. "Well, not exactly the same. I've changed shape since the last time I saw you."

"Yes, you have, honey. Be careful you don't gain too much weight."

So sure this was another one of Alzheimer's tricks and that her mother was confusing Wendy for someone else in her past, Tig said, "Mom, do you know who this is?"

Irritated, her mother rolled her eyes and said to Tig, "Would you mind seeing where my breakfast is? I'd like a few moments alone with my daughter."

"You already ate breakfast, Mom," Tig said pointedly, raising her eyebrows at Wendy.

Hallie looked at Tig. "I'd like a moment with my daughter, please."

Tig shook her head and dropped the quilt into a chair. She placed the plant and lamp on the bookshelf and sulked out of the room.

In the hall, she nearly walked into a woman just outside the door. Catching herself on the arms of the woman's wheelchair, she gasped. "Oh, excuse me!"

Unfazed, the woman said, "Would you mind wheeling me a few doors down to my room? I'm a little tired."

Tig straightened. "Sure. I'm not needed in there for a while."

"My name is Fern. Are you Hallie's daughter?"

"One of them," Tig said as she pushed the woman's chair.

"Don't worry. She'll forget her, too." Then, over her shoulder, Fern said, "Nothing else to do but eavesdrop around here." Tig turned the corner to Fern Fobes's room, her name in block letters prominently displayed. "Can you roll me over to the window? I like it best there."

Tig maneuvered around the obstacle course of a room containing a large walker, a portable oxygen tank, and the debris of the living, and settled the woman so that the sun from the window lit the soft, Marilyn-Monroe white hair. The apples of her cheeks were unlined and shiny, while the rest of her skin was scored and divided like a crazy, wind-torn corn maze. Her luminous hazel eyes glittered. "Hallie must be having a good day," Fern said, setting the brakes on her chair.

"Depends on which daughter you ask." Tig stared through the window into the grounds. The grass shone in the sun, and Tig suddenly longed to be outside.

Fern said, "You can wait in here if you like. I have a few minutes before my next pressing engagement. Sit for a minute."

Tig slid her lips into a polite smile, started to refuse, changed her mind, and sat in the ugly faux-leather armchair. "She never remembers me, which has been hard for sure. But my sister hasn't been around for almost two years and she recognized her immediately."

"I'm sorry about that."

"It's not right."

"That's dementia for you. Nothing right about it. You know what they say: it ain't personal, it's business? Alzheimer's is all personal."

Tig examined Fern's face again. "It's funny you should use that phrase," she said, thinking of the radio show for the first time in twenty-four hours. "It fits a lot of situations."

Fern nodded. "My husband died of Alzheimer's. Well, no, he died of liver cancer, but he had Alzheimer's, too. During his last years, he called me Patty. He and I were married fifty-two years. He went to his high school senior prom with Patty."

Tig shook her head. "How did you handle that?"

Fern smiled shyly. "When he talked about her, I called her 'Peppermint Fatty' and 'Fatty McFatty Pants,' my granddaughter's favorite, and I pinched him when he called me Patty. I was hoping for a negative feedback loop. A little nursing home Pavlov."

Tig laughed. "How did that go for you?"

"Not well. The nursing staff told me I had to stop. He was on a blood thinner and bruised easily. Oh, don't look so shocked. Tell me you don't feel like shaking your mom now and then."

"I'd rather punch my sister. But you can't hit old ladies or pregnant women. It sucks." Then, looking at Fern, she added, "No offense."

"None taken."

"I'm feeling better now. I guess I should go." She stretched to shake Fern's bony, soft, bird of a hand and in the doorway said, "Can I get you something from the outside world next time I come?"

"Let me think a little. I guess I could use an economy-sized pack of condoms." Fern laughed and said, "Just kidding. By the way, I believe you saw my son a bit ago, dark hair, attractive. He takes care of all my external worldly needs. He comes in after dinner a few times a week. He's single. Said he thought you were pretty."

Distracted, Tig said, "Okay," because at the far end of the hall, she spotted Wendy at the nurse's desk, looking impatient. She turned back to Fern and said, "I'll stop in the next time I come," then moved quickly down the hall.

"What's up? Why are you out here?"

"She was getting tired."

With dripping sarcasm in her voice, Tig said, "Yeah, those ten-minute visits are a real endurance event. Next time, we'll give her a PowerBar."

"Look, I just thought the first visit shouldn't be too long. From what you've said about her, I didn't know if she could handle more."

"Did she seem like she couldn't handle more?"

Wendy said, "She's better than I expected. Let's bring her home."

"You spend ten minutes with her, and my two years mean nothing."

"Maybe I remind her of home. Of living outside this sterile hospital."

"It's called having a good day." Tig walked through the exit, shaking her head, leaving Wendy to catch up.

"I'm just saying."

"I didn't just throw her in this nursing home without talking to a host of gerontologists, physicians, and other counselors, as well as seeing several other places. You'd know what a huge process it was if you'd been around."

"Now who's being a bitch? I'm just trying to have a discussion. Maybe we could move her back home now that I'm here, just until I find something better. Save some money."

"This place is free, moneybags." Tig wrenched open the car door.

"Why is it free again?"

"I don't know why. Mom had it all taken care of and paid for years ago."

"Don't you think you should figure out why? And it'll be free for how long?" Wendy walked to the passenger side, looking at Tig over the roof of the sedan.

"Listen, big sister," Tig said icily. "You think because she remembers your name that means something? It means nothing! None of it means anything. The only thing that means anything anymore are the memories we have of Mom, and keeping her safe. Leave the finances to me. I'll figure it out."

Tig dumped herself into the front seat of the car and took a breath. She grasped the steering wheel and, white-knuckled, yanked it ferociously. The effort seemed to tap her stores and she sat breathlessly.

Wendy tapped on the window. "Tig. Unlock the door."

A golf cart inched across the path just in front of the car. A nursing assistant in scrubs and a shrunken stub of a man sat in the front seat, unaware of the temper tantrum happening to their left.

Wendy knocked again on the window and pointed to the door handle. "Unlock the door."

Tig popped the locks and Wendy quietly entered the car.

"I liked it better when I was the big sister."

Tig said, "You can step up any time."

"There's not room at the top. You'd have to move over or step down."

Tig started the car and the two women buckled their seat belts. She heard her sister sigh quietly. Wendy said, "She did say one thing that was odd, you know, besides treating you like you were the bellboy."

"Yeah? What was that?"

"She said the daisies were from Daddy."

• • •

In her mother's old room at Tig's house, cardboard boxes, black garbage bags, and plastic bins cinched the bedroom, with the only open space in the center of the room. Old manila files, scarves, and photographs lay on every horizontal plane. A twin bed with a seafoam green chenille bedspread occupied a windowless wall. "There's hardly room for a person in here," Wendy said, pulling on her tennis shoes.

"When Mom moved in, I didn't store everything she owned. She loved to sit and sort through her files from the clinic. Sometimes she'd talk about her favorite animals. I thought it might stimulate her memories. Our school files are in here, along with her wedding pictures and old letters. We'll make room for your stuff this week. The only thing I've got going on is practice for the show."

"I saw a promo in the newspaper."

"Jesus, I'm a nervous wreck about it." Then, changing the topic, Tig said, "Did you call Phil? Tell him to send your stuff?"

"Did you call Pete?"

"The one who gets left doesn't do the calling."

"Did you learn that in counseling graduate school?"

"Yes, in the master class," Tig said with a grunt, hefting a plastic bin and uncovering a ruddy stain on the carpet. She bent, ran her hand over the stiffened patch. "This is what finally convinced me to move Mom. I came home to several bloody handprints and wads of paper towels, starting in the kitchen and leading like a breadcrumb trail to Mom. I found her asleep here on the floor, a half-eaten apple in her wounded hand, and Thatcher pacing nervously. It was like a scene in a Hollywood slasher movie that ended in a nap and a snack for the victim."

"God, poor Mom," said Wendy. "She'd hate to know this was her life."

"I know." A glimmer of metal in the indentation where the bedpost met the carpet caught Tig's eye. "What's this?" She lifted a tarnished silver ID bracelet from the floor. "This isn't mine. It must be hers. There's an inscription. It says, *If I could tell you.*"

Wendy took it from Tig. "I've never seen her wear this."

"Me, either. Maybe she dropped it and that's why she was on the floor." Tig looked at the bracelet for a long moment and then tucked it into her pocket. "I'll bring it to her; maybe she'll have a moment."

Wendy pulled a sweater over her shoulders. "I'm going for a walk. Maybe stimulate labor. You should call Pete."

"Leave it, Wendy."

"What's he doing in Hawaii, anyway?"

"He's studying ultra-endurance athletes. Male and female. He's not waiting around for a call from me. He'll be surrounded by fat-free, gorgeous triathletes. He'll find someone who can run the Andes Race with him."

"You could go to Hawaii."

"Could you just stop? I'm moving on, Wen. You're here now; the show starts tomorrow." Tig sighed. "When he was here, I was so often irritated with him. Now, I miss him, but if he came back, I'd probably be irritated again. It was the same when Mom lived here."

"Sounds like a pattern."

"What pattern?"

"Absence makes the heart grow fonder. Except where your sister and boyfriend are concerned; absence and presence are both irritating."

Tig blinked at her sister. "It's weird, you know, because I miss you when I don't see you."

"No, you don't."

After a minute Tig said, "No, I don't."

Chapter Ten
Is That Fair?

Jean Harmeyer bent in front of Tig and fiddled with her padded headset, trying to catch Tig's gaze as it nervously flitted from the acoustic tiles, to Macie at the telephone console, and to the note cards in her lap. Jean finally grasped Tig's shoulders.

"I don't know about this, Jean. What if I say something that makes me lose my license? I've been so stressed. I can't be trusted verbally. What if I choke and get a kind of counseling Tourette moment?"

"You are going to be fine. You're rested. We've been practicing for two weeks. This is the same, only in real time, on the air, and with an audience." She smiled, gesturing to the smattering of people in the airy, well-lit auditorium.

Tig glanced out into the space and counted roughly twenty-five fidgety people in a room that could easily hold two hundred and fifty. She tried on her most winning smile, then forgot it upon seeing a man in the front row painting his nails blood red with the concentration of an eye surgeon.

"What if no one calls in? Do we have to go the full hour and a half, or can we go to music or something?"

"Tig, I've been at this for a long time. People will call, if the promos did their job."

"If?"

"The billboards, radio announcements, and bus spots have been out there for two weeks. We've had calls already. Trust me."

"That's easy for you to say; you don't have a mic on you."

"I may not be actually on the radio, but I do have people I answer to. A lot depends on this for me." The briefest skittering of anxiety flashed across Jean's face. "But I'm not nervous, because I have you in this chair. I may be a terrible judge of character in romance, but I have killer instincts where radio is concerned. You're going to be great." She squeezed Tig's shoulders and added, "This is your calling."

Tig noticed Macie with her thumbs up, dressed optimistically in a kind of goth fräulein costume complete with knee socks and platform Mary Janes.

Jean said, "This is your chance to kick some counseling ass."

"I told you, I'm not going to do that. I can only do this if it is a professional thing."

"Just remember, there are a lot of words in Webster's dictionary. If I know you, you'll have a good balance between the colorful ones and the professional ones." As Jean walked away, she tossed over her shoulder, "Make sure you stray in the direction of the rainbow, Tig. Radio is entertainment, you know."

In the minutes before the final sound check, opening music, and first caller, Tig made a list in her head. Things that precluded being a relationship expert included:

Losing the love of your life.

Not realizing you were losing the love of your life.

Jean picked up her own headset and said, "Okay, everybody, we're about to go live. Best behavior, now. Watch the *On the Air* and *Applause* lights."

Tig brushed her sternum with her fingertips and waited for the lights to go up.

The theme song blasted from the overhead speakers; "I Can't Go for That (No Can Do)," vintage eighties Hall & Oates. The music faded away, trading places with a prerecorded announcer's voice.

"And now, under special arrangement, unedited and unrated, the show where you step up to the plate and swing, and we decide if it's fair or foul—it's *Is That Fair?* Sitting in the ultimate relationship-umpire seat, in her debut performance as the voice of sanity and reason, please welcome Dr. Tig Monahan!"

An ovation of canned applause from the speakers was joined with a smattering of studio audience clapping. Earlier in the day, Jean had sent the interns and technicians outside to round up pedestrians returning from the downtown farmers' market, promising them doughnuts and coffee if they came in for the show. Now the stragglers who had traded their free time for fried dough sat with faint white powder on their lips, looking for the relationship dynamo so enthusiastically guaranteed. Skepticism clouded their faces as they watched Tig fidget.

Tig immediately regretted the skinny cigarette pants and sleeveless top she'd chosen to seem nonthreatening. She should have borrowed Wendy's stilettos. She opened her mouth to greet her mostly unseen listeners, but before she could clear the cotton from her throat, a voice arrived in the studio.

"Okay, can you hear me? Am I on the air?"

A loud screech of feedback filled the studio. Tig jerked her head up and pulled the headset away from her ears.

Macie, all business and refined diction, belying her Halloween getup, said, "Yes, please go ahead, caller. You are on the air with Dr. Monahan. Please turn your radio down and continue."

"Oh, yeah, okay. Yeah, the radio's off now. Yeah. I've never done this before. Called into a show. You know, like, live and all."

Tig recognized the Wisconsin-lifer accent, Scandinavian vowels, and nasal twang. She pictured the caller dressed in a powder-blue cardigan, her high school sweetheart's diamond on her left hand, tiny and clogged with twenty years' worth of memories.

"Go ahead; I'm here to listen. Tell me your story."

"Yeah, okay. So, I've been having a lot of trouble sleeping lately. I guess it's that change of life thing you read so much about. Um, that's what the doctor said."

"Good, you've seen a doctor. That's good." Tig nodded with sincerity.

"Uh huh, so, the doctor gave me something to help me sleep and I've been taking it every night. Oh, and I feel so much better. It feels really good to sleep."

"Well, that's great," said Tig, looking over at Jean, anxious to move this caller into something more interesting and relationship-oriented than insomnia. Glancing at Macie, she widened her eyes. Macie nodded, gestured for her to wait for it.

"Sleep is good. Anyways, I forgot to take it the other night, y'know, cause it's new n' all, and I woke up in the middle of the night to my husband, y'know, having, um . . . sex with me. Like, he thought I was asleep."

Tig jerked her head back to Macie, who nodded feverishly.

The caller continued, "So, what I want to know is . . . is that wrong?"

The man in the front row stopped buffing his nails and the audience collectively put down their coffees.

Tig tilted her head. "Are you saying that while you were asleep, your husband thought you were sound asleep, and he engaged in intercourse?"

"Yeah, that's right. I was dreaming about grocery shopping and well, you can imagine my surprise! The thing is—he is my husband and all. He says everyone does it. Y'know, because there's such a big difference in drive 'tween men and women. He says no reason for me to get all worked up if it's gonna be over that quick."

There was a quick burst of laughter from the group.

Tig said, "Well, how do you feel about that?"

The woman hesitated. "I guess from a time management sense it should be okay, and I hate to be stingy. But . . . ." The woman clicked her tongue loudly into her telephone. "I don't like it one bit. I mean, it's my Private Pocketbook and all. I don't think he should be fiddling around in my area without me telling him it's okay. I mean, what the heck, why should he have all the fun, and I have all the mess?" As if remembering her place as the patient, she said, "What do you think?"

"I think you're absolutely right. I think at the very least, your husband owes you a giant apology and you should consider filing charges."

"Filing charges?"

"Well, at the very least, counseling!"

"Oh, no. I couldn't do that. It's not like we haven't done *it* before."

Tig considered this. The woman's need here was less about outraged litigation and more about setting boundaries and reasonable behavior.

"I think your husband needs a time-out. He should move his pillow onto the couch and have to submit written permission to re-enter the bedroom. I think you get to decide when you've forgiven him. I also think you two should talk to a counselor so he can understand what was wrong with his behavior, even if you can't exactly say why. If that doesn't work, try a shock collar."

The caller giggled and a fumbling sound came through the studio's speakers. The woman spoke away from the telephone. "See, Brady, I told you it wasn't right. I told you to keep the Governor away from the Mansion when I'm sleeping."

There was a burst of laughter from the audience. Then, into the phone, the woman said, "Thank you so much. I just couldn't ask my friends about this, and all I needed was someone to tell him it wasn't right."

"Tell Brady he shouldn't need someone else to tell him it's right or wrong. He should listen to you, because what you think is what matters."

The audience nodded. Tig glanced into the studio. Posture had improved; attention was focused on the stage. Macie hit the canned applause button, and the phone lines lit up like a Christmas tree.

The next call came from a young woman who lived in Baraboo, Wisconsin. Six months pregnant and married only a year, she needed someone to talk to before she sat her husband down with her concerns.

"I don't go out anymore. I'm so tired at night. I'm a third-grade teacher, and after a day with the kids, all I have energy for is correcting papers and dinner."

Tig considered the caller's statement. "I've never been pregnant myself, but my sister says it's exhausting."

"It is! But I don't want to stop my husband from going out every once in a while with his friends before the baby comes. There won't be much time for that later, so I always say okay. Lately, though, he won't wear his wedding ring. Says it bugs him when he plays pool or darts."

Tig looked at the audience. Two women in the center of the auditorium shook their heads with disapproval, and a mousy woman in the back row sat straight up in her chair. "Is that a problem for you, the fact that he goes out without his ring?"

"Yeah. I hate it. I think he's strutting around acting all single, while I'm walking around with this big billboard of a belly advertising that I'm anything but. Why shouldn't he have some kind of sign that says *I'm taken*?"

"I agree with you."

"You do?"

"Absolutely. If it makes you uncomfortable, he should honor that."

"What if he doesn't?"

"Well, you can always take it to the jewelers next time he takes it off and reduce it a half size. Then he won't be able to take it off. You get the added benefit of him thinking he's put on weight. That'll reduce his swagger a little."

The crowd laughed.

Tig added, "I'm just kidding about fiddling with his ring. Just tell him that if he can't respect this small request from you, then you're not sure how this marriage will move forward with such stingy roots. Tell him Tig said so."

It was silent for a minute on the phone. The woman seemed to be juggling the phone. "Okay, can you repeat that? I'm writing it down. So far I have, 'if you can't respect this small' . . . what did you call it? Request? Oh, that's a good word."

Tig repeated her previous statement and the woman hung up, but not before asking if she could send Tig some of her amazing rhubarb pie in thanks.

After several more calls, the last refrain of the theme song played and coupons were given to all the audience members for a buy-one-ticket-get-two-friends-in-free deal. Jean, Macie, and Tig sat together and debriefed while the sound technicians and interns tidied up.

"You were amazing!" Macie exclaimed. "I knew you could do it."

"When I'm right, I'm right," said Jean.

Tig smiled briefly, then frowned. "I just don't know about all this."

"What are you talking about, Dr. M? You're a natural." Macie's eyes shone with renewed admiration and warmth.

"I don't think I should be weighing in as if relationships are a glib piece of cake. I don't know the whole story, nor am I getting both sides of the stories. What if something happens?"

"Wait, are you saying you think it might be okay to have sex with your wife while she is sleeping?" Jean shook her head.

"Or how about the guy whose wife would only have sex after she'd had a full professional mani-pedi?" Macie said. "What was that about?"

Jean laughed. "Hangnails can be vexing in the throes of passion. I think telling him to go to cosmetology school or make the sex more interesting than a trip to the spa was perfect."

"That's what I mean," Tig protested. "That's not good advice. It may be good radio, but I'll never work as a therapist again in this town."

"Are you kidding? Did you see how many calls came in?"

"Just because people ask for it doesn't make it good for them. The mullet was a very successful hairstyle back in the day, but we know how that turned out. There's a whole generation of people with hidden senior class photos and buried family portraits."

Macie nodded. "Smart people, foolish choices."

Jean said, "Why does therapy have to be like going to the dentist? Why can't people laugh a little while they're making their relationships better? And don't get me started on the PC terminology."

"Language is important," Tig said.

"Sure, when everyone understands it," Jean said. "I had this one counselor who told me that I had to identify my faults and own them before my marriage could get better. Own them? They're my faults by definition; how can I own them anymore?"

"They meant acknowledge that you have faults."

"So why not just say that! Besides, how is *owning* my faults going to fix my husband's sleeping around? Are they saying that if I'd have admitted that I'm wrong more often, my husband would lay some pipe at home for a change? What I'm saying is that I need real language. Real directions."

"I can't change the language of the profession."

"But you can!" Jean said. "And I like how you tell it like it is. Listen to this: I called my insurance to take that cheating bastard off my policy. If he gets any warts, I'm not paying for burning 'em off, unless I get to cauterize 'em myself. Anyway, the guy on the other line told me to wait for the *marital transition* to progress. I said, 'Marital transition; a.k.a. divorce, you mean?' He actually got uncomfortable."

Macie nodded and said, "I can't keep up. Yesterday at the co-op a woman sneered at my banana, saying that clearly I wasn't a locavore."

Jean said, "What the hell is that?"

"Think globally, eat locally," said Macie with a smile.

"Shit, another thing to feel badly about," Jean said. "I eat an orange and I'm not supporting the Wisconsin farmer. Just wait, scurvy will be on the rise and then the cost of oranges will skyrocket."

Macie put her headset back on and said, "Local farmers get thrown under the bus for citrus. News at six."

Tig said, "All right, you two. I get it. I'll give this a try. What the hell, I'm unemployed, right? That's not very supportive of the economy."

"You're in a *job transition* right now," Jean said. "Embrace it."

• • •

As much as Tig wanted to talk to Pete about this new success, she knew that her status as an on-air relationship counselor would not impress the man who knew Tig was an imposter. The full irony could collapse the conversation. What Pete didn't realize was that, in the grand scheme of relationships, it was easy to point to absolutes as to why a relationship works or not. Try to be faithful, prioritize, trust, and communicate, all so important, but it was the smaller conflicts that often derailed people from the happy road to the fiftieth anniversary. Arguments about who should pick up the milk after work, unload the dishwasher, and replace the toilet paper could kill the passion. Add to that the larger considerations of whose job is more important and where will the kids go to daycare, and Waterloo can ensue.

Later, perched on a footstool in her mother's old room, amidst cartons, shoeboxes, and manila folders, Wendy smiled at Tig.

"You were great today."

"You listened?"

"I had the radio on while I worked on this room. They're delivering a crib tomorrow."

"Did you like the guy whose wife refuses to acknowledge his low sperm count?"

"What was his motto? 'Shoot to get hot, shoot to stay hot'? People are hilarious."

"God, I know. I love that I don't have that confidentiality clause anymore. I love that I can talk about all of this."

"You could start your own private practice today and rake it in."

"I doubt it. People don't want tough love in person. I'd never get any return clients."

"Do you care? I mean, maybe traditional counseling isn't where it's at anymore. Maybe it's time for a change."

Tig bit her lip. "To be honest, I don't know. How many years did I imagine I would be happy doing the same thing every day?" Halfheartedly, she moved aside a box of lace doilies and handkerchiefs embroidered with violets. "Maybe that's what Pete was really thinking. Maybe the prospect of every-day-forever sent him packing."

Wendy sighed. "It appears, little sister, that we just happen to have chosen very one-dimensional, one-hit wonders who can't go the distance. Better to know now than in five years."

"I thought Pete was different. Why do you imagine we pick men who leave?"

"Imprinting."

Tig gave Wendy a sidelong glance and opened a box of faded yellow letters.

"I took a reading comprehension test in, like, eighth grade, and there was this thing about ducklings imprinting. Whatever they see when they hatch, they will immediately identify with it, even if it's an animal of a different species. We imprinted on a father that was there a short while and then gone forever."

"He died. I don't think we can blame him for leaving."

"I'm not blaming him. I'm just looking at facts. You don't know that imprinting isn't the same for humans." Wendy dusted off an old photo box, pulled out a couple of pictures, and brushed them with her fingers. "Did you ever get anything out of Pete? An explanation? Something?"

"It happened fast and we haven't talked since. He just said he wasn't excited about me."

Wendy frowned. "As in sexually?"

"Don't you wish? Then you could be the hottie of the two Monahan sisters. No. Just in general." She thought about it for a minute, then added, "Maybe he meant sexually, but I don't think so. We were good there, I think." She tugged at a handful of photographs.

Wendy flipped through the pile like a dealer at a casino. "What did you guys fight about?"

Tig remembered their conversation, Pete's exasperation. *Your mother and sister are number one and one point five on your list of importance. Your dog is probably, like, two and I'm barely number three. I'm competing neck and neck with your job.*

Tig shook the memory away and said, "He didn't feel prioritized," and hoped that would be enough to satisfy Wendy so they could stop talking about it. She shuffled through the envelopes in a shoebox, pulled out a couple and replaced them. "I've been meaning to show you this. Mom saved all her old letters from Aunt Edith. They aren't very interesting. Every single one starts with a weather and season report and then a comment about her health. Sometimes that's all there is. Listen. *Dear Hallie, Sunny and seventy degrees today. A little rain forecast for tonight. Sore feet.*" Tig opened another envelope and read, "*Dear Hallie, Ladybugs out. Don't you love summer? Arthritis better.*" Tig pulled out another one. "Then there's this one. *Dear Hallie, Cooler tonight. Frost likely. Fall would be my favorite season but it has such a bad reputation hanging around winter like it does. I wish you would reconsider. He's lovely. I see why you call him the Goat. Bunions killing me.*"

Wendy put down a pile of canceled checks mixed up with the photographs. "What?"

"That's all there is. 'He's lovely. Bunions killing me.' Did Mom call Dad 'the Goat'?"

"I never heard her do that. But she always loved goats. Remember how she used to say, 'Don't ever underestimate the working animal. Before there were coins, goats were traded for silver because of their value. Work hard, girls.'"

Tig shook her head. "As if we needed that reminder. But here's the weird thing. The date on this letter is September 1974."

"That was two years after Dad died."

Tig folded the letter and put it back into the shoebox. "So who was Aunt Edith talking about? Did Mom date?"

"I can't really imagine that. Must not have been very important if we never heard about him."

Tig groaned. "I'm going to go see Mom. You coming?"

Wendy didn't answer right away. She looked around the room. "I should have come sooner. To help you here. This sorting is a huge downer. I'm really tired."

"So you're not coming."

"Don't be that way."

"What way? Hoping for a little help, but being disappointed and frustrated?"

"Bossy, demanding, and parental."

"Shut up, Wendy."

"Very professional."

"Haven't you heard? I don't have to be professional anymore."

• • •

At Hope House, Hallie stood rocking in front of the picture window. Her tortured face reflected back into the room, stark and worried in contrast with the peaceful darkness of the outside grounds. With her arms folded in front of her, she kneaded both her elbows.

"Mom, calm down. It's me. It's Tig."

"Is he coming to pick me up? Where's Shiloh? C'mere girl." Suddenly, she moved nearer to Tig, despite the arthritis in her hip, the chronic pains in her feet. Her gray hair, no longer in tidy combs, stuck out like dandelion wisps around her face. Her purse lay on her bed, upended and deflated amidst tissues, an empty wallet, a hairbrush, and a weekly pill keeper. There was an abrasion on her forearm.

"What's that on your arm, Mom?"

Her mother turned away and paced back to the large window in her room. She pressed her hands on the glass, her eyes frantic and searching. Suddenly, she folded her arms together and scratched at the raw skin on her forearm. Tig approached and quietly said, "Mom? Stop scratching." Gently, she redirected her mother's hands and tried to make her meet her eyes.

Struggling feebly against her daughter, Hallie said, "Is he coming?"

"Who, Mom? Dad?"

With tears in her eyes, Hallie said, "No! Yes. Your father."

In the reflection of the window, superimposed against the sorrowful night sky, Tig saw Wendy in the doorway, the light of the hallway around her. Smoothing her mother's hair away from her face, she said, "Mama, look who's here." Wendy took a tentative step forward and Thatcher pranced from behind her into the room, her tail like a metronome tick-tocking a rapid hello.

Hallie bent at the waist, the stubborn hip slowing her descent. "Shiloh! Good girl." Loyal Thatcher, recognizing her alias, gave her doggie smile and went straight to Hallie's ear for a taste and identity confirmation. Satisfied, Thatcher sat and winked as Hallie massaged her ears.

"I'm tired, old boy, so tired. But I have so much work to do. I have so much work to do."

"No, Mom, not tonight. We're here now. Work's done."

"So much work to do," her mother repeated, but more slowly and with less conviction.

Tig touched her mother's shoulder and steered her to the bed. "It's late." She patted the covers. "Here, Thatcher. Up here, honey." The labradoodle jumped onto the rumpled blankets and settled herself onto Hallie's legs.

Hallie said, petting the dog, "Good boy, let's take a look at you." She sighed and positioned herself around the animal, shrinking herself down to fit.

Tig glanced at Wendy. "I didn't think you were coming."

"I wasn't going to. I planned to take a walk. Thatcher wouldn't move so I said, 'You wanna go see Grandma?' and she hopped right up. I figured I'd better bring her in for a visit. When I was here last week, I saw the woman at the end of the hall with a cat."

"I don't know why I never thought to do that. Mom's a wreck at night."

Wendy leaned against the wall of the corridor. "I've never seen her so . . . haphazard."

"The move set off her sundowner syndrome."

"It sounds like it would be a good thing, doesn't it? Like a restful retreat at sundown."

"It's a misnomer. The sun goes down and every worry or anxiety she kept hidden all those years bubbles to the surface and pops through. Can you imagine the shit that's going to come out of me? Usually it takes a lot more to calm her down. It never occurred to me the 'he' she wanted was Shiloh." Tig gestured with her head toward her mother, "You see why I didn't want to leave?"

A soft snoring sound wafted into the hall. Tig saw her mother's head propped up on a pillow, her mouth open to the ceiling. Thatcher did the same.

"Her younger self would be mortified if she saw this," said Wendy. "She was always so careful about appearances. All those years watching what she ate, exercising."

Tig said, nodding, "Her medical history was super simple. Before here, she wasn't on any meds."

"She's going to live a long time." The reality sat between them, the implications staring them down. One look at her sister, and Tig knew Wendy felt as relieved and afraid as she did.

Wendy sighed and said, "I don't suppose we can leave Thatcher here."

"I'll stay."

"You should have gone to Hawaii."

As she continued to stare at her mother, Tig said, "It's better this way."

"For who, Tig?"

"For Mom."

Chapter Eleven
Stoke That Furnace, Sparky

Tig fiddled with her collar, pressed it smooth, and adjusted her necklace; a slim chain with the word *Peace* stamped on a silver charm.

"Nervous?" Jean Harmeyer handed Tig a pen and legal pad while Macie placed a water bottle on the small table next to Tig's chair.

"Always."

"Good. You thrive on it. It makes you fierce."

"That's ridiculous."

"Whatever you say. You're the star."

"What's my hair doing?"

"Relax, they can't see you. It's radio, remember?"

Tig released a little cardboard laugh. "There are people in the audience. They can see me."

Jean said, "Maybe I should put makeup into our budget. You do look a little terrible."

"I've been spending a lot of time at the nursing home."

Macie spoke into her headset from the control room. "Take some time off, Dr. M. This will be here when you get back. We've had some good shows. Look how manymore people are here."

"I can hear you, Macie," said Jean. "She cannot take time off."

With the house lights up in the red-seated auditorium, Tig saw what looked like a Whitman's Sampler of people: all colors, shapes, and sizes were present. A man in a Packers hat and camouflage hunting jacket lounged next to a fussy, tidy man dressed like it was picture day in elementary school: blue vest, loafers, and hair gel. The female college-student population was well represented in plaid flannel pajama pants and flip-flops. Theirs was the casual beauty of youth made complete with a messy ponytail and fresh-from-the-pillow skin. A smattering of seasoned professional women sipped coffee and sent mobile e-mails.

Tig checked the time and said, "Let's do this." The recorded music swelled along with the opening announcer, and Tig's nervousness fluttered around her chest and into her carotids. She flushed and the audience sat up in their seats.

The first caller was a man. "I can't get my wife to stop telling her friends about everything in our lives."

Tig jotted a note on a legal pad. "Tell me more about that."

"She's got no filter. Once, I overheard her telling someone on the phone that I prefer boxers over briefs. I mean, I go to the parish fall festival, and I never know if the person I'm talking to knows about my hemorrhoids."

"Oh, I doubt she goes that far."

"Really? I have a red cartoon devil shoveling coal tattooed in an extremely intimate location. Last week, I ran into my wife's friend—not her best friend, mind you—and she said, 'Stoke that furnace, Sparky.'"

Laughter erupted from the crowd, and the women who came with their girlfriends nodded knowingly.

Tig said, "Well, I can tell you straight up, if you don't like it, she shouldn't do it. Have you talked about it?"

Exasperation flooded the telephone line. "Sure, I have. She says I'm being too sensitive. I told her, 'How would you like it if I told everyone your nickname was Whiskers in high school?'"

There was a collective gasp among the women. Heads shook as if to say, *Traitor!*

Tig said, "You two have to set up some ground rules. Like everything in your private square, shoulders to crotch, is illegal conversation for playgroup or a staff meeting. Anything that might be considered sensitive in your medical chart cannot be discussed. Add to that your bank account, bedroom Kama Sutra, and anything else you want. If you have a collection of tiny president saltshakers and you don't want it talked about, add that to the list. Come to an agreement."

There was a moment of silence on the line. "That sounds great in theory, but how do I hold her accountable? What if she does it anyway?"

"Well, that's the problem, isn't it? I'm here to say whether it's fair or not, and how to make it more fair. That's the definition of an agreement." Tig paused a minute and added, "You send her to me."

The caller hung up and the *Applause* light flashed. Behind the glass in the booth, Macie pulled an enameled chopstick out of her hair and chewed on an end.

Tig said, "Hi caller, are you there?"

It was quiet on the line. Tig looked at Macie's intense and worried face.

"Caller?"

"My husband uses prostitutes."

Without missing a beat, Tig said, "Is there more you want to say?"

"What more is there?" The caller made a sound Tig couldn't identify.

"Are you laughing?"

The woman's voice, high-pitched and sad, said, "No, I'm sorry. I just found out."

"You're very upset."

The woman sniffed in answer. "He says I just don't understand."

"What's to understand? You want him to stop. He should stop."

"Yes."

"Tell him."

The air changed in the room, the connection died, and Tig looked around the studio at the listeners. She brushed her hair back.

"A relationship is sacred," she began. "Whatever that relationship is, whether it's with your hairstylist, your mail carrier, your spouse, it's a sacred pact. If you want it to continue, you can't cross the line and expect the person on the other side of the fence to cross it with you. If you suddenly stop tipping after a haircut or begin putting your recyclables in your mailbox, the people on the receiving end will be confused, disappointed, wronged. You have to define what the relationship is based on. Kindness? Fidelity? Casserole dishes with Bisquick? Find out, be consistent, check in. Build relationship equity."

It was stone quiet in the room.

Tig glanced at Jean, who nodded an almost imperceptible 'go on.'

"You can't go with the 'don't ask, don't tell' policy. Ask. Then ask again. Then make sure you tell a thing or two while you're at it. If you get it all out there on the table, in the open, then the rest of it is choice and prioritization. My mom always said that when it comes to relationships, it's important to pay as much attention to what people do as what they say. Only through their actions will you truly know where you stand."

A woman in the front row began madly texting someone. The call lights lit up and Tig steadied the microphone. "Hello. You're on the air."

"There's this woman. I want to talk to her about something. I think I'm starting to understand her."

Tig immediately recognized Pete's voice. Her eyes darted to Macie, who was in conversation with Jean.

Tig stuttered, "I—well . . . ." She saw the exit sign and considered its message. She locked eyes with an expectant-looking woman in the audience, and remembered her role, the part she had agreed to play for money: Tig the strong, Tig the funny, Tig the answer lady. Not the part she felt at the moment, Tig the wreck. She remembered seeing Pete's baseball cap that morning behind the closet door, thought of his straw-like, chlorine-fried blond hair, and recalled the feeling of homesickness that nearly swamped her ability to get ready for the day.

"Go on," Tig said.

"I liked everything about this woman, but . . . ."

Tig thought of her mother's fearful face, the new tremor in her hands. The people in the auditorium waited for the serene, nonjudgmental response from the resident expert and gazed at Tig with quiet expectation. Narrowing her eyes at Pete's unseen face, she said, "What? She wasn't exciting enough? Let me guess, you were not *in* love? Did the hot sex turn to tepid grocery shopping? Is that it?"

"No," he said quickly. "The problem is that she's so busy taking care of everyone else in her life that there's little room for me."

"Maybe she was busy doing what she had to do, instead of doing what she wanted."

"She didn't need me."

Tig opened her mouth to insist that she did need him. But that insistence clogged her throat. People whispered in the auditorium. Macie and Jean stared at Tig.

"You didn't need me, Tig."

Realization lit up Macie's face. She fingered the dog collar at her throat and leaned over to whisper to Jean. Jean turned her head and stared.

Tig said, "Yes . . . ."

Macie hit a button. The theme song blasted out of the surround-sound speakers, cutting off any qualification Tig might have offered. *Yes, you are right. Yes, I did.*

A loud voice-over announced a commercial break, followed by a buzzing of conversation among the audience. Jean bolted out of the control booth and strode over to Tig.

"What was that?"

Tig brushed her face with her hands. "Are we almost through?"

"How are you feeling?"

"How manymore calls?"

"We'll fill in with some cream puff call-ins, then complete the hour with music."

"That was more than I bargained for."

"He said he needs you. That call sounded like love."

Tig stared at Jean. "You think it's love to take a very private conversation into a public forum?"

With a pointed look, Jean said, "That's what we're doing here. Did you miss that?"

Tig looked away.

Jean said, "I bet he didn't think it would take such a serious turn. Hearing it over the speakers gives everything weight. A broadcast almost forces things like threats of divorce and proposals."

"Maybe he's thinking, 'Tag, you're it.'"

"Cut and run." Jean smiled.

"Coward."

"I'd be afraid of you, too, if I wasn't your boss."

Macie knocked on the booth's glass window and gestured at her watch. Jean made her way back inside the small soundproof room.

"Okay, I can do this. I'm ready."

The *On the Air* sign flickered. Macie sat ready with a caller, but was interrupted by a loud unfamiliar voice in the auditorium.

"Well, well, well, if it isn't the relationship bitch I keep hearing so much about."

Newman Harmeyer stood in the open doorway at the back of the studio, his words bounced down the aisle like runaway basketballs. The audience gasped.

He turned to them. "Ladies and gentlemen, did you know that Dr. Monahan here singlehandedly ended my twelve-year marriage? Why doesn't somebody call and ask about that?"

Newman lumbered closer to the stage. He was so disheveled that Tig wouldn't have recognized him on the street, dressed as he was in gray sweat pants and a plaid hunting shirt buttoned inaccurately across his belly. He stumbled during his rapid descent down the aisle.

Jean stood at attention in the booth and Macie, unschooled in radio crises, was frozen in place, staring.

Tig walked to the edge of the stage. "When you decided to have an affair, you effectively ended the marriage, whether you knew it at the time or not. I mean, unless that was in your vows. I promise to love, honor, and screw around as long as we both shall live and my wife doesn't find out."

Newman shouted, "She means nothing to me. Jean, she was nothing."

Tig shook her head. "I hope that's true, for your sake, Mr. Harmeyer, because I doubt your lover will enjoy coming back to be your 'nothing' again." She pointed to the *On the Air* sign.

With rapt attention, the audience watched the drama play out on stage.

Newman turned and yelled at the booth, "Jean! Jean, don't do this. Let me back into the house."

Behind the glass in the booth, Jean pointed and Macie switched over to music. The tension in Jean's jaw was visible even from where Tig stood. Stiff and unyielding, she walked out of sight.

"Jean." Newman's face smeared into a mass of sorrowful confusion. He mumbled her name again, and Newman's bravado slipped off his shoulders, down his arms, and seemed to drip from his fingertips.

Touched, Tig walked down the steps of the stage and said, "Mr. Harmeyer, let's get you into a cab."

He allowed himself to be guided up the corridor between the array of faces in the crowd, some compassionate, others sour. He stumbled once and muttered, "I love her."

Tig supported his arm and said, "I don't think it seemed that way to Jean."

He wrenched free and shoved her aside. "Fuck you."

Tig lost her footing and banged against the theater wall.

"This is your fault. Your fucking fault." He advanced, his arm drawn back.

Two men in the audience started in his direction.

"Newman." Jean Harmeyer's voice boomed from backstage. Newman froze and looked for his wife's face. Without showing herself, she said, "Go wherever it is you're calling home these days."

Cowed, Newman frantically searched the room, dropped his arms and left more steadily than he had arrived, muttering, "I don't have a home."

Out of the shadows, Jean walked to the front of the stage. All heads turned her way. "Well, that's all, folks. Tell your friends. Never a dull moment on *Is That Fair?* with Dr. Monahan. And remember, relationships are loaded guns. Don't operate them without a safety."

While Jean spoke, Tig moved quickly onto the stage and out of sight. Conversation broke out in earnest. Cell phones were dialed and Tig, Jean, and Macie took refuge off stage in the green room. Macie said, "Holy shit, you two. What do we need callers for?"

• • •

Tig lifted each leg slowly, and climbed into her car. The radio week was over. She rummaged for her phone in her bag, took it off vibrate, and for the thousandth time considered calling Pete. She squinted at the screen. Five missed calls. There was voicemail from Wendy.

"Hey, I don't feel so good. I'll call you from the hospital."

Tig sat up straight.

The second call from Wendy sounded scared. "I'm in labor. I can't get through at the radio station. I just threw up."

Tig fastened her seatbelt, started her car, and pressed the next button. Two hang-ups. She listened to the last message.

Weak-voiced and weary, Wendy said, "Hey, you're an aunt." A male in the background said something. Wendy responded, "No, I'll take her." Back on the line she said, "I'm at St. Mary's 212."

• • •

Tig rushed down the hall of St. Mary's birth suites and opened a darkened room. The baby, like a tiny wrapped burrito with a striped hat, was parked next to the bed in an open Plexiglas rolling crib. A tiny, ruddy heel peeked out from under the swaddling. Wendy, curled on her side and covered with a sheet, looked too small to have delivered a whole human being, even this tiny one. "Isn't she pretty?" Tig stood over the infant, tugged the white flannel blanket under the infant's chin. Wendy went on to say, "She looks like a bush baby when her eyes are open."

When Tig saw her sister she started. Bloody red masses colored both of Wendy's irises. "What happened to your eyes?"

"I broke blood vessels when I was pushing. Thankfully, it went fast. I was only in labor for a total of three hours."

"The entire time my cell phone was off."

"It gave me something to swear about in labor."

"I'm really sorry, Wen. I thought we'd have more warning."

"You and me both." Wendy's eyes filled with tears.

Tig sat on the bed. "I'm so sorry I wasn't here."

"That's not it. The nurses were great. It's just that I don't know how I'm going to do this without totally screwing it up." She grabbed Tig's wrist with icy fingers. "Promise me you'll help. Promise me you won't let me hurt her."

"Of course you won't hurt her."

"I could drop her. Or forget I have her."

"You won't." Tig brushed her sister's face with her hand. "You're exhausted. Go to sleep, now."

"Don't you want to know what I named her?"

"Yes, tell me."

"Clementine. It's a cartoon name. Like ours, and we turned out all right. Right?"

Tig smiled. "Right. Clementine. It's perfect."

"Will you stay until I fall asleep?"

"I'll stay as long as you need me."

In minutes, Wendy was lightly snoring. Tig was about to leave when her phone rang, the sound muffled by her pocket. She looked at the screen. It was Pete. She almost answered it. She almost did. But she didn't have the energy, and put the phone back in her pocket. Tig took her sister's hand, then touched her niece's foot. The baby's foot looked for all the world like a tiny new red potato with peas attached.

She swallowed hard, feeling her eyes well with tears in the quiet hospital room. Tig grew up knowing she would be a mother, like she knew she would learn to drive or go to college. It was only just recently that she had begun to acknowledge that there was another variable in the equation of adding a human to the world: she needed a plus one.

She'd always been a loner. When Wendy graduated from high school without college plans, Tig remembered feeling cheated. All of her friends' siblings had decorated their graduation caps with their prospective colleges—UW-Madison, USC, Notre Dame—but not Wendy. She'd glued flower petals over the top of her mortarboard and said, "I'm a free agent. I can't commit." Tig knew what that really meant for herself: she'd have to spend more time living under the shadow of the mercurial Wendy. The beautiful, free-spirited Monahan sister. The one *Most Likely to Travel the World*. When you are the sister *Most Likely to Balance Your Checkbook*, you are easily overlooked in the most unfair of ways. "Excitement" was what most people wanted, apparently. Excitement and unpredictability.

Clementine made a little pigeon coo in her throat that touched Tig in an immediate and alarming way. The sound seemed to fill her own throat with something she would describe later to Wendy as necessity.

"You make that sound again, Clementine, and I'll whisk you away and raise you as my own."

• • •

Hours later, she collected Thatcher from her house and drove to the nursing home. In the parking lot, Tig rested her head against the seat and considered going home, sleeping for a week. Suspended from the rearview mirror was the bracelet she had found in her mother's room.

She pulled it down. *If I could tell you.* She undid the clasp, placed the bracelet around her wrist and admired it, then fished her phone out and finally dialed Pete. It clicked over to voicemail. Tig opened her mouth, meaning to tell him she loved him, longing for a simple response. Instead she said, "Hey, I'm an aunt," and hung up.

Chapter Twelve
Stray Dog List

Tig searched the St. Mary's parking garage with Wendy's keys in hand. She pressed the lock/unlock buttons as a locator, and used the insistent beeping sound to find her sister's car. Inside, Tig pulled the visor down, looking for the parking garage ticket. A dried bundle of rosemary with a flattened green velvet ribbon fell into her lap, revealing a glossy photo of Phil beneath it: perfectly straight teeth, a thick head of hair, and the facial bones of a Grecian created the unlikely image of a terrifically handsome man who didn't want children.

Tig flipped the photo over and read, "There's rosemary, that's for remembrance," written in blue ink and signed with a cursive P. She replaced the bundle, which was apparently given to her sister to combat any post-relationship amnesia, and started the car. Now her sister held the ultimate genetic forget-me-not bundle, she thought.

Wendy waited in a wheelchair with a nurse at the hospital's exit, Clementine already tucked into her car seat on the ground next to her. Tig hopped out of the driver's seat and helped Wendy and Clementine get settled. Considering the triathlon of labor, delivery, and recovery, Tig said with a healthy degree of wonder, "You look good, Wen."

Wendy shifted on the doughnut-shaped plastic pillow in the front seat. "That's because you can't see my ass. If you could, you'd re-admit me." Tig accelerated and the car locks thumped shut, sealing the three safely and completely together as they moved forward as a family. "I thought we could stop to see Mom before we go home."

Wendy crumpled in the front seat, her head resting on the window. "What? No. No way. My milk hasn't even come in. We're going home."

"Just for a minute. She's your mother."

"I'm not Wonder Woman."

"Just for a second?"

Wendy turned and glared at Tig. "When you get pregnant, you can deliver in Mom's shower if you want. We are going home."

"Maybe tomorrow, then."

Wendy said, "I feel like I've been hit by a bus. God, my ass is killing me." She repositioned herself and the plastic pillow farted. Wendy shook her head in disgust. "The baby cried all night. I tried feeding her, but nothing happened."

"Did you call for help?"

"Yeah, the nurse came in and tried to shove my breast into the baby's mouth. She said my breasts were pendulous."

"Pendulous? God. What did you say?"

"I told her to fuck off."

At home, Tig nosed the car into the driveway. Wendy unbuckled and gingerly moved to the edge of her seat. With a puff of exertion, she stood and walked up the path, leaving Tig, the baby, and all of the post-baby hospital debris behind. At the door she ungracefully yanked her underwear from her rear end.

"Come here, little one." Tig hauled the safety seat out of the middle of the car. "God, this car seat is heavy."

So as not to wake the sleeping infant, she maneuvered carefully and followed her sister into the house. Wendy was already under the covers in what used to be her own mother's twin bed. At a loss, Tig glanced around the room, saw the crib still in its box. The place looked anything but ready for a baby.

"Wendy," Tig whispered. "Wendy, I'm going to leave her in the car seat, right here on the floor."

Her sister rolled on her back and said, "No, put the seat in bed with me."

Tig considered this and decided it was not the worst idea; the baby would be closer to Wendy, safe from any rolling around on her sister's part, and easily gotten to. She hefted the seat onto the bed and said, "Okay, she's right here. Wendy."

"Yeah, I hear you." Then she rolled onto her side and touched her daughter's foot, a decidedly protective move from an exhausted mother.

"You two get some sleep. I'm going for supplies and to check on Mom. I'm taking Thatcher."

"Whatever."

Thatcher stood at the door, eager and willing. As they approached Hope House, Thatcher sat at attention in the front seat, as if to say, *We humans are going to visit Grandma.*

At Hope House, Tig said, "Stay, Thatcher. I'll be right back."

Male and female voices fluttered out of her mother's room. Tig froze at the doorway. Her mother sat knee to knee with Dr. Jenson. Her mother's face could only be described as beatific.

"Oh, Dan," she said. "You're so sweet to me."

The hair stood up on Tig's arms. "Excuse me," she said.

The doctor jumped like a teen in the back of a convertible with the police spotlight illuminating undone buttons. He dropped her mother's hand and backed away.

"Tig, hello."

Unperturbed, her mother said, "We're going for the Christmas tree today."

Tig's gaze darted between them.

"She thinks I'm your father."

"Don't let her think that. You're not my father." Tig turned to her mother. "Mama, this is Dr. Jenson from the hospital."

Immediately, Hallie frowned and looked from her daughter to the doctor and back again.

"I . . . I . . . I'm so tired." Her hands dropped to her lap and she worked a frail tissue that had fallen from her sleeve.

Tig looked into her mother's eyes. "Wendy had her baby, Mom. It's a girl; isn't that wonderful? You're a grandmother."

Hallie said, "A girl? A girl what?"

Tig petted her mother's arm. "A baby girl. Wendy was pregnant, remember?"

"Wendy? Pregnant? No, that won't do. What will your father think? He'll say I didn't watch her enough." Looking over her daughter's head, she searched Dr. Jenson's face and said, "Dan? What's happening?"

In a soothing voice, Dr. Jenson said, "Hallie, it's all right. Everything is fine. Remember the Christmas trees you used to have in your clinic?"

"One for the cats. Another for the dogs. They were donated. Who did that, I wonder?" The wrinkles in her forehead melted away. Tig sat back on her haunches and watched them talk about the past, a time when her mother was in charge and competent.

"Excuse me, I'm sorry to interrupt." An unfamiliar nurse walked into the room with a syringe and a glass that looked like juice. "Hallie needs her B_{12} shot. It'll just take a minute and I'll get out of your way."

Tig and Dr. Jenson moved to the hallway. The privacy curtain rustled. Tig said, "I should know better. I'm a fricking psychologist. It seems like I always get her worked up."

"Alzheimer's is a trickster. One day reality therapy seems the way to go, and the next the only way to keep them calm is with validation. It's a dance they always get to lead."

"I wanted to tell her about Wendy." She looked into the doctor's face. "My sister. You met her the other day. She delivered a little girl.

The old Mom would have been thrilled. I wanted to tell someone. You know, that I'm an aunt."

Dr. Jenson said, "Your mom was always hard on herself, too. It's wonderful news about your sister. How's she doing?"

"Cranky, but that's usual. The baby is beautiful. So, you were friends with my parents? Good friends?"

"I'd like to think so, yes."

"What was my dad like?"

"I knew your mother better. Your father was someone I knew in a secondhand way. My brother and he were always horsing around. Your dad was really good at sports." He paused. "Your mother and he were good together. She loved him."

Tig took in this information, none of it new and on a whim said, "Was he funny?"

"They had charisma. That's what you noticed about your dad and mom. They were funny together, engaging. They had great stories."

Tig brushed a lock of hair off her forehead, and the silver bracelet glittered and slid down her wrist. Dr. Jenson gestured at it and said, "That's a pretty bracelet."

She smiled and lifted her wrist. "Just another mystery of my mother's. I found it in her stuff. It's engraved." She tilted the silver tile. "I don't know where it came from. I never saw it before."

"'If I could tell you,'" he read. "If I remember right, that's the beginning of a poem of some sort." He shifted his weight and looked away.

The nurse emerged and stepped between them. "She seems ready for bed. I'm not sure visitors are a good idea right now."

Dr. Jenson said, "I'm expected back anyway. Tig, nice to hear your news. Give Wendy my best."

Tig nodded and then said, "I'd really love to get together. Talk about my parents sometime."

The tall, distinguished man brightened and nodded with enthusiasm. "I'd love that. Soon!" He touched the pager on his hip and turned away.

Tig hesitated, and finally decided the nurse was right and it was time to leave. She took two steps and stopped just as Fern Fobes pushed herself out of her doorway. She wore a dressing gown and white canvas tennis shoes with the backs tamped down. "Did I hear right? Are you an aunt?" She dabbed at her nose with a tissue.

Tig nodded, gazing into her mother's room.

"Congratulations. Your mom may not fully understand what's happened, but that doesn't make you any less of an aunt. I hope you're celebrating a little."

"If you mean by buying baby supplies and grocery shopping, then yeah, it's a real party."

"Get me a diaper for this nose, will ya. It hasn't been dry since my husband was alive," Fern said. "Speaking of husbands, that Dr. Jenson is a real looker."

"My mom thinks he's my dad."

"That's nice for her, I bet. He's so devoted. He comes every day. The only person who comes that regularly for me is the nurse with my stool softener. Some people have all the luck."

"He comes every day? I come every day, but I don't always see him."

"Evenings usually. After you head out, or before you come again."

Tig frowned. "For some kind of therapy? I wonder how that's being billed."

Fern skillfully navigated her wheelchair next to Tig. "Come on; I'll roll you out. You better get some sleep. Don't you have a show tomorrow?"

Tig brightened. "Are you listening?"

"Yes, madam. All us oldies listen. My son Alec does, too; he needs a good laugh. You're kind of a celebrity around here"

Tig snorted. "A pretty dubious one. Did you hear the last show? It was like a feeding frenzy."

"Best thing on the radio since *Yours Truly, Johnny Dollar.* Sometimes my son is here when you are. You two should hook up."

"Hook up? Really?"

"Isn't that what you people do these days? Isn't that like get a coffee? Watch a movie?"

"Not exactly, Fern."

At the front door of the facility, Tig and Fern stopped to look at the birds through the glass, busy and oblivious to the other odd birds flitting on the human side of the glass. She watched a chickadee lift a wing and peck furiously at an unseen irritation. "I'm not sure if I can keep it up, the radio."

"Taking care of everyone in the world is a big job."

Tig laughed. "Not everyone in the world. Just the people who call in."

Fern tilted her head and said, "And your mother, sister, and now a niece." She lifted her almost weightless gloved hand and placed it on Tig's hand. The only place on Fern's face free of wrinkles was at the top of her cheeks right under her eyes.

"Fern? Can I ask you a personal question?"

"Certainly, my dear."

"Why are you here? You seem so, well . . . well."

Fern opened her mouth, started to speak, then sealed her mouth shut, burying her lips. She took a breath and said, "Oh, you are good. I'll give you that, Dr. Monahan." She chuckled and released Tig's hand.

A puzzled grin crossed Tig face. "What? What's the joke?"

"You're not going to add me to your stray dog list. Oh, no. I'm keeping my complaints to myself." Rotating her wheelchair like a pro, Fern turned away from the front doors and shook her head. Without turning to look Tig's way again, she said, "You almost had me there."

• • •

Tig walked up the steps of her house, balancing newly purchased baby items. She dropped the jumbo pack of infant diapers onto the stoop, and shoved the front door open and wrestled the rest of the baby loot inside. Out of the first bag she pulled little plastic prong-plugs that would soon go into all the electric sockets. She rummaged through another bag, found the toilet lid lock and bumper pad meant to soften all of the hard edges in the house. Tig tilted her head and listened. A mixture of mewling cat and sorrowful wails streamed down the hall. She rushed to the bathroom, where she heard the shower along with terrible racking sobs.

"Wendy? What's going on? What's wrong?"

Tig pulled the shower curtain, exposing Wendy and the baby in the shower, soaking wet and both of them howling. Wendy had her back to the water, shielding the seriously perturbed newborn. Clementine was still encased in a pink onesie, now sopping wet. Her red face and tiny nasal cry would have been heartbreaking if not for the louder crying that came from her mother. Tig grabbed a fluffy towel and folded the baby into it. "Oh, honey. C'mere, sweetie; come to your auntie." In the shower, Tig saw her sister cradling her breasts while water streamed over her shoulders and deflated tummy.

"Don't look at me," Wendy cried, turning her back on her sister. "I'm hideous."

"That's what this is all about? Your body being 'hideous'?"

Her sister let out an anguished moan. "No! Clementine's been crying since you left. My milk finally came in and now my boobs are so big she can't get them in her mouth. They feel like they're about to burst. I called the nurse and she said to stand in the shower, that it would help with the pressure. I couldn't leave the baby out so I tried to take her onesie off. That just made her madder. I've gotta go back to the hospital. I can't do this."

Jiggling the baby, Tig said, "I'm going to calm her and dry her off. You stay in there as long as you need, then we'll get her fed. Geez, it's steamy in here." She flipped the switch to the bathroom fan and it roared into action. Clementine took a few shuddered breaths and, maintaining her prune-like worry, she stopped crying. The room seemed oddly quiet without the infant's colicky complaint.

Wendy said, "She stopped. What did you do?"

"Nothing. I didn't do anything but turn on the fan." Tig shut the fan off and the baby squirmed, placed her knot of fist into her mouth and screwed her face up like an old man's sourpuss. Tig quickly turned the fan back on. As it sputtered, the baby's face unwrinkled. "Oh my God, she likes the fan."

"Thank the Lord." Wendy shut the shower off and wrapped herself in a towel. She sat on the toilet, soaking wet and dripping. The towel dropped to her waist, revealing eggplant-like breasts that contrasted with her white sternum and sculpted clavicle. "I tried to milk them like the nurse on the phone suggested. That didn't work. And the baby wouldn't stop crying long enough to latch on."

Content to stare wildly around the little bathroom, with the fan ringing in her ears and wrapped in her aunt's arms, the baby seemed harmless and simple. "Why don't you try now?" Tig handed Clementine over, the corner of the swaddling dropping in the handoff. Wendy tucked the infant's head closer to her breast. "My nipples look like planets."

"I read they become darker and bigger so the baby can see them better."

"Well, that's an okay idea, but try fitting a planet into a coin purse."

"People have done it before today, Wen."

"Okay, baby, open up."

Miraculously, upon feeling Wendy's breast on her cheek, the baby opened her mouth and clamped on. Wendy let out a low growl and her upper lip twitched. "What'd that book say about this pain? Shhhiiit. Everyone goes on and on about how wonderful nursing is and nobody talks about how much it hurts."

"I don't know, Wen. I've never done it before."

"Do you think it's just me? That there's something wrong with me?"

"No, I'm sure it hurts everyone in the beginning."

"Why then? Why would this hurt so much; what could the purpose possibly be?"

Tig pulled another towel out of the linen closet and draped it around Wendy's shoulders. The face of her niece was partially submerged in her sister's breast, a dark blue vein drawing a line connecting mother and daughter. Tig folded the baby's tiny arm into her swaddling and whispered her fingers over the top of her head. "I imagine it's getting you ready for the caring that's going to hurt so much more later on."

Chapter Thirteen
Splash Some Water on Your Face and Get on with Your Life

Tig paced backstage through the obstacle course of soundboard equipment, ropes, and old metal folding chairs. Jean Harmeyer fiddled with her headset, and Macie tried to clean the back of Tig's dark blouse with a lint brush. Tig said, "It's been six weeks. Clementine is still crying all day and Wendy is a mess. She barely gets dressed and almost never showers. If she isn't nursing, she's running that damn pump at all hours of the day and night. We've got enough frozen milk to feed that baby into high school. Wendy looks like Skeletor."

"Colic. Mine had colic, too. Nearly killed me." Jean picked at her French manicure. "Nothing you can do but wait it out. I was lucky. It only lasted three months, but my neighbor's kid screamed for a year."

Horrified, Tig said, "A year? Wendy will never make it. Shit, I'll never make it!" Tig looked at her watch, counting the minutes before the next broadcast. "It was almost easier living with my mom. Sure, half the time she put the dish soap away in the fridge and I worried she'd wander away and never return, but at least she was quiet. The only time the baby is quiet is if she's nursing." Tig scratched her forehead. "Maybe Wendy will wander away and never return."

"Hate to break it to you, but you wanted her here." Jean patted Tig on the shoulder.

"I like a lot of people in theory."

Macie strolled over to hand Tig her headphones. "When my sister was nursing, she fed her a bottle every now and then. Just to give herself a break." Macie's black hair was parted in the middle and braided. She wore burgundy fingerless gloves and a frilly black, almost transparent shirt displaying a red bra underneath.

Tig looked her over. She said to Jean, "Is scary girl over here right? Can you do that? The La Leche legions won't come and get you?"

"I did it. But I sure didn't talk about it." Smiling prettily she said, "Breast is best, y'know." Looking at the clock and the crowd, she said, "The show is catching on, Tig. Ratings are good, the execs are happy. Looks like you've got a new career."

Tig gave Jean a halfhearted thumbs-up and said, "Awesome." She slid her fingertips under her eyes, making sure no residual makeup or fatigue hid there, and got ready to give her last bit of energy to the show.

Jean clapped her hands. "Okay, troops, let's make this a good one. Not too many surprises, just good radio."

Tig waited for the lights to go on and off, followed closely by a voice: "He loads the dishwasher like a total moron."

Tig touched her headset and raised her eyebrows. "That's your complaint? Dishwasher loading?"

"How hard is it to load a dishwasher? Glasses on the top. Plates on the bottom. It's not rocket science."

"So, tell him you'll load the dishwasher and then you get to do it the way you want it done."

"Oh, no. That's just what he wants. He wants me to take it over, like everything else in the house."

"As I see it, you have three choices. Do it yourself, give him free reign to do it any way he wants, or figure out what's really bothering you."

"That's it? That's the big advice I get from the relationship expert? Glad it was free."

Tig turned her head to the gasping crowd. "Well, there is another option."

"Yeah? What is it?"

"Splash some water on your face and get on with your life. It's clear your problems have nothing to do with the dishwasher. It might have something to do with calling your husband a very disrespectful name, or that you have a tantrum if your glasses get washed on the bottom shelf. Either way, figure it out on your own time."

Tig gestured to Macie to disconnect and turned to the crowd.

"It's brutal at our house right now. We have a colicky baby and I'm exhausted. But even if I wasn't so tired and short-tempered, I think we can agree that calling names, mandating behavior, and manufacturing small issues to cover larger ones is never okay in a relationship. Sometimes it's hard to see when we are doing it, and sometimes all we need is a little reality. And that's exactly what we're here for on *Is That Fair?*"

The theme song played, and the audience applauded and tapped their feet to the music. Tig knew she had just described herself. But the show was off and running, and she didn't have time to reflect.

"Is this Dr. Monahan?"

"Yes, how can we help you today?"

"My husband is having an affair." It was a simple statement made in a girlish voice.

"I assume this is not okay with you, since you're calling," Tig said quietly.

"We were high school sweethearts. I've only ever been with him, and he me, or so I thought. For twenty-one years, I was wrong about him."

The studio fell dead quiet.

"Tell me more," Tig urged.

"He wants to move out. Says he's in love. She's nineteen years younger than me. Him." The woman took a sip from a liquid. Swallowed. "We have two children. He wrote a letter to me with bullet points on how I was such a bad wife, it forced him to find someone else."

There were murmurs in the crowd. Discussions in the back row. Women telling their own stories, stories of their best friends. War stories.

"I don't know why I called. You can't help me."

Tig almost shouted, "Wait, caller! Are you there? Don't hang up."

The woman cleared her throat and said, "Go on."

"You're right. I can't help your situation, but maybe we can help how you think about yourself. What he's done is not fair. He's broken your marriage agreement and decided to absolve himself from all responsibility by making you the fall guy. I can lay your mind at ease today. Your marriage didn't end because of you, no matter what his list of bullet points says. The fact that he would write a list like that tells me all I ever need or want to know about him."

"But, he said our sex life was . . . ."

Tig interrupted the woman.

"Were you solely in charge of your sex life? No! So cross that one off the list. In fact, I bet you have the list in front of you."

"I do."

Tig could almost see the woman obsessively smoothing the sheet, trying to iron the problems out on her own.

"I give you permission to cross out everything on that list that wasn't one hundred percent your duty. It won't take you long to draw a line, with a permanent marker, through every last one of his complaints. When you're done, don't throw it away. You're going to need it to remind yourself that you were not the only one in charge of keeping your marriage afloat." Tig took a breath and said, "Are you still with me?"

The woman's voice, a little stronger than before, came through the headset. "I am."

Tig raised her head and addressed the auditorium. "You know, experts say that the incidence of heart disease in the population is one in two. Ironically, that is the exact same proportion of the population that divorces. Affairs, broken relationships, shattered promises: this is the other heart disease, one we don't have any medication for."

The crowd laughed.

"Caller, I do have some advice to give, if you haven't already heard enough."

"Go on, it's okay."

"Get a good counselor, someone who you like and is on your side. Make nonnegotiable dates with that therapist. Circle your wagons, call your friends, and get a good lawyer. With that husband, sounds like you're going to need one."

There was more applause. Tig continued. "If he comes back and wants to do some repairs, it's okay to try again. I'm not leading the charge for a divorce. There's always room for forgiveness. You know . . . ." She winked at the crowd and added, "Until there's not."

The theme song built to cover the coming commercial break, and Tig took a breath to relax. She sipped her water and looked at her watch. She was beginning to recognize some regulars in the crowd. She waved at a nice-looking man holding hands with an elfin woman. They had talked to Tig before the show, saying they were using her show as pre-marriage counseling talking points. There was a group of four women who occupied the middle seats and came every show, bringing what looked like sushi, chocolate, and possibly wine. They were like a cheering section, and Tig fully expected signs and body paint before the year was out.

The music surged again and another caller came on.

"I'm the punch line in all my wife's jokes."

Tig raised her brows. "Can you give us an example?"

"Yeah, we walked into a party and my wife pointed to me and asked her girlfriend, 'Does this ass make me look fat?'"

There was an explosion of laughter. Someone in the crowd shouted, "Did it?"

Tig laughed herself. "I'm sorry. We just didn't expect it to be that funny."

"How about this one. We were out with a group of friends and the conversation turned to how no one has time for sex anymore. And my wife chimes in with: 'We'd have a lot more sex, but there's so much I could do with that ten minutes.'"

More laughter from the crowd, especially, Tig noted, from the central female contingent.

Tig diplomatically said, "She's obviously a very funny woman."

"Oh, she's hilarious; that's the problem. Everybody excuses a good joke. When we use walkie-talkies on the ski hill or at Disney, my wife insists that my handle is Tiny Dancer. Inevitably, I'll be having a nice conversation with some person, y'know, while waiting in line. And boom, here comes my wife's voice: 'Tiny Dancer, come in Tiny.' I think we all know what she's referring to."

Tig smiled in spite of herself. "Has she always done this?"

"Yes, but it's getting meaner."

"You know, mean humor is easy. I should know. I'm a genius meanie. Kind humor is harder. Challenge her. If she thinks she's so funny, why not try raising the bar."

"Maybe." The caller sounded unconvinced.

Tig said, "Have you told her it hurts your feelings?"

"No." Pausing, he fiddled with the phone. "She'd make a joke."

"There's your issue then, and I'm here to tell you. That's not fair."

She peered over her shoulder. Macie and Jean signaled that time was running short. Quickly she added, "And caller, you might want to find out what she's so mad at you about."

Someone from the audience yelled, "There's gotta be something." And the group nodded, everybody was on board.

Macie gestured, holding up one finger.

"I guess we have time for one more caller. Are you there?"

"Yeah, like, what I wanna know is, like, can ya get genital warts if you're, like, a virgin?"

Tig's eyebrows raised again. "Yes."

"God, that sucks. That's, like, so totally unfair."

"Totally."

The theme music swelled and loud applause burst onto the stage. Her eyes shining with success, Tig smiled out at the crowd and waved.

Jean's voice boomed through the microphone:

"Don't forget to tune in tomorrow for our bonus broadcast, where Tig will take more calls. Same time, same station, on *Is That Fair?*"

Macie and Jean walked onto the stage and Jean, in a rush of warmth, hugged Tig.

Macie said, "That was a great show, Dr. M. You should go out and celebrate."

Jean nodded and said, "Not too hard, though; we're back tomorrow."

• • •

Celebrating for Tig was a trip to the nursing home, where she considered staying the night while Hallie shred tissue after tissue, fretting about veterinarian mistakes long past. In the hall while looking for the nurse, Tig's phone rang. It was Wendy.

"Can you bring home one of those rotisserie chickens and some gas medicine for the baby?"

"The baby's name is Clementine." Tig could hear her wailing in the background.

"Shut up, Tig. I know what her name is."

Sighing, Tig said, "I just have to get something for Mom's anxiety and then I'll stop at the store."

Returning home was a mistake, the only mistake she made all day. Tig stepped over glasses, plates, tissues, and small bundles of dirty diapers on the way to the kitchen. Thatcher welcomed her with unhinged enthusiasm. "It's been that bad, huh?"

Thatcher sneezed twice and pressed her head against Tig's leg. The television in the living room was turned to a Spanish cartoon channel, and all the blinds were closed. Tig followed the sound of the bathroom fan and found her sister and her niece sleeping on the floor next to the bathtub. Clementine sat partially upright in her car seat. Wendy dozed, her head on the porcelain of the tub, the tip of her pinky finger inserted into Clementine's mouth. The baby suckled and slept. Tig frowned. The only way anyone could nap in that position, Tig knew, was if they were fantastically sleep-deprived.

Tig gazed at what should be post-baby bliss and saw her previously beautiful sister wearing the same grubby clothes as she had the last several days. Her hair had grown out of its stylish cut, and the cost of nursing the baby round the clock had sacrificed all of Wendy's pregnancy fat and much of her muscle mass.

On the sink sat the white paper pharmacy sack containing antidepressants Tig knew Wendy hadn't been taking regularly, despite the fact that Tig had taken the liberty of calling Wendy's physician and getting a prescription. Tig picked up the bag and saw it was stapled shut.

"I don't need them, Tig."

Whispering, Tig said, "I'm sorry. Did I wake you?"

"I'm never fully asleep." Repositioning slightly, Wendy said, "I don't need those pills."

"Trust me, Wendy. I think you do."

"Why? Just because I don't take a shower every day? Just because a few dishes pile up? I challenge anyone to do any better with a colicky, wakeful newborn, who appears to need more food than a linebacker for the Green Bay Packers." Wendy eased her finger out of Clementine's mouth.

Tig frowned. "Just think of it as short-term help for a short-term problem. The colic will go away. You'll feel better, then you can go off the meds."

Wendy's eyes filled like a flash flood. "I went off them when I got pregnant and vowed never to go on them again. I'm the cheerful sister. *Me.* I'm the fun one. The fun one doesn't need antidepressants. Quit trying to turn me into you."

"Nice, Wendy."

Tucking her knees to her chin, Wendy rested her head on her arms. "I just need sleep. I could use something more than a phone call from Phil, too."

"Oh, you've been talking?"

"Yes, we're not totally dysfunctional. I can't cut people out like you can, Tig."

Tig inhaled and exhaled slowly. "I'm not going to arm-wrestle you for the title of Sister with the Biggest Issues. Go to bed. I'll take over from here. When she wakes, I'll feed her one of the millions of bags of pumped milk you've stored in the freezer."

Wendy stood up in the same arthritic way as the residents of the nursing home. None of the healthy flush associated with new mothers bloomed on her skin, none of the joy. That week, Tig had noticed a mother in the audience holding an extremely small baby with the look of first-love infatuation reflected in her smile. Mother and infant gazed at each other as if no one else in the world existed for them. When Wendy looked at Clementine, it was as if her daughter were a crossword puzzle and Wendy couldn't figure out a four-letter word for mother-daughter bond beginning with L, O and ending with V, E.

As Wendy eased herself out of the room, Tig said, "I got this. Go to sleep. I'll wake you only if I have to."

"Thanks." Wendy sniffed and scratched something that looked like dried pancake mix off her sweatpants and shuffled off to her room.

As the door to the bedroom closed, Clementine opened her eyes, then her mouth; she furrowed her brow and brought her fist to her mouth. Tig rocked the car seat and gave her niece her finger to grip. This small offering seemed to change Clementine's mind. She searched the room for a place to lay her eyes and Tig centered herself in Clementine's view.

"Hi, girlie. Hi, sweetie. Mommy's going to take a nap. Aunt Tig's in charge. Can you give me a smile?" When Clementine dropped her chin and grimaced, flared her nostrils and pushed her tongue out like a drunk licking the salt from the tequila glass, Tig laughed. "Not quite, but I'll take it."

Over the next several hours, Clementine's crying jags were miraculously abbreviated compared to what they'd been over the past month. Throughout the evening, Tig used every last piece of information she knew about her niece. Clementine liked the low-flow clear nipples on her bottles as opposed to the flatter gold ones. She preferred the football hold and would pass liberal amounts of gas in this position. When using the electric swing, the high speed made her spit up, the lowest speed pissed her off to no end, and she would only tolerate the swing long enough for Tig to thaw half a bottle of breastmilk.

By eight-thirty, the baby care had exhausted both aunt and niece. Tig lay down in her own bed to feed Clementine what would hopefully be the final bottle for the night. She built a barrier between the baby and herself, creating a kind of walled security bed complete with terry-covered hot water bottle, every pacifier any child could possibly want, six diapers, a package of wipes, and a large bear with the choice of womb or heart sounds positioned close enough to hear but far enough to discourage suffocation. Tig didn't bother taking off her work clothes before she crawled in. Thatcher curled herself on the floor, the ready sentinel hoping to be of service.

Sometime in the night, her door opened. Tig, too tired to acknowledge it, turned on her side, resting her hand on Clementine's foot. Later still, she blinked as a car's headlights fanned the room, then faded into darkness.

Chapter Fourteen
Stage Fright

The crying came on so loud and fast that Tig sat up in bed and frantically looked around the room. Thatcher scuttled to attention and trotted away, looking over her shoulder as if to say, *Not again, I'm outta here.*

Tig cradled the baby and made her way to the kitchen. A bag of thawed milk sat on the refrigerator shelf, and she tried placing the screaming child into the swing. Clementine hollered louder.

"Let's see if we can get you fed, let your mama rest or shower, or whatever she's doing." She ran warm water over the packet of milk. Just as she poured the milk into the bottle, Clementine shifted in her arms and Tig watched most of the milk pour down the drain. "Shit."

Tig slung her niece onto her shoulder and reached for another bottle. She ran the water and called out, "Wendy, I could use your help out here."

Tig tried putting the now-screaming, red-faced baby, who looked disturbingly like Newman Harmeyer, into the football hold, but Clementine cried harder. Tig rotated her until she was able to get the bottle to her mouth. "There," she said, "there you are." The baby swatted the bottle with her fist and Tig almost lost her grip. She walked the length of the kitchen, and shoved her sister's door wide.

"Wendy, I was . . . ."

Wendy's bed was empty. Tig kicked open the bathroom. Empty, too.

"What the heck?" Trying again to keep the bottle in Clementine's mouth, she said, "Where's your mama, honey?"

Tig strode out of the bathroom. A small scrap of paper flapped on Wendy's pillow.

Don't be mad, Tig. I'm not leaving for long. I just need a break. I need to figure out if Phil still loves me. You're doing better with her than I am. At least she sleeps with you. There's plenty of milk. I love you. W.

Tig stormed out of the bedroom to the front window. "Jesus Christ." Wendy's car was gone.

The bottle dislodged from Clementine's mouth and the infant inhaled. Tig plugged the infant's perfect, candy-ribbon lips with the nipple and searched her purse for her cell phone. When Wendy's voicemail picked up, which Tig had predicted, she pulled the bottle out and let Clementine wail for at least thirty seconds before replacing the bottle, hanging up, and soothing her like only an angry auntie can.

• • •

Tig rushed into the studio, carrying Clementine in her car seat. Macie and Jean snapped to attention and watched as Tig fished a pacifier out of the child's rumpled jumper, disentangled Clementine from the straps of her seat, and rummaged in the diaper bag for a bottle.

"Can someone give me a hand here?"

Macie jogged to Tig and helped ease the diaper bag from her shoulder. Jean swiftly took Clementine and proceeded with a series of deep knee squats. The redness drained from Clementine's face as she gave herself up to a kind of disgruntled quiet.

"This is the only thing that comforted the twins. My ass never looked so good as it did in the first three months post-baby." Jean continued bobbing. "When's the sitter coming?"

Tig frowned at Jean. "I don't have a sitter. How would I get a sitter? I'm still wearing yesterday's clothes. Wendy took off and I can't get hold of her. This is the first time Clem's been quiet since five A.M."

Jean said, "Do you have one of those baby sling things?"

Nodding, Tig pulled a large, paisley-patterned piece of fabric from her bag.

"Macie, put this on. We can't have her screaming all through the broadcast. And I can't keep doing this. You'll have to walk her around. I'll screen the calls, and we'll figure the rest out after the show."

Tig helped Macie position the sling and slid Clementine in, tucking her tightly to her chest. Macie, dressed like a pierced Raggedy Ann doll with pigtails, striped sailor shirt, and hot pants, wriggled until she was comfortable and gave Tig a thumbs up, beginning her series of knee bends. The baby quieted again and grasped a black braid.

Jean shook her head at the ridiculous image. "You look part marsupial, part elementary school poster child for abstinence."

Macie stuck out her pierced tongue and lisped, "Shut up, Mrs. Harmeyer."

"Tig," Jean said, "You can't wear the same thing as yesterday. I have an extra sweater and some makeup here. Let's see what we can do with you." She pulled Tig into the wings and said, "What's your plan?"

Tig shook her head, incredulous. "My plan was to get to work. Beyond that, I am considering killing Wendy."

Jean brushed makeup onto Tig's cheeks and paused. "From what you tell me, this is what she does, so I can understand your outrage." Tig nodded, disgusted. Jean pulled out a lint brush and proceeded to dehair Tig's pants. "But consider this. Wendy has lost her partner, is faced with single parenting for the next eighteen years, has a constantly screaming child, and is, from what I gather, suffering from postpartum depression. I did something equally stupid around the same time."

Surprised Tig said, "You ran away?"

"Worse. I stayed."

"How can that be worse? You took responsibility."

"I dug in. I adapted. I didn't even try to solve the problem of a husband who ran in any direction but home. I gritted my teeth, didn't ask for help, and resented everyone who didn't have twins screaming in their ears."

"It's not the same. Besides, what could you have done?"

"I could have left, gone to my parents', nipped it all in the bud." Jean helped Tig into a pale pink cardigan and grabbed a hairbrush. "But instead I played the good wife, because I believed the bullshit line, for better or for worse. When you blindly make that promise, you're thinking worse is being laid off from work or maybe a car accident. It never occurs to anyone at the altar that worse could be blatant disregard followed by adulterous skirt-chasing. If I'd had the courage to get my butt on the road like Wendy is doing, maybe my future would have held a cruise for me instead of the divorce courts."

• • •

Twenty minutes later, the audience patiently waited for the start of the show. Occasionally, a wail erupted from somewhere in the studio but was quickly silenced by Macie. Tig checked her messages. No Wendy, and, as always, no Pete. She realized that with all the drama, and so little interaction with him, Pete had fallen off the radar of her life. She wondered if this was proof of how their relationship had worked, or if it was proof of its imperfection.

An intern from the college handed her a fresh double cappuccino, which helped warm her anger, the caffeine licking her drowsy wounds. In the control booth, Jean sat, ready to command applause, information, and commercial breaks. They were a three-women and one-irate-infant show.

Tig prompted the first caller, "Yes, caller. You're on the line." There was a shuffle and hang-up. Tig smiled. "Stage fright." The crowd laughed a little. Tig touched her earbud and adjusted her microphone. "Hello?"

A thin, girlish voice came through the speakers. Tentative. "I don't know if you remember me." The caller hesitated.

"You've called before?"

The caller cleared her throat. "I just want you to know that I don't blame you exactly. I just think you should be more careful."

Tig felt her stomach lurch. "Blame me for what? I don't understand."

"My husband died," the caller said. Then, correcting herself, added, "Killed himself."

Alarmed now, Tig said, "I'm terribly sorry."

"You said he should stop. You know, with the prostitutes. Several weeks ago. You said if I didn't like it, he should stop, so he did."

The frown cleared from between Tig's eyes. "Ah, yes. It was a very short call. I remember now."

"He stopped using prostitutes, but then killed himself. He didn't leave a note."

Tig inhaled. "My God."

"I'm calling to tell you I don't think it was your fault, but his family says differently. They're suing you, the radio station. I wouldn't have called you here, but your home phone is unlisted. I had to tell you before, you know, you get the papers. It only seemed fair."

Tig felt the faces focused on hers. Any words she might have said were lodged in her throat as she struggled to breathe and remain calm.

The woman spoke again. "He was troubled. He needed help. They say you should have taken more time."

Tig glanced at Jean, who gave her the cut sign, a straight finger across her neck. Tig shook her head vigorously.

To the woman, she said, "I can't imagine what you are going through. What that was like for you? Any of it."

"We have a two-year-old daughter. What will I tell her about her father?" The woman began sobbing. "I'll never know the reason. I mean, for the other women." The caller gulped and said, "He loved me. I know he did."

"That's what you tell your daughter, then. You tell her that he loved you . . . both."

The woman sniffed and took her time before speaking. "I think I caused this. Not you. Me."

Tig sat up straight. "Listen to me, because if what you're saying is true, I won't be talking to you again. People won't allow it. But I have this to say. Never in my life have I ever been successful in making an adult do something he or she didn't want to do. If your husband was trying to give up these women, he was doing it because he wanted to, because he loved you, because he knew it hurt you. Stop blaming yourself." She breathed and washed her hand across her face. "If you do, I might be able to as well, but I doubt it."

Clementine bellowed from the wings. Tig gazed out at the listeners, who began a respectful steady applause. Jean started the theme song button and the *On the Air* sign was extinguished.

Tig stood, turned, and tried to leave the stage. The wire from her headset held her in place as effectively as a mousetrap. She pulled the microphone from her head and dropped on the floor. The crowd's murmurings became louder as Tig bumped into the chair and spilled her coffee. She staggered off the stage and jogged into the wings. Jean left the booth and tried her hand at crowd control. Tig spotted Macie, who was rocking the screaming Clementine. Her braids were undone and Macie's face showed the strain of caring for the chronically unhappy.

Tig reached for Clementine. "Cover for me. I gotta get out of here."

"Dr. M? What are you going to do? About Clementine?"

"Stop asking me what I'm going to do. Everyone needs to stop asking me. Didn't you hear the show? I can't do this anymore. Tell Jean."

Tig grabbed the diaper bag and tenderly placed Clementine into her car seat. She buckled her in and exited the studio. In the car, the roar of the motor and the white background street noise quieted Clementine. Tig's phone rang in her purse, but she ignored it.

She drove past her house twice in indecision, hoping Clementine might fall asleep. On the third pass, the baby was quiet. Tig slowed and crept into the driveway, holding her breath while she slid the car into park, unbuckled her seat belt, and tried to open the car door without waking Clementine. When the back door hinge creaked, Clem gave a start, raising one fist and then dropping it in slow motion. Tig breathed a quiet sigh and unhooked the car seat.

When she inched her way to the front stoop, Tig had to place Clementine on the cement step and, like a pickpocket, slide her keys silently from her jacket pocket. Whether it was a tiny clink of keys or the lack of sustained movement, Clem screwed her face into a human pinwheel and began to cry.

Tig pushed into the living room with Clementine wailing like a tornado siren. Thatcher, surprised at being caught industriously cleaning her privates, stopped licking, held her leg up at attention and watched Tig wrestle the child free from her seat. "Up we go, Clem," she said, hoisting the almost ten-pound child high. She noticed the sweetish, not-unpleasant odor. "Oh, honey. Your diaper." This was so like babies. *You might need to think about a possible lawsuit, but a baby demands maintenance.*

She laid Clementine on the changing table, and grimaced as she eased down leggings and pulled the tabs loose on the disposable diaper. Between Tig's racing thoughts and her unskilled movements, Clementine screamed louder and Tig started to sweat. "Oh, God, Thatcher, it's all the way up her back." With great care, she wrapped the angry, covered-in-crap child in a swaddling blanket and dashed into the kitchen for scissors, thinking she would cut the turtleneck from the child. Thatcher watched as Tig considered what it might take to surgically remove clothing from a writhing baby and how that might sound in the ER after slicing the infant's ear. Instead, she peeled the shirt free, warmed the sink water, and hosed down the still-screaming child in the kitchen sink with the vegetable sprayer.

Her phone rang as Tig diapered Clementine. She ignored it and positioned the hot, already sweaty, screaming infant into the front pack. Remembering Jean's advice, she performed deep lunges, the kind a personal trainer would admire; first in place and then moving from the living room into the bedrooms and back again. The roller-coaster rocking seemed to quiet Clementine enough so that Tig could lunge into the kitchen, open the freezer door and, with a series of timed up and down movements, thaw the breastmilk in the microwave, transfer it to a bottle, and screw the lid on tight. When she finally made contact—rubber nipple to perfect lips— Clem groaned and refilled her diaper.

Clem set the pace for the next few days and nights. When she wasn't a twitchy bundle of sobbing infant, she was asleep with a placidly perfect face, a doughy, powdery sweet roll of a baby who looked nothing like the unglued colicky infant that Tig otherwise juggled to keep content. Whenever the baby slept, Tig would rub her eyes and tell herself to get up and do a load of laundry, but instead she'd stroke Clementine's perfect skin or arrange the binding of a blanket to brush her tiny chin.

If Tig was quiet and patient enough, Clem might open her eyes and stare with what looked like the wisdom of the universe into her aunt's eyes. Once she reached for Tig, and Tig, sleep deprived and emotional, teared up at the missed connection of whatever Clem was reaching for: mother, Tig, or cheek. Then she would remember the man who killed himself and she felt guilt like a fever she couldn't control.

This was the pattern of her days. Some days she was filled with love for Clem and forgiving of her sister; other days she was furious at Wendy for abandoning them. She was used to feeling the furious anger and could recall many times in their past when she'd wanted to throttle her sister. Once, Wendy had brought Tig to a party. Tig didn't know what to expect from the barn party, where the plan was to stay the night so no one drove home. She'd packed her retainer and a change of underwear only to watch people vomit, cry, and wander off with blankets into the loft. Tig had felt unsophisticated, grimy, and forgotten until someone tried to persuade her to hook up in his car. She told him to go find Wendy, she was always up for a good time, and he staggered off. She knew she should just take their car and drive home, but then she visualized her sister in need. She had remained until the end of the party, and so had her anger.

Now, in addition to this new love and old anger, came this ferocious guilt of hurting someone with her off-handed reckless ways. Maybe Tig was more like Wendy than she wanted to admit to herself, and that thought was truly exhausting.

Over the next two weeks, Tig gave little thought to Pete except in a dreamy, reminiscing way. She felt like she was on the bottom rung of Maslow's hierarchy of needs: her life was all about survival of the fittest. Her greatest desires were to eat something other than a granola bar and sleep through the night. She considered Wendy, felt a looping connection with her that comes with the beginning of understanding another person's struggle.

Tig called the nurses at Hope House to get reports about her mother and apologize for not visiting, but the phone calls were short and frantic and left Tig feeling even more scattered. She considered driving Clem to Phil's house, calling Child Protective Services, and drugging Clementine, but did none of these things. Finally, after spilling breastmilk on the floor one morning and watching Thatcher lick it up, she said, "Let's go, Thatcher. We're going to Grandma's."

Chapter Fifteen
I Have the Lethargy

"Dr. Monahan. Tig? Wake up! How long have you been here?"

Tig opened her eyes and looked slowly around. Pam Gibson, the head nurse for the night shift, stood over her, a gentle hand on her shoulder. Tig sat up, bumping a water bottle to the floor and knocking her reading glasses under the chair where she sat. Her mother slept soundly with Thatcher curled at her feet and Clementine between her body and a padded bed rail. "It's after midnight. They said you and your sister's baby were here with Hallie for dinner. I didn't realize you were all still here."

Tig said, "Yeah. We're still here." Tig checked on Clementine, tenderly touching her head.

Pam straightened and appraised Tig from head to toe. "How long have you been here? Is that your mother's robe you're wearing? And her slippers?"

"What day is it?"

"What day? We just finished Thursday. We're into Friday."

"I've been here three, no, four days. Where have you been?"

"I've been off. My niece got married."

"Oh. Congratulations." Tig dropped her head back and stretched, yawning. "I have to pee."

Pam stood to the side as Tig shuffled to the bathroom, the tie of the light blue terry cloth robe trailing behind her.

When Tig returned, she saw the room as it must look through Pam's eyes and shuddered. A bag of dog food rested against the wall, her mother's walker straddling it like a cage. Thatcher lifted her head briefly and slapped a cheerful, brief hello with her tail, then settled her head back onto Hallie's legs. Clementine sighed. Baby diapers, wipes, and rattles littered the windowsill, television top, and tray table. A series of bottles and nipples dried on the sink just outside the bathroom.

The room was a mess, but Tig cared about one thing only: Clementine was asleep.

"Shhh, don't wake the baby," she whispered. "It's a bitch to get her back to sleep when my mom is sleeping. She's the only one who can quiet her. Do you have an extra toothbrush? I dropped mine into the toilet yesterday."

Pam cocked her head and said, "Are you telling me that you've been here all weekend? Without going home?"

Tig sighed. "Yeah. No, we went home to get supplies."

"You're living here? My staff is letting you live here?"

Tig scoffed. "No. Kind of. But no, we just have extended visits. It's nice for the residents to have a baby around."

"You can't live here. You can't. It's illegal."

"Is it?"

"Isn't it?"

"We're not hurting anybody. In fact, this is the happiest Hallie and Clementine have been for a long time. Well, not that long. Clem's only, like, two months old." Tig laughed a little. "I'm really tired. Can we talk about this tomorrow?"

"Where's your sister?"

"You tell me."

Tig picked up her cell phone off the bedside table and idly looked at the screen. "Man, I should charge this thing."

"You can't stay here, Dr. Monahan. I'm sorry if my staff misled you, but I'm sure there is a policy against family camping out long term."

Tig's temper flared. "Really? Since when? You had no problem with it when my mom was having trouble acclimating. Nobody minded when I was here helping my mom calm down. Well, now I'm having some trouble acclimating."

"Are you pushing me to call security? Is that what you're saying?"

"C'mon, Pam. Just give me a diagnosis for the night. Painless baggie colon, antisocial liver disease, bad chi rising. I guarantee I have a diagnosis pending. It wouldn't be a total lie."

With a silent push, Fern rolled into the doorway. "What's a gal gotta do to get some rest around here?"

Pam started. "Mrs. Fobes. What are you doing out of bed?"

"Well, I can't sleep with all this yakking going on. Leave the girl alone and let's all get back to sleep."

"Oh, Mrs. Fobes. You and I both know you don't sleep at night. We're not keeping you up."

In her wheelchair, Mrs. Fobes fluffed up to her full hip-to-head height. "You wake that baby and nobody's going to get any rest. Can't you see Dr. Monahan needs a good night's sleep? One more night isn't going to matter. Leave her be."

Tig had already turned her back to the women and settled herself into the reclining chair. She curled on her side away from the door, reached through the bed rail and held onto Clem's foot. "Shut the light off when you're done, girls," she whispered.

From the doorway, Fern said, "She'll be leaving tomorrow now that the jig is up. Can you just give her tonight?" She sighed and added, "I can't begin to tell you how nice it's been to have an intact brain, baby, and dog inside this stuffy barn."

The words floated around the ceiling tiles, ricocheted off the prefab doors, and into Tig's ears. She stared at her sleeping mother, who looked almost normal with the baby in her arms and a live animal at her feet. She considered the jig being up. She stared a bit longer at their reflection in the window, held the stare with her mirror self, and slowly let her eyelids close.

• • •

The next morning, Tig woke to whispering voices. Her mother sat propped up in bed, the very picture of a new mother save for the wrinkles, white hair, and age spots. Hallie had on a housecoat, buttoned at the throat, and two pillows supported arms that cradled baby Clementine. A small fist held Hallie's pearls in her hand and the expression on both of their faces said rapture. The morning nurse, Serena, stroked Thatcher while feeding her cinnamon toast and calling her "good girl" repeatedly. In the doorway, Dr. Jenson stood quietly watching the scene.

From her vantage point on the reclining chair, Tig was able to observe him before announcing to the small group that she was awake. The formal tightness previously noted around his mouth had given way to a strange, unclear emotion. She had seen gazes of gratitude from Hallie's clients at the vet clinic and looks of respect, reverence, and trust, but this was different.

"Good morning, everyone," said Tig. Thatcher was the first to respond with a wag and a pant. "I'm sorry for sleeping so late. I have the Lethargy."

Dr. Jenson tore his gaze away from Hallie and laughed. "Is that like *the* cirrhosis or *the* gout?"

"Yeah, except without the death and toe pain. I only have a tired feeling, really, and my pants chafe."

"That's the exact diagnostic criteria for the Lethargy." Dr. Jenson took a step into the room. "Good morning, Serena. Hallie." Serena nodded and made room at the bedside while Hallie beamed into Dr. Jenson's weathered face. "I was at a conference all week. Did you miss me, Hallie?"

"I always do, Dan." Holding the baby forward, Hallie said, "Isn't she a beaut?"

"She sure is. May I hold her?"

Hallie frowned. "I don't know. You were never very good with babies. Remember when you almost dropped Tiglet on her noggin? If I hadn't been there, well, it could have been a disaster."

Tig blinked in surprise.

"I'll be careful. You can help me." Dr. Jenson sat on the bed near Hallie's leg, and reluctantly she nestled the infant into the doctor's arms. The baby seemed to be the weight that had given Hallie's arms purpose. Without her, Hallie twisted her rings, touched her hair, fixed the neckline of her robe, and tried to smooth the covers. Clementine had her own reaction. Her relaxed face contorted and she did a kind of sit-up while twisting her fists into her mouth. She inhaled a mammoth breath and let out a wheezing, piteous cry.

Hallie bit her lip. "Oh, give her to me. You're hopeless." Taking the child from the doctor, she deftly placed Clementine on her shoulder and checked her diaper.

"Mom," Tig said, embarrassed.

Dr. Jenson held up his hand to Tig.

Hallie spoke again. "Hand me a diaper and get me a bottle, if you want to be useful."

Tig rolled her eyes. A nursing assistant approached Hallie with a glass of juice just as Dr. Jenson placed the already prepared bottle on the tray table along with a diaper and baby wipe. Then he tilted his head in the direction of the hall, and Tig followed the doctor out.

"My wife and I were never blessed with children. I guess that's why I continue to work at sixty-two. With my wife gone, and no kids or grandkids, I am kind of hopeless."

Tig smiled kindly. "Hardly. You've been so good to us. I want to thank you for visiting my mom."

"It's my pleasure." His hands in his pockets, he leaned against the wall outside Hallie's room. "I understand you've been spending quite a lot of time here."

Tig looked down at her feet. She wore the slippers of a seventy-six-year-old Alzheimer's patient, yoga pants, and a University of Wisconsin Go Badgers T-shirt. "I'm in a bit over my head lately."

Dr. Jenson examined Tig. "Don't misunderstand me. I'm fine with you being here. I know Pam was surprised. You probably should have told someone what your plans were."

"Plans?" Tig snorted. "That's a big assumption, plans."

"Here's what I'm thinking, Tig. I'd like to use you and your mother as a kind of case study. That is, if you'll agree."

Tig said, "No way. I'm only interested in getting out of things these days, not getting into anything new."

"Just hear me out. I told you I'm working on non-traditional modalities to ease family transitions. I want Alzheimer's patients to dictate our treatment, to make the medical community fit client needs, not vice versa."

"Doctor, I appreciate what you're trying to do, but we're . . . ." Tig paused and cleared her throat. "I'm exhausted. I'm at the end of my abilities. This is all I can do."

Dr. Jenson raised his hands. "Let me be clearer. We are going to be as flexible as possible with you and your niece being here, but it can't look like you are living here. We are going to have you keep a notebook of hours visiting, Hallie's behaviors and moods, and staff and residents' interactions. This way we can call it research, and give you a little time to find your sister."

Tig closed her eyes. "It's a lovely thought. A lovely fantasy. But how do you have the authority to make this happen?"

"Do you know what the formal name of this place is?"

"Of course. Hope House."

Dr. Jenson said, "Thor Jenson's Hope House. Thor's my dad. Long gone now."

"So, you own the place?"

Tig threw her head back and laughed. Thatcher barked in response. Suddenly energized, Tig walked back into the room where her mother dozed and Clementine snored quietly in her bed-nest. She eased Clementine into her own arms and said, "C'mon Thatcher, it's time to go home and pull ourselves together. We can get back in time for lunch."

• • •

Tig paused at the front door of her house. The mail was piled up on the stoop; the Town Shopper fliers littered the lawn. She shoved the front door open, averting her gaze from the dust and disarray, and grabbed a brown paper grocery bag from under the sink. She shoved the mail in along with a novel she had been meaning to read. She passed over her makeup, grabbing an extra pair of reading glasses and leaving her contacts behind.

"Jeans for dress-up," she said as she packed a sweatsuit and several pairs of clean thongs, just for daring. "Get your ball, Thatcher. The grounds need a dog." She stopped in front of her old answering machine. She'd made a note to disconnect the land line, but before she could stop herself, she punched play.

"Your messages are full."

"Tig, this is Jean, call me. We have a lot to discuss."

There was a pause, and Jean's voice came on the line again, "Christ, Tig. The lawyers need to talk to you. Call me."

Several more followed: "I'm outside your house, Tig. Pick up."

Macie's voice respectfully intruded: "Dr. Monahan, Jean Harmeyer needs you to call her." And then Macie whispered desperately, "Call her! You know how she gets when she's mad."

Then Jean again. "I was at your house today, Tig. There's mail all over the place. Where are you?"

Finally Wendy's voice, both timid and defiant, resounded throughout the empty house: "Tig. How's the baby? I'm sorry. I need to talk to you. Call me. I'll pick up. I will." Tig hit stop and said, "Screw you, Pete, for not calling." Thatcher, thinking she was being called, came and sat at her heels. "C'mon. It's depressing around here."

With her arms full, she yanked the door open and walked right into a young man standing on her porch. "Dr. Tig Monahan?"

"Yes, that's me."

With a serious look, he handed her an envelope from Columbus County Circuit Court, saying, "You've been served," and the memory of the man with the ligature around his neck admonished her for thinking she could forget about him so easily.

Chapter Sixteen
Space-Shuttle Relationship Conditions

In the craft room with her mother and Clementine in her car seat next to her, Tig answered the woman on her right: "Emma, I think painting your chicks black isn't going to be seen as a protest against ceramics, but will most likely land you on an antidepressant."

Emma Mobry continued painting a shaky, glossy, black lacquer onto a series of porcelain chicks. She repositioned her nasal cannula and through pursed lips wheezed, "Back in black. Get it?"

Tig nodded. "I forgot you used to own a bunch of Harleys."

"Biker chick," she said. "Too many cigarettes and too many years ago."

Tig glanced over and saw a woman with her wheelchair facing the wall. "I'll be right back." As Tig approached, the woman mumbled and then chuckled softly. Tig touched the woman's wheelchair. "Beverly, why don't you join us at the table? You haven't even touched your vase."

Beverly glanced anxiously at the red emergency electrical outlet. Tig followed her gaze. "Beverly, the nursing staff would like you to participate, and remember, electrical outlets don't talk."

Beverly winked at the electrical outlet and said, "Of course, they don't talk, sweetie. Why would you say such a thing?"

Beverly waved over her shoulder at the red, plastic, shin-high outlet. Tig shook her head at one of the nursing assistants who untangled a resident's walker from an empty wheelchair.

The nursing assistant said, "It takes all kinds."

"I guess I should know, huh?" Tig squeezed Hallie's shoulder and said, "I'm going back to the room to get Clementine a bottle, Mom."

"Check my appointment books. I think Sherlock, the Jeffersons' Labrador, is due for his shots."

"All right."

In the room, Tig prepared a thawed packet of Wendy's milk that she had stored in the nurses' break-room refrigerator. She wiped her hands on her sweatpants and rolled up the sleeves of her navy hoodie.

"Where's Hallie's dog?"

A girl of about six or seven stood in the open doorway, her jet-black hair pulled into two loose pigtails that fell to her shoulders. She wore shorts and a T-shirt with *Do I Look Like I Care?* printed on the front next to a sarcastic-looking bunny pulling at his ears.

"One of the residents has her out for a walk."

"Do you live here, too?"

"No. I don't live here." Tig screwed a rubber nipple onto the bottle.

"You look like you do. You're wearing slippers."

Tig examined her feet. "Sure enough, I am. But I don't live here. I'm part of a research experiment for people with memory problems."

"What can't you remember?" The little girl pulled her gum from her mouth in a long, uneven string.

"Not me, honey, my mother."

"What can't she remember?"

"Me. She can't remember who I am."

"Who are you?"

Fern arrived in her wheelchair, propelled by her son. With a mildly cross look on his face, he said, "Erin Ann. That is enough questions." The girl turned and tried to squeeze next to Fern in her wheelchair seat. Fern reached her arm around her shoulder.

Tig smiled. "This must be your granddaughter. She's charming."

Fern smirked. "She's nosy, more like." She tickled the girl's chin. "Erin Ann, go get my walker. I have to go to physical therapy." The little girl scampered off and Fern continued, "This is my son, Alec." She winked and raised her eyebrows, a look that Tig knew she meant to be suggestive, but only succeeded in making Fern look demented.

Alec offered his hand. "I've seen you here many times. My mom says you've taken a leave from your job to help in Dr. Jenson's research."

"Well, part of that is right, I guess." Tig shook her head at Fern, who was busying herself with her support hose.

"Which part?" he asked.

"The part where Dr. Jenson is doing research. I'm fleeing life and apparently I'm just the data he's looking for."

"Time does seem to stop when you walk inside this place," said Alec.

"That's true. You get the feeling that no matter what else is happening in the world, dinner will always be served at five and be followed by a bran cocktail."

"Hear, hear!" said Fern.

"Ah, a place you can count on," said Tig.

"You'll have to excuse my daughter, Erin. Her mother was in a place like this. Hospice, actually. It freaks her out. She loses all her social graces."

"Fern told me of your loss. I was sorry to hear it."

Erin Ann returned, dropped the walker, and pushed her father out of the way. "I get to push Granny to her appointments, Dad. You said."

Fern grasped her son's hand briefly. "You two stay and chat. Bring the walker when you're done. I don't need it right away."

Tig and Alec watched as Erin Ann pushed her grandmother down the hall. Both heads were cocked to the right, the little one bobbing with effort.

"She has your hair, doesn't she?"

He smiled. "The rest is all her mother. Every last gene."

Tig said, "This must look nuts, me living here."

"I don't know. It makes more sense than what I'm doing, which is barely visiting." He slipped his hands into his pockets. "I wanted my mom to live with us. She wouldn't have it."

"No? My mom lived with me. I was happy to have her, but being an all-inclusive for the forgetful elderly is exhausting. Just keeping them dressed can be a full-time job."

"I assured my mom that as soon as she became a burden, I would slap her into a nursing home so fast her head would spin. She told me her head was already spinning and to sign her in."

"When I first met Fern, she told me to pick up a jumbo pack of condoms."

Alec laughed. "That's my mom."

He was handsome, Tig realized. Fern was right. Tall, broad shoulders, a dip to his eyes that made him look vulnerable. Vulnerable, she could not handle. Whoever she would date in the future would have to be formed like a diamond, able to sustain space-shuttle relationship conditions. Melting hot, freezing cold, dizzying speeds, and the inevitable gravity of reentry. There was no way Tig would subject this gentle man, this mother-lover and widower, to her brand of relationship.

Alec scratched his chin and said, "How did you pick this place?"

"My mom had a pre-Alzheimer's wish book. She kept a notebook her whole life with little comments to be carried out in case she wasn't able to help herself."

"Wow. That's kind of amazing. What other things were in that notebook?"

Tig looked to the ceiling. "Let's see. She wanted someone to pluck the hairs on her chin and wax her mustache; the only charities she wanted supported were for animals or children; and if rap music was ever on her radio, she wanted the radio to be thrown through a window."

"Not a fan of rappers?"

"Oh, the rappers themselves were fine in her opinion, but she thought they were too focused on their genitals and she didn't want that invading her chi."

"That was a pre-Alzheimer's request?"

"That could have been during her borderline period."

Alec said, "My mom went from gentle housewife to a sort of watered-down Amelia Earhart—ready to get up and go at a moment's notice. She bought a camper, got a passport, and started traveling. Then, when she got sick, she parked the camper and turned into the patron saint of sarcasm and inappropriate humor."

Tig laughed. The image fit Fern so beautifully. "My mom was on the same trajectory, but her synapses hijacked her along the way."

"How long will you stay, do you think?"

Tig looked away. "I don't know." She shook the baby bottle and said, "I'd better get this to Clementine before she realizes she hasn't eaten in a while."

"I guess I should deliver this walker."

They looked at each other for an awkward moment, sharing a kind of wireless connection that swooped and snapped between them. Tig said, "You can come to dinner sometime, if you like. You and your daughter."

"That would be nice. Where do you live?"

Tig said, "Oh, I meant here. Come to dinner with us at Hope House."

Instant mortification spread across his face.

"Or come to my house," Tig said quickly. "I live over in University Heights."

"Sorry, my wife was the social one. I am . . . ." He paused and looked at his hands, the bare ring finger. "Not."

Tig touched his forearm, felt his strong muscles beneath his light-blue cotton shirt. How long had it been since she had felt anything but the marshmallow consistency of Clementine and her mother? Pete's face flickered into her mind.

"I'm the one living in the nursing home. It's me who is socially inept. Friday night is lasagna night with fresh peaches and buttered bread. Four-thirty sharp, if you don't want to sit back by the kitchen." She turned her head. "Let's see how we do with supervision first, and then we can try the real world."

She winked and pulled her sweatshirt down around her hips, a mannerism she had picked up at the nursing home, sure to turn on the one non-resident male.

• • •

Jean Harmeyer looked fashionable and exotic next to the functional go-the-distance chairs in Hope House's party room and Tig's nursing-home-chic sweatsuit. "I can't believe we have to meet in your mother's nursing home," she said, clearly aggravated.

Tig marveled at Jean's smooth skin, slick hair, and fitted clothing. Not a trace of wattle on Jean's chin. Not a trace of stress. "You have great skin, Jean."

"What's wrong with you? What's wrong with your house?"

"It's being painted."

"That's ridiculous." Jean slapped her palm down on top of the large laminate table. "This has gotten out of control. You need to call your sister and tell her to get her ass home, then come back to work. And for God's sake, get a haircut and wear some actual clothes. What's with the sweatsuit? Unless this is a well-disguised spa and you're exercising every hour, there is no reason on earth to dress like that."

"Is that what the lawyers sent you to say?"

"No, the lawyers say lawsuits are a way of life. Either this ridiculous charge will be dropped or we'll settle. This probably won't come to fruition."

"Probably?"

"What difference does it make? Medical doctors are sued all the time. It doesn't make them bad people."

"What kind of therapist simplifies a very complicated emotional problem into a sound bite? I'll answer that, Jean: a terrible one."

"That man's death was not your doing. A suicide, by definition, is very personal. On top of that, his wife didn't give you any information and you didn't make any judgments. You didn't say prostitutes are wrong, give them up. You said . . . wait . . . I have it right here." Jean rustled through her file and pulled out a transcript. "You said, 'You're very upset.' She said, 'He says I just don't understand.' You said, 'What's to understand? You want him to stop. He should stop.'"

Tig felt her face redden with mortification. "I said, 'What's to understand?' Oh, God. The attention must have gone to my head." Disgusted, she mumbled to herself. "I can't believe I said that."

"Why the hell not?" Jean answered impatiently. "You were responding to a woman saying she wanted her husband to stop paying to screw someone outside their marriage. There isn't a person in this solar system who would have answered differently."

"He killed himself."

"Listen, Tig, I'm going to say something here that I might regret later, but you are overestimating your influence on other peoples' lives. And so, quite frankly, are the alleged victims' parents. You were a voice on the phone. It was his wife who asked him to stop, and his suicide wasn't her fault, either. It was the fault of the man who put a ligature around his neck."

Tig closed her eyes. She saw an imagined face, gray. A purple tongue. She saw an idealized woman, blond with a headband, holding the hand of a little girl in lace socks as they walked in on their husband and father slumped against a snowblower. A Honda. No, a Toro.

"No influence?" Tig felt a combination of misery, relief, and affront. "You and Newman would still be married if I hadn't reduced your marriage to a joke."

"Dream on! No, Tig. My divorce was my decision. I acted alone. You just opened my eyes."

"So if I'm so ineffectual, what's the radio show about?"

"It's about giving people a place to go, a bottom line in an entertaining way." Jean pushed away from the table and pantomimed holding a phone to her ear. "Is it okay to bang a prostitute while I'm married? No. Can I slip my willie into my wife while she's sleeping? Not so much. Okay if I screw my nanny when my wife has a migraine? You're a douchebag if you do!" Jean stood and walked to the window. "You're telling people what they already know. You are helping empower them to stand up for themselves—*you* are not the power."

"Not everyone knows that. I want to help people, not hurt them."

"You think you're helping people here? You think you're helping your sister? All you're doing is allowing your sister to shirk her responsibilities. Meanwhile, you're getting in the way of your mother ever acclimating without her precious Tig by her side. Even Thatcher has lost her sheen."

Tig looked away. "I'm doing my best."

Jean halfheartedly kicked the wall and turned. "I'm sorry." She cleared her throat and said, "I'm not a person with much finesse. I know that. Every last ounce of patience and kindness that's inside of me goes to my twins. The rest of the world gets my angst. You can thank Newman for that."

An overhead speaker announced a chair aerobics class in the recreation room.

"The show's on hiatus until I . . . I mean, until *we* . . . figure this out. Have you listened to our station during your time slot?"

Tig shook her head.

"We've got some woman who answers pressing scrapbooking questions. It's called *Snip and Share with Sue LaPere*."

Tig grimaced. "Not really."

Jean held up her hand. "I swear it's true. I just have to know, when did scrapbooking become a verb?" She made a disgusted noise with her tongue. "We aren't going to replace you. You are the show. If you don't come back, well, I'll let these speak for themselves." Jean reached into her oversized bag and dropped a large, bulky envelope onto the table.

"What are these?"

"Letters. They started coming in around the time of the last show."

"Hate mail?"

"No, you little idiot. Letters of support and gratitude. Offers to help. Letters from people who called and people too timid to actually pick up the phone. You want influence? You want to help people? Then get yourself back into the studio, because right now, it's you who is being an asscrack. You are most certainly not doing your best."

When Jean was gone, Tig scuffed back to her room, the pack of unopened letters under her arm. Her mother and Clementine slept together in a lopsided yin and yang symbol. She dropped the letters on her bed and the baby stirred, woke, and stared at her aunt. Tig noted the similarities between grandmother and granddaughter: barrel belly, wispy white hair, sky-blue eyes. She saw her sister's chin.

"Hey there, little chicken," she whispered. "How's my girl? I don't get to see much of you, do I?"

Thatcher wagged her way over and Tig scratched under her chin. "You, either, big girl. Are you ready to go home?" Thatcher dropped her ears. "Me neither."

Clementine gurgled and sucked her fist. Her clear-eyed gaze made Tig's throat ache and she swallowed, trying to hold back tears. "Your mommy is coming back, sweetie. Don't you worry about that. Your mommy will be back. And when she comes, we're going to punch her hard. Yes, we are."

A nursing assistant passing by the room stuck her head inside.

"She looks just like you," she said and smiled warmly.

Tig tried a smile, but her lips trembled and she returned her gaze to Clementine. She traced her finger from Clementine's forehead to the tip of her nose, finishing at her tiny, tented lip. "The big question in my mind is not if your mom is coming back. It's if Pete is, and if I'll get a chance at having someone like you."

Chapter Seventeen
Consider-It-All

The best thing about Hope House was the shower. There was none of that low-flow showerhead nonsense or a limit to how long a person could camp out. There was always a plastic seat nearby when standing and scrubbing got just too much to handle, and the hand-held nozzle was amazing for several reasons. Tig thought of Pete, of his strong hands, his full lips, and lowered the showerhead down her body.

"Isn't this your mom's shower?"

Tig gave a shout of surprise and dropped the nozzle. The water pressure kicked the showerhead around, sending a spray of water around the room.

Water hit Erin Ann directly in the face and she hollered, "Hey, you got me wet!"

Trying to simultaneously retrieve the bucking bronco of a showerhead and cover her breasts, Tig said, "Erin Ann. Shut the curtain. What are you doing in here?"

The girl wiped her face and said, "I wanted to ask you a question."

Tig grabbed a towel. "Can it wait until I get dressed?"

"Why? We're all girls. Even Thatcher is a girl."

"That's true, but some people don't like to have important conversations when they don't have any clothes on."

"My mom didn't care. She said that after you have a baby, you just don't care about that stuff anymore."

Tig turned off the water and wrapped herself with a towel. "I guess that's the difference. I haven't had a baby yet."

"You have Clementine."

"I don't have her, really. I'm her aunt, not her mother."

Erin Ann pulled the bottom of her pigtails apart to tighten them against her head and said, "Yeah, I don't get that."

"Her mother is coming back soon."

"My mom said she didn't want to miss a minute with me. But then she had to."

Tig blotted her hair dry and sat on the shower chair. She looked the little girl in the eye. "What was she like?"

"She was really pretty, before she got sick. She was a really good singer."

"Did she sing to you?"

"Yeah, her favorite song was 'Waltzing Matilda.' It had a lot of funny words in it. We looked them up."

"Does your dad know the words, too?"

"He can't remember them, so he makes up his own." Erin nosed the toe of her shoe into a puddle from the shower and drew a letter C. "It's not the same, but it's funny. How come you don't have your own baby? I asked my dad if you were old enough, and he said you were."

Tig smiled. "Did he? Hand me that robe, will you, please? I'm getting cold." Tig wrapped the dry material around her and modestly plucked the towel away from her body after she was completely covered with the robe.

"I know how people do it."

Tig dried her hair with a towel. "What, honey?"

"You know. *It*," Erin said with knowing emphasis. "Would you like me to tell you?"

Tig said, "Uh, no. I'm pretty clear on the mechanics of it."

"Tracy Smiley told us at recess and then got in big trouble for it. It's gross."

Tig nodded. "It totally is gross."

"People must really want kids."

Tig wrinkled her nose and said, "I know, right?"

"We're here for dinner tonight. We ordered a guest tray for me and my dad."

Tig brightened, "Oh, so I should dress up for dinner, since it's a special night."

"Um, I don't think you have to be fancy. You could wear what I'm wearing."

"I don't have a rock star T-shirt or shorts with diamonds on them. Can I just wear jeans?"

Erin considered this and angled her head as if to assess Tig's potential. "I guess." She turned to leave.

"Wait. What did you want to ask me before?"

Erin looked over her shoulder. "If you could be friends with my dad. He's super lonely, I can tell. I don't want you to be my mom or anything, just a friend to my dad. You're nice to people and good at taking care of them. My dad kind of needs that."

Tig put her hand on Erin's shoulder. "You're the kid, you know. You don't have to take care of your dad. That's not your job."

With a steady gaze and not a moment of thought, Erin said, "You're the kid, too, but you're doing it."

• • •

After dinner, Fern Fobes wiped her mouth with a napkin from a stash swiped daily from the dining room. Alec said, "Mom, you already have enough napkins and tissues to start a hot-dog stand. Why did you take more?"

"Oh, stop bothering me." Fern rolled her eyes at Tig. "Erin and I are going for a ride around the grounds in one of the golf carts later. I already talked to Jerry, that handsome nurses' aide, about it." Winking, she said, "We have a date."

"He's too old for you, Mom."

"I know. I'm branching out. Listen, Hallie and Clem are sleeping. Why don't you two go for a walk or something? I'll sit here. Make sure nobody hits the floor."

Tig brushed her hair back from her face. "We're almost out of our frozen milk stash. I have to go back to my place and pick some up. Get my mail."

"Go with her, Alec. You can help carry things. I don't want you sitting around flirting with Mrs. Templeton in 34A."

Tig looked at Alec. "We're not needed here, and it's only five-thirty—that's the nice thing about eating during the Early Bird Special. You have the rest of the night for bunion soaks and terrible television."

Alec nodded. "Let's go."

Without the nursing home residents, Erin Ann, and the constant interruptions of nursing staff comings and goings, there were highways of open air to fill between Alec and Tig. It was a quiet walk to the car.

"I know this isn't healthy, but it feels weird to be out of the nursing home and with my arms free."

"You don't have to apologize for stuff around me, y'know. Ever since Jennifer died, I try not to judge what people do or what they need at any given moment. You're helping your family. That's good enough for me."

"Thanks." Tig drove out of the parking lot and stared straight ahead. "My boyfriend is mad at me about all of this. He wanted me to go with him on sabbatical."

"Your boyfriend." Alec said this like a statement and suddenly the car felt overpopulated with Tig, Alec, Jennifer, and the word 'boyfriend' drifting between them.

"'Boyfriend' is too strong a word. 'Old boyfriend' would be more accurate. I haven't talked to him in, like, two months."

"He wanted you to travel and you felt like staying home?"

"I felt I needed to stay home."

The evening sun gleamed through the front windshield as Tig turned down her street. Alec dropped the visor. "When I was a kid, I had no idea how hard relationships were."

Tig braked and opened her car door, but Alec stayed still. "I have to say, I kind of understand the lure of the old folks' home," he said. "It's always a perfect seventy degrees, you never run out of toilet paper, and no grocery shopping ever has to be done for food to appear on the table."

Tig sighed. "Never having to grocery shop again would almost be worth being flashed daily by wrinkled Mr. Schrofnagle every time I go into the TV room."

Alec laughed and made a face. "Poor you, ugh. I sure wanted a place to go right after Jennifer died. But, as you know, you can't check out when you have a child."

"Not everyone ascribes to that theory."

"Oh, right. Sorry," he said with a wince.

"Hey, no, I feel the same way."

"Erin hates hospitals and medical facilities in general. I don't blame her. She likes to visit you, though, and Clementine. And Thatcher, of course."

"Thatcher makes everyone feel welcome."

"Erin has been putting the full court press on me for a dog."

"You won't get any nay-saying from me. Thatcher is my rock."

"I'm not sure I can take on anymore responsibility. When my wife was alive, I . . . *we* had a plan. We knew what we were doing. Now the wind could blow and we'd be gone."

Tig nodded. "I feel the same these days. Clementine and Thatcher seem like the cement holding me to this earth. A baby and a dog. How do you like that?" They walked up the front steps, and Tig inserted her key into the lock and shoved the front door open.

Unopened mail, cloth baby diapers, and unfolded laundry littered the room. The slightly sour smell of a neglected house wafted over them. The end-of-the-day sun poured into the bay window, highlighting the neglect. *Look here*, it seemed to say, *unemptied garbage, and over here, unwashed dishes. Have you ever seen so much dust?*

Tig said, "Wow. I didn't remember it looking this bad."

Alec pushed gently past her. "You should see my place. I imagine you keep the milk in the freezer. Do you have a cooler somewhere?"

"Under the sink."

Tig noticed the remnants of tape and an index card stuck to the face of the mantle clock, a fossil left over from when her mother roamed the floorboards.

The sound of the freezer opening and shutting moved her to retrieve a plastic grocery bag from the floor and start cleaning. In the bathroom, she looked in the mirror and shook her head. The bottle of antidepressants Tig had bought for her sister sat quietly, waiting for someone to notice the symptoms helpfully listed on the insert: *Lack of interest in pleasurable activities, persistent feelings of guilt, inability to cope.* Tig muttered to herself, "Between the sun and the pills, it sure is noisy in here." She looked at the bottle for a long moment and unscrewed the top. Considered the peach pills, jiggled the container, and put it back on the sink.

Tig joined Alec in the bedroom with the bassinet. "Wendy's room?"

"And my mother's before that."

"I love that little painting." Alec gestured to a small watercolor of a red barn surrounded by a raggedy tree and air so fresh you could almost smell the newly mowed hay.

"Yeah, the artist got the colors just right. It hung next to our front door for as long as I can remember."

Alec stepped closer. "I love how you can't tell what season it is."

Tig unhooked it from the wall and said, "I think I'll take it to my mom. See if it jogs her memory." She blew dust from the frame. With her T-shirt, she cleaned the front glass and some of the paper backing came free with her effort.

"Shoot. Look what I did."

"I can glue that down." Alec examined the edging and tugged at a small piece of paper. It fluttered to the floor.

Tig stooped to pick it up. With one hand she unfolded the paper and read its contents. "It's a poem, listen."

If I Could Tell You

Time will tell you nothing but I told you so.
Time only knows the price we have to pay;
If I could tell you I would let you know.

If we should weep when clowns put on their show,
If we should stumble when musicians play,
Time will say nothing but I told you so.

There are no fortunes to be told, although,
Because I love you more than I can say,
If I could tell you I would let you know.

The hum of the refrigerator continued. A dog barked and a semi truck drove down the street, rattling the windows on its way to the grocery on the corner.

"That's seriously beautiful," Alec said with reverence.

"I wonder why it was hidden in the back of this painting. Don't you think that's weird?"

"Maybe your father liked thinking she might find it one day and be reminded of the message."

"I don't actually think it's my father's handwriting. Even so, why hide a message like this, that time is the ultimate equalizer . . . that no matter what else there is in the world, time will always be there, tapping its foot."

"And love," Alec added. "I think it's saying love is timeless and 'I told you so' is the ultimate promise."

Tig blinked. "Why, sir, you are a romantic."

"More like a coward. In high school I was madly in love with this girl. Diane Riskitall."

"You're kidding me. Risk-it-all?"

"You're one to talk, Dr. Tiger Lily. Anyway, suffice to say, she never felt the same way. We were more like best friends, but I always wanted more."

Tig smiled at him and said, "Unrequited ardor, the ultimate teenage angst, since time isn't even acknowledged at that age."

Alec nodded. "When we graduated, I gave her a gold locket. Inside it, I taped a note that said, *Soon.* It was the way we said goodbye on the phone. We really were best friends and I never wanted to say goodbye."

"God, high school. That is so sweet."

"On the back of the note I wrote, *I love you* but I taped that side down, hoping someday she would loosen it and know, figuring by then we would both have a life and it would be a warm memory stretching across the miles."

"What happened to her? Did she ever throw caution to the wind like her name suggested and find you?"

"Nah, that's where the story ends. I heard she got married and teaches third grade somewhere. I don't know if she ever discovered the back side of the note."

"You know," said Tig, suddenly realizing, "the handwriting may not be familiar, but the title is." She pushed up her sleeve and showed Alec the engraved bracelet she wore on her wrist. "This was in my mother's things when we packed to move her to the nursing home." A thrill shot through her as Alec tilted her wrist to read the bracelet.

"'If I could tell you.'" Moving his thumb a gentle inch and without releasing her arm, Alec looked at Tig. "I wonder if whoever it was ever told her so."

She held the catch in her breath and noticed the heat in her arm spreading. "I assume it was my father, and I hope he told her." Almost challenging Alec, she added, "But that kind of thing does take courage."

Alec held her gaze. "After high school, I promised myself I wouldn't let opportunities to connect with people pass me by. I would read the signs better, have more guts."

Tig cleared her throat. "How's that going?"

"In high school, I didn't take into account daughters and mortgages. The fear of collateral damage."

Tig smiled in understanding. "Risk assessment."

Alec said, "I wonder if Diane aged and changed her name to Consideritall."

"If people did that, no one would ever do anything," Tig said, hoping Alec would know exactly what she meant.

Chapter Eighteen
Life Is Lame

After a surprisingly comfortable return trip back to the nursing home, Alec and Tig walked into Hallie's room. Tig's immediate reaction was panic. Then she suffered a hot sweeping fury.

Wendy stood in front of Hallie's bed, looking at grandmother and child. Their mother held Clementine, who watched her own chubby fingers with a cross-eyed look of concentration. A worried veil passed across Hallie's face.

"Well," said Tig, biting off each word, "look who's decided to come home."

Wendy, with equal parts joy, bewilderment, and sorrow, said, "She's not crying."

Her mother said, "Look who's here!"

Tig smiled quickly at her mother. "I see, Mom." Then turned her steel jaw to her sister. "Wendy."

"I started to call, Tig. About a hundred times."

"I wouldn't have answered. If you wanted to know about Clementine, you could just come home."

"Well, here I am, and I can see how happy that makes you."

Alec said, "I think I'll go find my mom and Erin. I'll see you soon." Tig mistakenly said, "Bye, Pete." Mortified, she closed her eyes. "Alec!" Walking to the door, she called after him. "Please don't hold that against me. I used to be a very normal person."

Calling back over his shoulder, he said, "I never liked normal."

Tig smiled and returned to the room. Wendy was trying to take Clementine into her arms. Tig could tell by the look on Hallie's face that her inner alarm was getting ready to sound. Tig eased her sister's arms back, whispering gently through a humorless smile, "Wendy, just wait a minute. You have to wait until she's asleep to take Clementine."

Wendy balked, desperation showing through the skin beneath her eyes. "What are you talking about? I haven't seen my daughter in weeks." She gulped a sob. "I've got to tell her how much I love her."

"Forgive me for not seeing the urgency here."

Wendy's eggshell façade began to crumble. Her voice, a thinning band close to snapping, vibrated. "I had to leave. Don't you understand?"

"No. Here is what I do understand. Your mother and daughter have some kind of amazing bond. Mom was the only one who could calm Clementine down when she started wailing with colic. And Clementine calms Mom. It's the perfect symbiotic relationship, except for it to work, we all had to come and practically live here at the nursing home."

Wendy stood back, astonished. "You live here?"

"No, but we might as well."

"You did this for me?"

Tig said, "No. I did it for Mom, Clementine, and me. When you decided to take off, I didn't know what to do."

As if finally finding some common ground, Wendy said, "I didn't know what to do, either."

"Yes, but you're a mother, you little irresponsible shit. You can't leave."

Wendy sat heavily on the edge of Tig's bed. She inched her hand over to the bundle that was her daughter nestled in her mother's arms.

Hallie shoved her hand away and pulled the baby closer to her chest.

Tig put her arm on her mother's leg. "It's okay, Mom. It's just Wendy. She wants to touch the baby."

Hallie snapped at Tig, "I know it's Wendy. Tell her to keep her hands off Tiglet. She's always aggravating the girl."

Tig and Wendy looked at each other. In spite of the bitterness boiling between them, Tig laughed.

Wendy squeezed her eyes shut and a tear scooted down her face. "I would have hurt her, Tig."

Tig moved away. "No, you wouldn't have."

Wendy said, "Yes. I would have."

Hallie shushed them, placing a finger to her lips.

"You were right," Wendy went on. "I needed the antidepressant. I started them as soon as I got to Phil's. I got in to see my old ob/gyn and he said what I was feeling was normal, given the circumstances. I know it was wrong to leave her without talking to you first, but I had to get out of there before I did something terrible. I knew you would take care of her."

"That is not enough, Wendy. And too much like what you've done for years. Leave everything to Tig, because her life doesn't really matter."

"I know it. But I'll make it up to you. I promise. Once Phil gets here and we get a place of our own."

Tig put both hands up into the air. "Hold on a minute. Phil's coming? You're getting your own place?"

"That's the good news. Phil wants to try. Says he was miserable. Wants to give the family a go." Wendy brightened, wiping her face. Tig yanked her sister by the arm and into the hallway.

"So that's it for good old Tig, then, huh? You're taking Clementine and you and Phil are going to . . . How did he put it? *Give it a go?* What is this? A carnival ride for him? No freaking way. I love that little girl. She's my family. You can't just treat me like I'm some unneeded foster family."

With an accusing finger, Wendy poked her in the chest. "You're treating me like I'm a crack addict. I'm her mother."

"If I'd called social services, this would have been a much bigger deal. You wouldn't be able to waltz back in and take her back so easily then."

Wendy's hands flew to her head. "I thought you'd be happy for me. God, I'm an idiot. You're only happy when you're taking care of everyone else's life so you don't have to focus on your own."

Tig's head snapped back as if she had been slapped. She opened her mouth to speak and found she couldn't.

Wendy began again. "Don't get me wrong, little sister. I'm grateful. More than grateful. Indebted to you forever. I know that. But I'm back now."

Tig said, "But that's not fair!"

"Guess what?" Wendy said, sniffing. "This ain't your radio show, and who said life was fair?"

"All right, you two. That's about enough." Dr. Jenson strode down the hall, his white lab coat snapping around his thighs. Tig and Wendy stopped speaking. Dr. Jenson frowned. "This is not the place for this; you both know better. You're upsetting the other residents."

Wendy scoffed and mumbled, "Other residents."

Dr. Jenson trained a disapproving gaze on Wendy and said, "Yes, Wendy. Tig has been performing a very valuable service here at Hope House. We have been collecting data on family impact in a healthcare situation, hoping this pilot will underscore the need for more data."

Tig cocked her head, all but sticking out her tongue at her sister. Dr. Jenson caught the movement. "Tig, I'm surprised at you. You, better than anyone, know we need peace and stability, not stress and strife in our hallways. If you have an issue, bring it to the conference room." The two women dropped their heads and gazed at the carpet. "Your mother always said there were no two people who loved each other more than you two, as long as you weren't in the same room."

Tig started to explain. Dr. Jenson put his hand up. "I heard what this was about all the way down the hall; I certainly don't need a reprise."

"We all heard." Fern made her way forward from her own doorway.

Dr. Jenson smiled. "Mrs. Fobes. Good to see you up and around."

"Thank you, Dr. Jenson. I'll take it from here." Then, with a wry smile, she said, "Did I not say this would happen? I told you so."

Apparently happy to go back to the comfort of science and prescription pads, he said, "Time will say nothing but."

Tig opened her mouth to call after him, but Fern said, "Listen, neither one of you is thinking straight." Fern wheeled herself between the two women. First, she addressed Wendy. "You can't come in here and yank Clementine out of your mother's hands and your sister's responsibility without so much as a second's consideration to what you will leave behind. For heaven's sake." Then she angled her chair closer and said, with the gentleness of age and understanding, "Tig, you didn't really think you could keep that baby forever, did you? She's not a kitten. And she has a mother." Fern gave Wendy a thin-lipped grimace, adding, "Albeit a challenged one."

Tig took a breath and snuck a sorry, protective peek at her sister. While Wendy had gotten her hair cut and colored and was dressed in real clothes, Tig could see her weight loss and the patches of eczema on the back of her hands that always showed up in times of stress.

With both authority and tenderness, Fern addressed Wendy. "Go on in there and spend some time with your mother and your child. Watch Clementine in another person's arms. Get to know her before you claim her. Once Hallie's asleep, you can take her and nurse her if you like. Plan to spend the night. It's going to be a long one for everyone."

She rolled her chair back. Looking between the two sisters, she said, "I'm going to take myself back home now. You two make up and don't make me come out here again. Tig, honey, when you're done, I need you to do something for me in my room." Fern propelled herself over her threshold.

Wendy said, "I don't think she likes me much."

"I suppose not much yet. But she will. Everyone likes you."

The words sat between them like a special delivery package of undeserved kindness. Wendy asked, "Do you think Clementine does?"

"Likes you?"

"Remembers me?"

"Don't be stupid, Wendy. Just show her your boob and all will be forgiven. It's called the mother advantage."

Tig walked to Fern's room. "The bio on your door says you were a labor relations specialist, but I could never picture it until now."

Fern wrestled the black gloves she always wore off her hands. She had her teeth involved and was clearly losing the fight. She straightened and gestured for Tig's help. "I was never a labor relations specialist."

"What?" Tig said. "That's what your biography says. Labor relations specialist, accountant, and community theater actress."

Fern grunted a little as Tig pulled at one of the fingers on the gloves. "I was a homemaker. For that job, you have to be skilled at mediation, finances, and acting if you're going to succeed at marriage and motherhood. I put in the time. Can't I be a little creative with my history?"

"Sure. I guess. But why?"

"The generation that works here, they value titles, experience, and achievement. I may not have been the CEO of my own accounting firm, but I want them to wipe my heinie like I was."

Tig pulled the glove free and gasped at the swollen shiny surface of Fern's hand. "Fern. What happened to your hand?" It had the pale, waxy appearance of a mannequin's hand. Tig tried to warm it in hers.

"Correction, hands. And feet, abdomen, chest and legs."

Fern continued cataloging her affected areas: "Esophagus, colon, and lungs, too, if you really want an inventory."

Tig held Fern's hands and pressed them together between hers. "What is it? What do you call this?"

"Scleroderma, the diffuse form." When Tig shook her head slightly, not comprehending, Fern said, "It doesn't sound that bad, does it? Like a little ointment might do the trick. But it's a nasty disease."

"Tell me," Tig said, still trying to warm Fern's fingers.

"You know when you have a pencil with one of those hard erasers? Like it's old, no longer flexible? Always rips the paper when you try to use it and leaves crumbles behind?"

Fern waited for Tig to nod, and continued. "That's what my body is turning into. A hard, thick, band of connective tissue. It has something to do with autoimmunity."

"What does it mean, Fern?"

"What do you think it means, dear heart? I am going to die from it. Probably sooner rather than later—from complications." Fern rolled her eyes to the ceiling and said, "God, at least I hope sooner. I just have a few more things to take care of and then I'm checking out."

"You don't mean that."

"Well, yes, I do." Fern patted Tig's hands and did a pretty good impression of John Wayne in his cowboy incarnation. "There are worse things than dyin', missy."

"No, don't joke. I didn't know."

"You're just like Alec. He's got this constant cheerful 'life is good' goal. I got news for you kids, sometimes life is lame and that's just the way it is."

Tig started to speak, but Fern interrupted her. "I called you in here to get you out of your sister's way."

Surprised by the hairpin turn, Tig swallowed hard. "I thought you were on my side."

"Oh, I am. And I'm also on Hallie's, Clementine's, and Wendy's sides because—and you already know this—we're all on the same side. That's what Dr. Jenson's been trying to accomplish here, in his own tortured, noncommunicative way." Fern clicked her tongue, "Men. I swear. I spent my life wishing I could live in a menses hut like they did in biblical times. No men. Just nurturing women all speaking the same language. Lucky me, I finally get to do that. A nursing home is essentially a post-menopausal hut, but it's run by a man." She shook her head in disgust.

Tig smiled.

Fern said, "Have you figured him out yet?"

"Figured who out? Who? Pete?"

Fern, without changing her expression, appraised Tig for a long moment and changed the subject.

"Did I tell you? Alec took me over to Erin Ann's school the other day. She goes to that Lutheran day school. They had a Grandparents and Special Person morning. It was lovely. We had homemade *lefse* and *krumkake*. Erin sang this song, 'My God is an awesome God; He reigns from heaven above.'" Fern waved one damaged hand over her head. "I don't remember the rest. Erin likes to change the words and, you know how badly she wants a dog; she sang, 'My dog is an awesome dog.'" Fern smiled and said, "One of the teachers got really mad about it. Pulled Alec aside and told him Erin needed more 'limits at home.'"

"Oh, brother," Tig said.

"Right. You know what Alec said to her? He said, 'You don't think it's limiting enough to lose your mother at seven?' Then he said, 'If my daughter finds something funny in a day overshadowed by loss, she can sing any damn thing she wants.'" Fern whooped. "Oh, you should have seen her face."

Tig smiled. "That's fabulous. Alec's a great dad."

"When we left that afternoon, I saw that teacher get into a car with license plates that said SUPA MOM. Now, Alec sings 'My dog is an awesome dog' to Erin whenever she's stressed and he wants to let her know he loves her just the way she is."

"Here, Fern, let me help you into bed, get your feet up and warm."

"No! You aren't paying attention. SUPA MOM is caught in the trap of rules and rights. You're in that trap, Tig. Say what you want about your sister. She did what she had to do, let it be dammed how it looked or what people thought. She saved herself so she could be a mother."

Tig shook her head. "But she left in the night. She was a coward."

"So we don't agree with the mechanics of how she did it. But she wasn't a coward." Fern wrapped her hands in her lap robe. "When Clementine hears the story later in her life, I hope she hears that her mom was willing to do the impossible, which was to put herself first so she could be better for others. She can be a narcissistic little snipe, your sister. I hardly know her, but I know that much. Still, she's smarter than you in some ways."

Hurt, Tig stood and withdrew, putting her chair back next to the chest of drawers.

Fern tilted her head in concession. "Sorry. I'm not mad at you. I just don't have a lot of time to mince words anymore. Just call the nurse; it's her job to put me to bed. And you go find my son; he needs a kick in the butt, too."

Chapter Nineteen
Time's Fun When You're Having Flies

From the doorway, Tig watched as Wendy shut off the overhead light above their mother's bed and lifted her child to her breast. Clementine drowsily raised her hand to her mother's face. Wendy guided the tiny hand to her lips and kissed the pudgy fingers. Clementine finally settled her fingers on her mother's nose. It wasn't a Mary Cassatt *Mother and Child*. It was better. More real. One might want perfectly placed reunion kisses, but sometimes a nose-hold will have to do.

Tig stepped from the voyeur shadows. "I'm heading back to my house for the night. Let you guys get reacquainted."

Holding Clementine's gaze, Wendy nodded.

"I'll be back tomorrow. Come on, Thatcher. Let's go."

Thatcher wagged her tail without lifting her head.

"Oh no, you're not staying; you're coming with me, you old traitor." To her sister, she said, "Mom's been feeding Thatcher off her dinner tray." Tig added, "The diapers are under the bed and the bottles are . . . ." Tig didn't finish her sentence. "Never mind, you don't actually need the bottle, do you?"

Wendy said quietly, "I've been pumping like mad for this moment, and I'm talking a really low level of med . . ." she stopped, looked at Tig and reached for her hand. "Thank you, little sister."

Tig squeezed Wendy's hand. "If Mom wakes, give her Clementine."

• • •

At home, Tig woke with a start, fumbled for Clementine, and came fully awake to her aloneness. She peered at her clock: 3:16 A.M. She propped herself up with pillows against her headboard and looked around her bedroom, the only place mostly untouched by either her mother or Clementine. It was not a perfect haven, though, with Pete's memorabilia scattered around the room. Before, when she took inventory of his things, they felt comforting, like maybe he'd just left for a run and would return sweaty but calm. Now, they stuck out as harbingers of what she'd lost being stubborn and refusing to deal with her feelings or lack of feelings for him. A Milwaukee Brewers baseball cap dangled on the bedpost, and a pedometer lay on her dresser next to an entry form for the Chicago Marathon, now only a couple of months away. The walls of her bedroom were pumpkin-colored, and when she and Pete had painted them, they had joked that they would dream in cinnamon and clove and wake up craving pie.

On impulse she grabbed her phone and dialed. As it rang, she glanced at the clock. It was after ten P.M. in Hawaii. His phone was sure to be off, given Pete's early bedtime, but Tig waited anyway, just to hear his voice. He always sounded like he was just about to tell a joke or start laughing in his voicemail message. Tig remembered reading an article about how just hearing your lover's voice could provoke endorphin release and feelings of well-being.

A woman's voice said, "Hello?"

Tig snapped the phone shut, checked to see if she had dialed correctly. It was one thing to lose Pete to Hawaii, but quite another to lose Pete to a Hawaiian girl. Surely a beauty, a surfer with muscular thighs and hair thick with sea foam. A Title Nine catalog model with lean biceps and teeth as straight as a row of white corn. She grimaced and screwed her face into an expression where tears would surely follow. Dry-eyed, she searched for the photo she now kept under her mattress and pulled it out. She studied Pete's unguarded face, his scruffy beard, his angular jaw. There it was, in the pit of her stomach: regret. A knobby macadamia nut of longing, but for what? For Pete? For his uncomplicated view of a life comprised of eating, exercising, making love, and working?

She dropped the photo onto the bed. How quickly he'd found her substitute. He'd once said Tig was his home. His home apparently was an Airstream or Winnebago motor home, not one of substance, of roots or staying power. She touched her lips and thought of Alec. He felt more solid, dependable. Could she be attracted to both sides of the coin? Was this why she couldn't get a handle on her feelings for Pete?

With both hands, she raked her fingers through her hair and the silver bracelet she wore yanked at a section above her temple. To untangle it, she undid the clasp and slid it free. *If I could tell you.* She ran her thumb over the engraving.

"My dad sure loved my mom," she told Thatcher. "I have to admit, Thatcher, it's kind of nice to be in the house with just you. No fear of Mom leaving in the middle of the night, no screaming Clementine, no fights about marriage or divorce or anything else."

Restless, Tig turned on the television, skated around the channels. She stopped briefly at a show where real people talked about their addictions and how it ruined their families. A woman with pitted skin and very few teeth cried while she tried to find her crack pipe.

"See, Thatcher. We're not that bad. I know right where my crack pipe is." Thatcher yawned. "You'd have laughed if you were Pete. The Pete before the Hawaiian girl." She picked up her phone and held it for a long moment, dropped it, shut off her television, and stared at the overfilled envelope Jean had given her. Upending the entire lot of printed e-mails and a few letters onto her bed, she spread them out and selected one written on thick card stock in Tiffany-box blue. The penmanship was straight-A material.

Dear Dr. Monahan, I just want to say that you have made a big difference in my life. It sounds ridiculous as I write this, but I never considered fair or unfair in marriage. I've always just tried to adapt and get along. I think of myself more now. We have more fights, but at least I feel more like this is our marriage and not just another one of my husband's annoying commitments.

Tig tilted her head. "Wow, Thatcher. This one likes me." She selected another note, this one written on yellow legal-pad paper.

My wife bugs the crap out of me about the dishwasher, too. I asked her what she was really mad at. And she told me. She said I was nicer to the dog. She's right, I guess. I'm trying to scratch her more behind the ears now (figuratively). Thanks. Al Zankman.

Tig raised her eyebrows and reached for a stack of what appeared to be printed e-mails clipped together with a black metal clip.

Thanks, Dr. Monahan, you rock.

Dr. Monahan, you hit the nail on the head the other day. Marriage is like that game, Deal or No Deal. If you don't shape up, it's just the No Deal part.

Hey, Dr. M, Nice touch with the drunk guy. Don't let him get you down. You're doing good.

Where's Dr. M?????

Tig sifted the papers through her fingers, feeling the hum and crackle of support. Near the bottom of the pile she found a handmade card decorated with a frog with an expandable ribbon tongue and what may have been a hand-tied fly. Written across the front, in an especially frilly hand, was the phrase, *Time's fun when you're having flies.* Tig opened the card and read: *My husband doesn't take his ring off anymore. Now, how do I fix the rest? What next?*

Thatcher snored. *What's next?* Tig stood, intending to brush her teeth and lock up for the night. She stopped as headlights swept through the room and died on the back wall. She peeked through the beveled glass window in her front door. Alec's face appeared, fragmented. His features rearranged and softened as she opened the door.

"Hi." She tightened her robe.

"I know it's a ridiculous time, but sometimes, Erin Ann wakes in the middle of the night and can't fall back to sleep. For some reason, driving around helps. She's sound asleep in the back seat. We brought you something to bring to your mother tomorrow."

"I'm up. I think I'm on Hope House's medication schedule." She gestured Alec inside.

"I thought this might help." Alec pulled a baby doll out of a wrinkled brown paper bag.

She laughed. "Where did you get that? And help with what?"

"Erin Ann is too old for it now, and I thought maybe your mother might like to hold something now that Wendy is back."

"Oh."

The doll was the heavy, loose-limbed type. Her face was daintily painted in pastel blushes of peach, sea blue, and shell pink. Her lips were permanently pursed to accept a bottle. She blinked demurely at Tig.

"She's got that one lazy eye, but I don't think we should hold that against her." Alec pressed an invisible switch hidden in the doll's pajamas. The baby began to vibrate slightly and coo.

The sight of Alec's careful face and the baby doll's heft brought stinging tears to Tig's eyes. Noticing her discomfort, Alec said, "I can't take credit for this. It was Erin's idea. She said she saw another resident at Hope House with a doll."

Tig sat heavily on the arm of the couch and stroked the doll's hands. "She's lovely. Thank you. I'll bring it with me tomorrow when I visit. I can't promise I won't sleep with her tonight."

"Lots happened today. I'll let you get some rest." Alec turned.

"Did you get new glasses?"

"Yes. Erin said I looked like Harry Potter, and that wasn't a compliment."

"Would you like a cup of tea, or maybe a hug?"

Alec sucked on his lower lip. "I don't think I've ever been offered those together like that before."

"I'm a little unorganized."

"It's hard to be the one left behind, isn't it?"

"I'm frankly disgusted with myself. Losing your wife, now, that's a loss that deserves checking out for a while."

"So, in your world, Tig, you only get to grieve if someone dies?"

Tig didn't speak because she found she really couldn't.

Alec said, "I'm going to take that hug and go home. Erin wants us to paint toenails and do hair in the morning." Taking her in his arms, he said, "Chicks. Such high maintenance." Tig rested her head on his chest. With one arm holding her, he rhythmically stroked the back of her head with the other hand. After a moment he began a hum that turned to words she could only just make out: "My dog is an awesome dog . . . ."

Chapter Twenty
Wrestling Intruders

Unrelenting drapes of rain crashed onto to the blacktop and streamed into the gutters. Tig shook herself in the entryway of her old clinic and made her way over to the reception desk. Macie waited for her, smiling, resembling Thatcher's barely contained enthusiasm.

"I saw you on the schedule to see Julie." Macie pulled gently on her eyebrow ring. "It's so good to see you."

"It's good to see you, too, but you hardly look yourself."

Macie poked her head forward and lowered her voice. "Things are changing around here. I got the vibe that they'd prefer a more conservative look." Macie made quotation marks in the air over the word *conservative*. She had cut and dyed her hair into a sharp blond pageboy and wore a vintage housedress with lacy collar. "The goth look is so yesterday anyway. I'm wearing camo underwear just to keep my edge. Are you here to get your old job back? They'd give it to you in a minute. People discovered this was your clinic and they call for appointments all the time."

Tig shook her head. "No, I don't think so."

Macie sat at attention. "Does this mean you're going back to radio? I only ask because Jean's mad, but not so mad she wouldn't put you back on the schedule."

"I don't know what I'm doing yet. Is Julie available now?"

"Yeah. Go down the hall to the right, second d . . . oops, you know where she is." Macie laughed uncomfortably.

Just before Tig turned the corner, Macie called out. "Dr. Monahan, it's an honor working with you. I just wanted to say that."

Tig waved, knocked once, and walked into her mentor's office.

"Thanks for coming in." Julie came over and gave Tig a quick hug. "You look well. Too thin, but a little more rested." Julie gestured to the chair in front of her desk.

Tig said, "The place looks the same."

"Did you expect it to look different?"

"I wanted it to. So I could feel differently, maybe feel like I want to be here."

"You don't?"

Tig said, "I'm not sure. I'm going to Hawaii for a while. I don't know for how long." She crossed her legs. "The radio show didn't go well."

"That's not what I heard."

"Macie."

"No, it wasn't just Macie who told me about the show. My patients listen, too."

"They're not exactly qualified."

"You don't think so?" Julie leaned forward. "I tuned in. You're a good therapist, Tig." Julie rolled her chair close. "That's why I was prepared to offer you a portion of your job back. A job share. But I'm glad to hear you're taking some time to find your feet."

Tig dropped her shoulders. "I think Pete leaving me set something in motion that might otherwise have stayed dormant forever."

"Possibly. But I think issues are selfish little itches. They want attention and they don't exactly wait around for a good time to ask for it. Have you considered what role you played in ending that relationship?"

"He moved . . . to Hawaii. What could I possibly have done about that? He appears to have a girlfriend there." Tig scowled at the memory. "It was a sham. All of it. My mom was just starting to deteriorate. He couldn't take the heat, so he left. The question is how I missed such a gigantic flaw." Tig stood and walked to the window, staring out at the rain. "I'm getting out of this dreary place for a while."

"I wonder if Pete had a similar impulse."

"I can't tell which is more offensive: you suggesting I'm impulsive, or you saying if I'd been sunnier, I'd have kept my man."

"I'm not going to fight with you, Tig. And you know I am not saying either one of those things."

"Then what, Julie? Just say it!"

"Did you read in the newspaper about that fifty-year-old nurse who killed an intruder in her home? He had a hammer, but she wrestled him down and apparently strangled him with her bare hands. Her neighbors said she didn't even need to be comforted afterward. She was an emergency room nurse."

Frustrated, Tig said, "I feel like I'm in a made-for-TV movie where the karate master gives advice to the grasshopper. Could you be anymore obtuse?"

Julie stood. "It's hard for people to get close to you because you're so busy wrestling intruders. One crisis after another keeps you so busy, a quiet cup of tea with conversation never can happen. Relationships need some sit-down time."

"Why is it that every time I'm in this office I want to have a temper tantrum?"

"Let's make another appointment and then you can tell me."

"That's why I can't do this anymore," Tig said, touching Julie's nameplate on her desk. "I can't wait to let people figure things out on their own. I'm not like you anymore. I want to slap people."

"Not every therapist has the same technique. With experience, successes, and failures, you adjust your therapy style. I think you are adjusting."

"I've gotta go. I didn't come here for therapy."

"What did you come for?"

"I don't actually know. Maybe I came for permission. Permission to go to Hawaii. Permission to leave and figure out if this relationship door is opened or closed, and do it where there is sun."

"You don't need anyone's permission."

"I think I've been waiting for someone to say, 'Go to Hawaii and figure this thing out with Pete.' I don't think I've entertained the idea of going there until right this minute. But I've got to go and look Pete in the eye and see how both of us are feeling while in the same zip code, Hawaiian girl or no."

Tig stood and looked at Julie who said, "I'm not going to say it, Tig. You have to give yourself the permission to go."

Tig nodded, collected her purse and raincoat.

"Before you go, I have something for you from Mrs. Biddle." Mrs. Biddle, from what seemed to Tig a lifetime ago. The woman who lost her daughter to cancer and couldn't even manage a load of laundry.

"She wanted me to tell you something." Julie shuffled through a small stack of pink memos on her desk and read: "'Dr. Monahan, I made chicken almondine and my new dog's name is Mug. He's a pug.'"

In the hallway, head down, hands in the pockets of her raincoat, Tig fingered Mrs. Biddle's note. It felt like a diminutive cheer. *Goooooo, Tig!* Engrossed in her thoughts, Tig would have walked right by Jean Harmeyer, who stood at the front desk, if Macie hadn't said, "I called her."

"Come back to the show, Tig."

"No. It's not right."

"What if we make it right?"

"How?"

"I don't know. Let's take what we started and make it into your dream job."

Tig jerked her coat open. "I don't know what my dream job is. Or my dream man, or my dream sister. I can't keep doing this."

"What do you mean, doing what? Living, Tig? This is living."

"It feels miserable."

Impatiently, Jean placed her sunglasses on top of her head. "Um, yeah, Tig that is living. Did you think the definition of living ended with a smiley face and a series of exclamation points? We're not a teen's notebook here." She slipped her computer bag over her shoulder. "Your problem, Dr. Monahan, is that you don't know what you want."

"You're wrong. I do know what I want." Tig clenched her teeth and for the second time in thirty minutes she had an epiphany of certainty and action. "If you want me back, then call the woman whose husband killed himself. I want to do the show, but I need to talk to her first."

"Well, this is out of the blue."

Tig nodded. "I just now realized that's what I need."

Jean shook her head, "I can't legally do that."

"Call her, Jean. I can't move forward until I talk to her."

"You don't understand. I think we have her family convinced that you didn't have any part in his death. If you talk to her, it will look like you do. Or you'll say something that will implicate yourself."

"I'll talk with you about the show if you do this for me." Wrapping the belt of her raincoat around her waist, Tig said, "Now, I'm going to Hawaii, to wrestle an intruder and figure out what else I want."

Chapter Twenty-One
I Like You Just Fine When You're Not Around

Tig realized she had a lot to do after announcing to everyone who still talked to her that she was heading for Hawaii. She needed to search for flights, pack, tell Wendy, notify Hope House, and call Pete. For a moment in her living room she considered not leaving at all, and letting people think she'd gone on to confront her problems, get her man back. She laughed at what a ridiculous notion that was. What an impossibly silly, overly Hollywood notion it was to think a grand gesture could restore trust and return a man to his rightful owner. How unrealistic it was to get on a plane and expect all would be well. And before she thought anymore insane thoughts, she grabbed the grocery bag with the baby doll from Alec in it and walked out her front door. It was a perfect time to visit her mother. Fern was in warm water therapy. Wendy, upon greeting Tig, left to drop off the breakfast tray, and Clementine was happily imitating a tiny, hairless, panda baby: nuzzling her fist, burrowing her face, and clucking quietly in Hallie's arms.

"Hey, Mom. I have something for you."

Her mother turned from the big picture window and smiled. "I'm glad to see you. I think this kitten is going to be all right."

"I think so, too, Mom."

"Have any of our afternoon appointments come in?"

Tig withdrew the doll. "This one needs to be looked at."

Hallie tilted her head. Tig flipped the hidden switch in the doll's back and cradled the bundle in her arms.

"What do you think is wrong with her?"

"She's a stray. She just needs some love."

Hallie frowned. "Can't you see my hands are full?"

"I can see that, Mom. Would you like me to take that one?"

Exasperated, Hallie said, "Obviously."

Tig carefully traded Clementine for the nameless baby doll, snuggling each bundle close.

Hallie knit her brows together, hefted the doll, and looked uncertain. She lifted the arm and said, "I don't know." Tig didn't speak. Hallie shook her head side to side, frowning. "I don't know."

Tig drew in a breath. "She's sick. That's all. You know how they get."

Her mother snuggled the doll a little closer. She tucked her limbs into the blanket. "This one is going to take some time. This one looks as bad as the McGuires' cat, the one with the twisted bowel."

Wendy walked into the room and Tig turned, placing a finger to her lips. She slowly handed Clementine to her sister. "Do you think you can help this kitten, Mom?"

Resolved, Hallie raised her eyebrows and gave a little nod. "I can sure give it a try."

Tig released a relieved breath to the ceiling. "What are you going to call it?"

"You can't name them. They may not make it. I learned my lesson with the last one. Now, go on. This one needs some rest, and it is way too noisy in here."

Tig ushered her sister out the door.

With admiration, Wendy said, "Nice."

Tig ignored her. "I'm going to Hawaii and you have to move into my place to take care of Thatcher. And don't even think of saying no."

Wendy quickly bobbed her head up and down. "I'll do it. Don't worry about anything. And when you get back, we'll all get together. You, Phil, me."

"Just live in my house. Bring Phil in, too. I don't care. Let him see what it's all about so he really knows."

"Don't be mad at us, Tig."

"I don't know who to be mad at. I'm getting out of here. I've got to talk to Pete."

Wendy reached out to touch her sister's arm. "I think that's a great idea. Don't worry about anything."

"Thatcher needs a walk every day."

"Right."

"Tell Fern and Alec where I am, and be sure Erin Ann knows that I'll bring her something back from the Big Island." She continued the list, backing up down the hall.

"Dr. Jenson needs to keep an eye on our bill. The payments are mysterious enough. I don't want there to be a mysterious lapse too while I'm gone."

"Yep."

"Oh, and Wendy, get Mom to name the doll."

• • •

When she'd called Pete, she cried into the phone, "I miss you."

When he exhaled, she could almost see him rub his hands across his scar. "I miss you, too," he'd said. "When are you coming?"

Tig boarded her flight with a full fifteen minutes to spare. She'd packed her breeziest clothing. Light cotton dresses, flip-flops, beachwear. She even brought the swimsuit the Asian store clerk had called her Hot Mama suit. A red bikini with strings. "Purple not your color; you go with red. Get your boyfriend to sit up. Take notice."

Breezy clothes for a breezy girl. The kind of girl who would take off at a moment's notice. A Wendy kind of girl, Tig thought.

A middle-aged man in a yellow golf shirt and khakis smiled politely as he settled a computer briefcase under the seat in front of him and pulled out a newspaper. A Wendy kind of girl might say hello. Instead, Tig pulled the inflatable travel pillow from her carry-on bag and started to blow it up. Would a Wendy kind of girl plan far enough ahead to have an inflatable travel pillow? No, she said to herself. I'm a more evolved breezy kind of girl. Breezy with benefits.

The act of inflating the pillow and herself exhausted her, so Tig slept. After a zombie-like plane change in Seattle, she leaned her head the other way and snored through cart service. When the plane touched down on the Big Island, the grandmotherly woman across the aisle said, "First time on the islands?"

Tig nodded.

"Well, you're sure rested for whatever it is you're going to be doing here. Mahalo."

Tig wiped her mouth with a crumbled in-flight magazine insert and said uncertainly, "Mahalo."

By the time Tig deplaned, she had her wits about her. Pete stood in the baggage claim area, scanning the crowd. He had two flower leis around his tanned neck, draped over his red bandana shirt. Tig was touched by both.

Pete placed both leis around her neck. "Aloha."

Tig said, "Can I just say 'hi' and 'bye'?"

"It won't take long to feel like a native here. It's infectious; you'll see." Pete was like a kid bursting to talk about the first day of school.

"I took some days off. My grad students can handle things. There's so much we can do now that you're here. I want to fly to Maui and mountain bike down Haleakala, and then head over to Kauai and hike on the Napali coast. I thought today we could snorkel and check out the Ironman route."

Tig put her hands up. "I thought you said things move more slowly here. I'm here for three weeks to start; let me regroup for a second."

He took her shoulders and bent down so they were face to face. "Sorry. I'm so glad you're here. Are you tired?"

Tig looked around, hoping not to see the older woman from the plane. "Exhausted."

Pete chatted easily as Tig watched her travel brochure of Hawaii come to life. Palm trees waved as if it was nothing to be a towering tree over an azure ocean. It was as if watching sea turtles float like hubcaps in the water all day was a way of life for everyone. No big deal, mahalo.

"I rented this convertible for us so you could get the whole island experience," Pete said, smiling and showing every one of his stunningly white teeth. Tig felt a splash of wet on her cheek and looked around. The sun was still shining but a sprinkle of rain hit her hands and shoulders. A rainbow appeared on the horizon.

"It rains for five minutes every day and then it's over. If you keep your eyes peeled, you might see a double rainbow."

Tig smiled. "I feel like the island is trying too hard. It's already the prettiest girl at the prom. She doesn't have to show so much leg."

Pete laughed and reached for her. Tig touched the rough calluses on the palms of his hands.

"I've missed you, Tig."

"I've missed you, too," she said, and for a wonderful, carefree, breezy moment, Tig let herself imagine what a life like this might be like. Pete pulled into a hotel turnabout.

Tig said, "I don't have to stay here. I mean, it isn't necessary."

"My place doesn't represent the island adequately."

When they entered the room, Tig felt his expectation in the rushed way he laid out her bags. "Could we just take it easy today? I just want to see the beach. Eat."

He dropped the last bag by the sliding doors in front of a full view of Waikiki Beach and looked into her eyes. "Of course. This trip is for you. I'll admit, I was so angry at you, and then I felt terrible for pushing you all the time. Now, I'm just so glad you are here and I want you to see everything all at once."

Her mind wandered to her mother, the doll, and then to Alec. She recalled the woman's voice when she'd called Pete. It was a sweet voice: *Hello?* She forced her attention to the man in front of her. Pete. She felt the remembered roughness in his beard as he kissed her; took in the faint smell of chlorine that never left him from the years of training in a swimming pool. He had a way of cupping the back of her head, sliding his hand to her neck that raised goose flesh where his fingers made contact. He placed the palm of his hand against her heart and looked into her eyes. They made love on the bed with the sea winds blowing across their bodies, cooling and lifting away the layers that that had built up over their time apart.

When they were finished, Tig lay on her back and Pete ran his fingers over the notch of her shoulders.

"You're thinner than when I left."

"No one was around to feed me."

"I meant to go more slowly, Tig. But then I saw you."

Miraculously she slept again, and when she woke it was dark. Pete sat on the balcony drinking a beer and speaking quietly into the phone. Tig wrapped herself in the bandana shirt and said, "You got food."

He put his phone away. "Takeout from the restaurant beneath us. I was just talking to one of my grad students. I want you to see the lab tomorrow. There's a lot to tell you about."

Tig bit into a shrimp. "It's too good to be true, here. It's like the theme song for a show called *Happily Ever After* is playing all the time."

He guided her onto his lap. "I've been thinking a lot."

"A lot has happened. Wendy came home, had the baby, and left again."

"I heard."

"You heard? How?"

"Macie."

Tig exhaled. "Shit." The Christmas-like lights of a large ship floated across the blackness. Then she gave a tiny shrug. "It's hard to be mad at anything in a place like this. It's like being angry in a dream where a witch materializes and quickly turns into a flowering plant; nothing feels real."

"She means well, and I wanted to know." He took a sip of his beer and said, "There are things you should know, too."

Tig placed her hand over his mouth. "No."

Speaking around her fingers he said, "It's not bad news, Tig. You look like you're bracing for a hit."

"Not tonight, Pete. Just let me be here with you, eating shrimp and feeling this breeze. Anymore sensory changes and I might short-circuit."

Pete concentrated on her face and smoothed her forehead with his thumb. Placing his arms around her, he hugged her and stood. Without speaking, he led her back into the bedroom.

• • •

The next day, Pete gestured with a wide sweeping arch, indicating the large windowless storeroom. "This is my lab." Laughing a little, he said, "I know it's not much. Space doesn't come cheap in Hawaii and the university has very little to begin with."

Tig glanced at the folding tables, laptops, and portable machinery that cluttered the room. "There sure are a lot of outlets."

"Bravo, you have discovered what makes this lab a highly competed-for space." He walked to a cart filled with equipment and said, "We're mostly a mobile lab."

"We go where the athletes go," said an extremely tanned woman with the defined shoulders and the biceps of a professional jar opener. Tig considered her voice, tried to match it to the one in her memory. *Hello?*

Pete turned to Tig. "This is Geri. She's a native on loan from the university here."

"Yep. I volunteered to work with Dr. Pierpont. I've followed his research and think what he's doing with nonsteroidal anti-inflammatories is thrilling. I used to take, like, five ibuprofen before every marathon. Now I know better. I'd like to keep my kidneys." She smiled and displayed one of the prettiest smiles Tig had ever seen outside of a primate lab or *Sports Illustrated Swimsuit Issue.*

Tig smiled and shook her hand, feeling very unfit, very untanned, and very out of the loop.

"I'm Bobby." A tall, wiry man with dreadlocks loped over to where they stood and put out his hand. Tig took it and wondered if he needed a catcher's mitt when he played lab softball, or if his bare hand qualified.

Pete patted Bobby on his shoulder. "This here is our own genuine defector. His hair turned into that mess the first week here and he says he's not going back to Minnesota."

"I'm never wearing a coat again." His skin was flawless, caramel, and luscious. The striations in his long, sinewy muscles could almost be numbered. He was an anatomy lesson awaiting students.

"You do look like you get outside a little," Tig said.

Bobby pulled his hair back and secured it with a longer, matted, beaded piece of hair. "I took up surfing. I try to go before and after work every day. I'm teaching Pete. He's a natural."

The door behind them opened and a woman walked in holding a grocery bag and a six-pack of a red energy drink. There was no debating her beauty. Tig shook her inner head with chagrin. Blonds; they always got a leg up. Casual, surfer-girl perfect, and smart, too, if she was working in Pete's lab.

Pete turned and gestured to the woman. "This is Willow."

Tig smiled. *Of course you are.* "What a perfect name for you."

"My mother was a hippie even after hippies were out of style." She came to stand by Pete and pulled an unseen piece of lint from his hair.

If Tig had been a dog, the hair on her neck would have stood at attention. She took a step back. "This is a far cry from what my graduate school education was like. We spent our days inside racking up counseling hours, and our nights in the library. I should have chosen something more adventurous."

Willow smiled. She had a small gap between her front teeth that made her look even younger and almost accidentally beautiful. She clearly couldn't help her looks. With a surprising generosity of spirit, Willow said, "You're one of us now." Addressing the group, she said, "Should we go for a run?"

"Sometimes we all go for a run to clear our heads for a brainstorming session," Pete explained.

Tig narrowed her eyes at Willow, wondering if she detected the least bit of territory protection coming from the woman. If there was any, Tig couldn't see it. She both liked and disliked her immediately. Pete announced to the group, "You all go. Tig and I are heading over to Kauai to hike and camp."

• • •

After flying, boating, and hiking most of the day, Tig and Pete rested under a tree dripping with moisture near a waterfall. "Did you ever imagine you'd be listening to the waves in a place as close to heaven as this?"

Tig examined the twin blisters open on the arches of both of her feet. She slapped at a mosquito on her chin. "If I were a billy goat, this would be total heaven."

Pete laughed. "You did well today."

Tig scoffed, "Oh, shut up. I did not. It took us the entire day to hike four miles, and my hips, calves, and feet are killing me."

"You made it."

"You should have warned me. I'm not Willow, or the muscly one. I can't just walk out of the nursing home onto a cliff. Mortals have to train. This hike is like running the stairs at a football stadium over and over again."

"Better views here." Pete nudged her and said, "You just don't push yourself. If we moved here, we could do this all the time."

"I think the iodine in that water is affecting your brain. Move here? I don't think so." Tig hadn't meant to say exactly that, or at least not in such an abrupt way. Pete stiffened. The sound of frogs chirping seemed to take over. Tig sat up. "Oh God, I'm sorry. You're serious."

"Why do you do that? Discount what I'm saying like I'm a child? I've been here two months. I love it here."

"I'm sure you do. You're among your people—beautiful, doting ultra-athletes living in uber-paradise. But this isn't real."

"It is to the people living here. It could be for us, too."

"Was this your plan? Change my geography and work my ass off so I'm too tired to fight?"

"You're never too tired to fight, Tig."

"Sorry if I'm not Willow Namaste, the mistress of peace and tranquility."

"I'm not in love with Willow. I'm in love with you."

"My family is in Wisconsin. Yeah, the weather sucks and you can't surf anything but the Internet, but family trumps any other consideration when choosing a place and settling down."

"It's your way or the highway, is that it?"

In the shade of the dripping tree she saw sadness and defeat on Pete's face. She could see what he must have looked like as a child:

cowlick by his forehead, dirt on his chin, a bird with a broken wing in his hand.

"Pete," Tig put her hand on his chest. "I'm here. Can't that be enough for now?"

The soft crash of the ocean hitting the beach washed the air between them, and Pete said, "Okay, I'll leave it. I was stupid to bring it up. You just got here." They listened to the roaring water, allowing the angry falls to fill in their conversation.

"So how was taking care of Clementine?" The question hung in the air between them. It might have been a question about being an aunt, or it might have been a question about being a mother.

Tig sat back in the ruddy sand. "All my college friends are on their first and second kids. This was my first experience with being a full-time mom. It was exhausting, but entirely engaging. It kept me from dwelling on anything for too long. Surprisingly, it only made me want to have a family more than less." She paused. "It's really glorious here."

"I know. I wanted to call you, tell you about it, but I worried we'd fight."

Tig shook her head, knowing it was true. "You know what Oscar Wilde said about relationships, don't you? 'If you don't fight, one of you isn't necessary.'"

"Well, that just about makes us indispensable for each other, doesn't it?" Pete said. "Did Oscar Wilde actually say that? I don't think that's right. It was probably someone from *The View*."

Tig gave a little snort. "You know, Pete, relationships and family are great in theory, but in practice they're a whole different thing."

"Meaning what, exactly?"

"When I think of you, I only remember the good things, the simple things in our relationship. The blue of your eyes. How your hand feels in mine. How much you love Thatcher. I forget that you're a genetic mutant who binges on exercise and calls it a workout, while I call getting out of bed an endurance event. I forget that you love travel, and I'm a homebody. That I love a good snowfall, and you get cold watching a Christmas movie. I don't know why I can't accept those things, why we fight all the time. Because the truth is, and don't be offended, I feel like this with everyone. I like you just fine when you're not around."

Chapter Twenty-Two
Worry Is What You Do When There's Nothing to Be Done

Tig pushed open the door to Pete's lab. "I've brought lunch."

Willow and Bobby looked up from laptops and smiled the dazzling smiles of youth, fitness, and American dentistry at its finest.

"Pete and Geri are meeting with race officials, but they'll be right back." Willow brushed back her hair from her face and strolled over as Tig placed drinks and takeout containers on one of the tables.

"I brought a little bit of everything. I wasn't sure what people liked."

"Bobby," Willow said, "She brought the curry you like."

Bobby gestured with two enthusiastic thumbs up.

Willow said, "Well, Tig, you've been here two weeks. What do you think?"

"It's fabulous."

"I'm not talking about Hawaii."

Tig stopped fiddling with the lunch containers and looked at Willow's face.

Willow bit into a spring roll. "Geri's got a huge crush on Pete."

Tig tilted her head. "And you?"

Willow laughed. "No way. I don't go for men who are in love with other women. It's a turnoff." After opening a sauce packet with her teeth, she said, "When Pete first came, all he could talk about was Tig this, Tig that. Tig would love it here. Tig likes pineapple. Tig has a radio show. Then he calmed down and became kind of sad."

"My mom isn't doing very well. I couldn't come."

"Oh, I know. We heard all about it."

"So is Pete—uh, interested?—in Geri?"

Willow shot Tig a very grownup, *don't be silly* look. "Pete likes a challenge. He's all about running the race, solving the puzzle. He's not attracted to the sure thing. He values something only after working for it." She smiled. "I'm not telling you anything you don't know."

"I can't stay too much longer. I have to get back."

"Pete's doing amazing work here. Making a lot of connections in the Ironman world."

"I get it, Willow." Tig put her hand to her head and said, "I'm sorry, I don't know what's wrong with me. I'm just not a don't-worry-be-happy kind of person. I'm a keep-your-nose-to-the-grindstone kind of person. And that kind of person can be pretty crabby at times."

Willow said, "I understand. The sun and fun attitude on the islands can make for as much peer pressure as a frat party. When I first came here, I felt super guilty whenever I was in a bad mood. Like you had to be just as cheerful as the weather every second of the day, or you were ungrateful."

"Exactly! I've felt that since day one," Tig said. "It's a tremendous amount of drag on your serotonin reuptake. I'm afraid that anymore time spent here and I'll be completely out of positive brain chemicals. I'll be like a person in ecstasy withdrawal. Like I have to get out of here before I drink the Kool-Aid."

"You'd get used to it and take it for granted like the rest of us before long, I promise."

"I suppose," Tig said, unconvinced. "Hawaii was just a sabbatical idea at first. He completed the application process and we talked about Hawaii like it was the moon. A pretty, silver dream. I was in the middle of caring for my mother. Of losing my mother. Of course I fantasized about Hawaii. When his sabbatical was approved, Hawaii became part of his teaching contract, but it was still just an idea for me. I feel like I okayed the thing just by talking about it. I don't think I ever intended that. My mom may not have her mind, but she also may not have many years left. I've got to get back home."

"You gotta tell Pete what you just told me."

"I don't know how to leave, or tell him anything."

"Yes, you do," Willow said. "I'll back you up if you at least show him how to use soap. Half the time he smells like a camel."

The outer door pushed open and Pete strode in with Geri on his heels.

Tig smiled and looked more closely at Geri than she had before. Maybe it was unrequited love she saw in Geri's eyes instead of ownership.

"Everything is set at the race site. I got a press pass for you, Tig, and our mobile unit is getting rigged. In one week, we go live." Smiling at Tig, he said, "Can you believe we're coming up on fall? It's seventy-five degrees today."

"You can quit selling it, Pete. You win. The weather is fabulous; the people are beautiful; there are no negatives. It's paradise."

Pete put his arm around Tig's shoulder and hugged her. "I'm glad you see it my way."

Tig's phone rang. She fumbled in her purse.

The caller ID said *Mom*.

With alarm, Tig said, "Hello?"

The hesitant voice of a little girl said, "Tig? It's Erin Ann."

"Erin? What're you doing? Is my mom okay?"

"Yeah. I took her phone to call you. It's Grandma Fern. She's really sick. Can you come?"

"Where's your dad? Can I talk to him?" Tig turned her back to the others.

There was a long pause. "He's here. He doesn't know I'm calling. I think she's dying. She looks like Mama did."

Pete, Willow, and Geri stood quietly, listening to the phone call.

"Fern was fine a week ago when I called. I'm sure she's not dying, sweetie."

"She's barely ever awake. My dad and I come every day."

"Put Wendy on."

"No. I don't want Wendy." Starting to cry, Erin said, "Can't you come? I need you. Everyone does."

"Everyone?"

"Wendy cries a lot; your mother fell. She's got two black eyes. Grandma Fern is gonna die. Please."

"My mother fell?" Alarmed, Tig paced. "I call every day. Why didn't someone tell me? Don't cry, honey. You keep my mom's phone. Put it in your pocket. I'll call you back."

She hung up the phone and looked into Pete's eyes. What she knew, he knew. She was leaving.

• • •

At the airport, Pete said, "You don't have to go." The tropical breeze ruffled his hair. "They didn't call you about your mom because she's fine. Didn't Dr. Jenson say so when you talked to him?"

"You could come with me, Pete. Let the kids collect the data. You've done the hard part. Let them finish it." The look in his eyes told her this would not be happening. Putting her hands up, she said, "Okay. All right. Be patient with me, Pete. I promise to consider Hawaii. I just have to get back home now. At least now I know what I'm missing by not being here."

He shook his head in frustration. "Wendy is never going to grow up if you keep rescuing her."

"My mother fell on her face, Pete." As if to herself, she said, "Besides, it's not Wendy I'm going back for. It's for Clementine and my mom. It's for Fern and Erin."

"And Alec?"

"I didn't tell you about Alec and Fern to have you toss that back at me." She fiddled with a luggage tag. "He's my friend, Pete."

"A friend with a ready-made family."

Her head snapped up. "That was a low blow. What about you and Willow, or Geri? They've got no family. No issues at all, from what I can see."

"I'm not shopping for a relationship based on the size of their entourage, Tig."

"Exactly," Tig said, clicking the handle to attention on her carry-on luggage. Softening, but still anxious, she placed her hand on Pete's forehead and smoothed his hair back. She touched his scar. He pulled his head away. Tig, hurt and insulted, said, "Go on back to your worshipful flock. It's a simple relationship, as long as everyone understands the terms. All admire man-boy Pete while he runs in the opposite direction."

The sound Pete made was not loud; in fact, Tig couldn't have said where it came from. His strangled throat, his twisted heart. She had already turned her head away, so she didn't see his face when he said, "Pardon me, Dr. Monahan, but I think you have me confused with yourself."

• • •

As much as she had slept on the way over, Tig found there would be no rest on the way home. Dark, anxious anticipation filled her stomach on the red-eye flight from the first connection to last. Spending two weeks in paradise had done nothing to erase the worries. Thoughts of her mother's imagined, injured face, the blood on the carpet in her own house. Fern's stiffened hands. Pete's rough beard, his hardened words, his hands. Uncomplicated Alec with his own sad history. The man who committed suicide, though faceless to her, followed her everywhere with a blaming finger raised.

She could hear her mother's voice from the past addressing Tig's anxiety over an unfairness or a troubled relationship. Her mother would say, "Tiglet, this high drama is over when you say it's over. Just pull out. Stop playing along."

Unable to disengage that easily, Tig would cry, "But I want to be happy. What if I make a mistake?"

In her signature, practical way her mother would say, "Stop making happiness some kind of concrete goal. It's a side effect. It's a secondary happening, but not the main event. Happiness is what you feel when you've been kind, fair, or loving in the face of hardness. It is the feeling of light that comes after behaving in the way you ultimately want."

But that was the problem, Tig thought. What did she want?

Tig brushed her hair and applied lip gloss on the way from the airport to Hope House. She took in the vivid change of scenery. The succulent greens had changed to boisterous yellows, reds, and oranges. The smell of mossy pre-fall Wisconsin filled the car.

Once inside Hope House, Tig strode to her mother's room. Hallie sat holding her baby doll, gazing serenely out the picture window onto the grounds. As Tig approached, Hallie smiled. "I don't feel like seeing animals today; call Mrs. Tyson and tell her I'm taking a personal day." Her eyes were ringed with dark blue, red, and yellow—garish and stark against her pale face. Tig reached out to touch the bruises. Her mother pulled back and glared at Tig.

Pam Gibson walked up. "I heard you were here. Welcome home."

"I leave and this happens? Look at her."

Hallie started to fidget.

"Where was Wendy? How did this happen?"

Unfazed, Pam said, "Wendy was here, Tig."

Hallie started to fret and rock the baby doll. "There, there."

"Why wasn't she helping my mom?"

Pam crooked her finger. "You are upsetting your mother, Dr. Monahan. Come with me."

Tig looked at Hallie, who frantically patted the baby and looked worriedly from the window and back. "Get Dan. I need Dan."

Touching her mother's shoulder, she said, "It's okay. I'm sorry. It's okay." She placed a cool hand on her forehead.

Her mother ceased her rocking, but her eyes darted around the room. "I need your father."

"I know, Mom. It's okay."

"Let's step outside in the hall and talk." The nurse strode out the door and into the hallway, stopping only to see that Tig was following.

Right behind her, Tig said, "Tell me what happened."

"She was on the toilet and dropped her doll's blanket. When she bent to pick it up, she bumped her nose against the safety rail mounted on the wall next to the toilet. She didn't break her nose, and she appeared to have no other injuries, but when she woke the next day she had two black eyes."

"Why didn't someone call me?"

"What would you have done, Tig? Your sister was here. Dr. Jenson came. We had it covered."

"I'm her daughter! I should have been told."

"Her other daughter, Wendy, didn't want you disturbed. Give her some credit for handling it."

"I can't help but feel that I was off getting a suntan while everything over here was going to shit."

Pam pulled herself up. "That is offensive, and belittles what I personally do here. You are not some good-luck talisman who keeps everything running perfectly as long as you're around. This is a nursing home, Dr. Monahan. People don't usually get younger here. We do everything we can to fight against the discomforts of aging. If you think you can do better, take your mother back home. Be my guest."

Pam turned on her heel and marched away. Watching her go, Tig muttered, "Score one for Hope House."

No longer filled with outrage, Tig walked to the nurses' desk where Alec stood, arms folded, concentrating on the compassionate face of a nurse. She touched his arm gently. Delighted surprise flitted across his face, momentarily followed by concern. "What are you doing here? I thought you weren't due back for another week."

"I thought it was time to come home. How's your mom?"

He sighed and gave Tig a brief hug. "Not well."

Tig accompanied Alec down the hall. In Fern's room, Erin popped up from her chair and ran to Tig.

"You came!" She buried her head into Tig's stomach, holding her tight. The unbridled enthusiasm and girdle of warmth from Erin, coupled with her own fatigue and worry, made Tig's eyes smart. Over Erin's head, Tig was alarmed to see the shell of Fern Fobes. She looked as dry as the leaves Tig had kicked through on the front path to Hope House. Parched and tiny. Flat on her back with her white hair brushed up on her pillow, Fern's mouth was open and she seemed to breathe in a way that was all unsatisfying nerve impulse and had nothing to do with rejuvenation and life.

Tig guided Alec into the hall with Erin still clinging to her waist. "What happened?"

Alec shook his head, baffled. "She told me she wanted to die and made me sign a Do Not Resuscitate order. Then she had a long talk with Erin."

Tig knelt down and looked Erin in the eye. "What did she say, honey?"

With a watery breath, Erin said, "She said that she was getting really sick and pretty soon she wouldn't be able to go to the bathroom or breathe alone. She said that her body has been her best friend for eighty years, but now it needs to rest. She said her body is really tired."

Tig pulled a strand of light brown hair away from Erin's face and secured it behind her ear. "Oh, I'm sorry, sweetie, that must be so hard for you."

Alec hugged his daughter close. "The nurse said her skin is starting to mottle. That's not a good sign. Her blood is pooling. I can't see how this happened so fast. Now I don't know what's keeping her here. At this point, I wish she would allow herself to go. I can hardly bear to watch it. It's just too close to losing Jennifer."

Tig stood up. "Maybe you need to tell her it's okay to go. That you will be fine."

"Do you think she can still hear? That it will register with her?"

Erin Ann wandered back to Fern's bedside and tentatively touched her hand.

Alec said, "She's gone through a lot, that little girl."

Tig stepped into Alec, holding him close. After a moment, he said, "I don't know what I'll do without my mom." Tig heard a gurgle in his throat and realized he was crying. "She's always been there." Stepping back, he palmed his face and gave a little self-conscious sigh. "Of course she has, right?"

Tig smiled. "I understand. Some parents go on cruises; others, like yours and mine, they never miss a baseball game and hold your baby even when their mind is off in the 1960s. I'm not sure which is better."

"The second one looks better on paper."

"Yeah. Still, being the one who's always there isn't what it's cracked up to be."

"I'm glad you're here."

"I didn't mean how that sounded. I want to be here."

Alec leaned against the wall and looked over Tig's shoulder. "I've always been afraid of the freak accident. You know: the car crash on vacation, a fall in the shower. Sudden death. God, worry is a waste of time."

"Worry is what you do when there's nothing to be done. You can't be in the car with your teen, so you worry about your teen in the car."

"Yeah. I worried when my wife was on the road if it snowed. I worried that if she traveled, her plane would crash. Apparently, I should have been worrying about my wife's pancreas." Shaking his head, he added, "And my mom's connective tissue."

"That's exhausting to even think about."

Alec studied his daughter, who was now sitting with her knees tucked under her chin, playing a handheld computer game. "I'm mostly sorry for Erin. Look at her, so at ease with death at such a young age."

Tig folded her arms. "I don't think that's a bad thing, Alec. Think about it; you don't really live life if you don't know the value of it. You learn the value of things when you realize you could lose them. Think about all the people who finally give up smoking or steak after they have their first heart attack. Erin will always know how precious life is."

Alec looked at her admiringly.

"God, don't look at me like that," Tig said. "I'm only smart about other people. I've got absolutely no insight where my people are concerned. Or myself, either. You met me living in a nursing home, remember?"

"That was the one happy accident that's occurred lately."

Tig smiled. "Don't start worrying about my connective tissue."

Walking into Fern's room to be with his daughter, he said, "I might, and there's not a thing you can do about it."

Chapter Twenty-Three
A Little Night Music

With half a dozen leis wilting in the back seat next to her luggage, Tig passed the University of Wisconsin Hospital, the remodeled strip mall, and the bagel shop close to her house. She dialed her phone.

"Jean, I'm back. I've been thinking a lot. If you set up a meeting with the woman whose husband killed himself, I'll tell you my idea for some changes in the radio show with the goal of trying again. That's my deal. Take it or leave it." Tig dropped her phone into her purse and drove up her driveway. The sight of her red door, the golden leaves of the maple tree, and Thatcher's head in the front window was as effective as a Welcome Home banner at making her feel, well . . . home.

Inside, Thatcher scrambled to her side, sneezing and doing what Tig called the doggie-hello dance. *That was the longest ten minutes of my life. So glad you're home, your crotch smells exactly right.* It was the same welcome she received if she was gone for a month or an hour. Thatcher never discriminated. Her philosophy was if you came home, you deserved a parade.

Tig looked around. The place was spotless. The notes for her mother were all gone, along with the remnants of adhesive and dust that went with each. Her mail was stacked in a tidy basket on the hall table next to a mix of orange, red, and yellow mums. The house smelled of lemons, cinnamon, and fresh air. Wendy rounded the corner with Clementine tied to her in the baby sling.

"Bienvenido a casa." Wendy smiled, bending her head to her child. "I told you your aunt was coming. Look Clem, it's Auntie Tig."

Tig peeked at her niece. Stroking the baby's face, Tig felt a rush of uncomplicated pleasure. "I thought you'd be at Mom's."

Wendy smiled back. "I wanted to make sure the place was ready for you. Come see." Tig followed Wendy, noticing small changes along the way. The frayed carpet in front of the sink had been replaced with a vibrant rug woven with reds, oranges, and blues. The old singed potholders that had hung over the stove now matched the rug. The counters were clean, the microwave wiped free of smudges, and the coffeemaker bubbled.

"I hired a cleaning woman. Come see Clem's room."

No longer a makeshift baby-holding area, the space had been arranged into a cozy living spot for a girl to grow. "I hope you don't mind. Phil painted. Do you like the color? It's called Sweet Pea Green. I found the crib dust ruffle at Lost and Found, that little consignment store downtown."

"It looks great, Wen, like we stepped inside a magazine. So things with Phil are good?"

"It's a long story. How is Pete?"

"That's a long story, too."

A slice of quiet sat between them until Wendy cleared her throat and said, "Do you really like the place?" Wendy beamed like a six-year-old looking for approval on a handmade birthday card.

"I do, Wen. What's not to like? The place hasn't been this clean in years. How'd you do all this with Clem? Phil must have really stepped up."

"It wasn't that hard after Clem stopped crying." Wendy addressed her child in baby talk, "You did, didn't you? You stopped crying." To Tig she said, "We have a little routine now. We get up and eat, take Thatcher for a walk, get started on our lists, nap a little, and start over."

"And Phil?"

"He's gone." Wendy blinked rapidly and inhaled.

"That was fast. For good?"

Wendy nodded hard. "Just couldn't do it." With her chin up, she said, "I'm not interested in any half proclamations, any 'we'll sees.' All in or all done is what I'm saying these days."

"Does he want to be in her life in smaller ways?"

"I don't care if he does. What would that message be? I like you, but not enough to put you to bed every night or go to your parent-teacher conferences on a regular basis. That's a pet owner, not a father. I might ask him to sign over parental rights. We grew up without a father, you especially."

Tig said, "The people who always use that argument are the ones with the most problems. I mean, Wen, we sat right here, in this room, looking through a mystery box trying to figure out who our mother was after we made some dubious choices of our own."

"All in or all done." Wendy's voice cracked on the last word.

"You okay?"

"I found I can't like someone who doesn't love Clem and want to spend significant time with her. Look at her, Tig. Just look at her." A fat, silent admonishment sat unspoken between them and Wendy dragged her head up to look at her sister. "You had every right to want to kill me. I can't explain how I could leave her with you. It was like there was a freight train going through my brain and I was trying to deal with everything else around that sound. If I ever did get a chance to sleep, I would wake feeling like cold water was swirling around my neck. The night you came home, I had a thought that I just couldn't deal with." Wendy coughed.

Tig stroked Clementine's head. "I did time with the colic version of her. I know. She was merciless."

"No. Let me say this. I wanted to stop her. Put my hand over her mouth." Wendy coughed again.

Tenderly, Tig said, "Wen, I know. I should have always known. I just couldn't see past my anger at you. I really need to work on that. I'm only a therapist when I'm working. I'm terrible in my life."

Wendy tried to take a deep breath and gasped a great gob of air that sounded like what pain would sound like if it could speak.

"You're not alone. I brushed up on postpartum depression. I developed a hypothesis of my own: New moms are in over-achieving mode. They want to do it all right—parenting, partnering, preparing for every possible danger. They assume when something isn't going well, it's their fault, and if they just try harder—sleep less, dig in—all will go well. I think the unspeakable thoughts that vault into the brain are a way of getting our attention. As if the sane part of the brain is hitting you with the next best thing to a two-by-four. The thought is so terrible you can see it for what it is. Not right. Sick. Before that, moms think they have to be Martha Stewart and make a fondant-covered caterpillar cake for the baby's first-month birthday and color-code the nursery—which is its own sickness, no offense, Martha."

"So you think my brain was firing off warnings, and I wasn't paying attention until it fired off the mother of all warnings?"

"It's an idea. A shot over the bow with the roots in low serotonin reuptake"

Straightening Clementine's collar, Wendy said, "I should have listened to you. But to be honest, I was sick to death of listening to you."

"I'm sick of listening to me."

A car accelerated up the hill outside the house. Thatcher walked to the front window, her nails snipping at the hardwood floor.

"I boxed up the rest of Mom's things and brought some of them to the basement. The rest I took to Goodwill. But I found something you need to see."

In the living room, Wendy slid a small, unadorned cedar box off the mantel and handed it to Tig. "It was wrapped up in a box of dresses you probably never had a reason to unpack. Apparently, Mom had a romance some time after Dad died. And it wasn't fly-by-night."

Tig's eyes narrowed. "I've been wondering. Do you remember her ever talking about it?"

"Never, but wait till you see what's in there."

Tig cracked the lid open and peered inside the box. At the top of a small pile of papers lay a photograph of three people. Hallie Monahan—timeless in her khaki shorts and bare feet. A simple white sleeveless shirt and shoulder-length chestnut hair completed the vision. Her hand was extended, once and forever giving orders, orchestrating in the middle of the music. It was the mother of Tig's memories, the mother whose soft hands comforted her at night and whose voice whispered aspirations at the end of a challenging day: *You're smart and beautiful. You have it all.*

On the back of the photograph, the year 1971 was written in their mother's hand. Tig said, "That's the year before Dad died. I wonder if he took the picture."

"Look at who else is in the photo."

"Who are the other two?"

Clementine fussed, a soft sounding percolator of hunger. Wendy opened her shirt. "Keep looking."

To the side, the space of a missing person away from her mother, stood a couple. The woman had a sunny head of frizzy curls, a seventies perm gone bad, and high-waisted short shorts. She laughed into the camera, oblivious to the man next to her, who was clearly enthralled with Hallie's antics. He had a full head of hair and an athlete's body.

"Who are they?" Tig said, then jerked up her head, eyes wide. "Dr. Jenson! And that must be his wife. He told me they used to spend time together." She looked closely at the photograph again. "I don't know if I'm more surprised by the young and handsome Dr. Jenson, or the look of adoration on the face of the young and handsome Dr. Jenson."

"Yeah," Wendy nodded.

"Mom was pretty." Tig placed the photograph aside and picked up an envelope, heavy with something bulky inside. She found, wrapped in a piece of unlined notepaper, several wingnuts strung together with a piece of twine. Penned in the now familiar hand from the poem behind the painting were the words *I'm nuts about you*. Tig looked at her sister and raised her eyebrows.

Another envelope contained her father's obituary, and Wendy said, "The day Mom turned to steel."

Tig read from the clipping. "'Dan (Danny) Monahan passed away September 9, 1972, at the age of forty-three. Loving husband and best friend to Hallie Monahan. Devoted father and adoring fan of Wendy Monahan. Memorial service Saturday,' etcetera. Leave it to Mom, this obit was the business end of sorrow."

"Who's this other obituary?"

"That's Dr. Jenson's wife. Judy Werner Jenson. It was several years after Dad, but she was ultimately about the same age as Dad when she died."

Tig scanned the newspaper clipping. "I knew they didn't have children. It says here she lost a battle with breast cancer. Man, she was young when she died."

"They must have been good friends."

"Tig. Wake up. It wasn't the woman Mom was friends with. It was Dr. Jenson. Think about it. Look at the picture. Why do you think he visits her, has her in his nursing home?"

Tig's hand dropped to her lap. "What?"

Wendy raised her eyes to the ceiling. "For Christ's sake. How can you not see it? He still looks at her the same way as he does in the photograph."

Tig examined the small, yellowed picture in her hand. It did seem like there was an invisible arrow connecting Dr. Jenson's gaze to her mother. "So you think he's still in love with her?"

"You've seen them together. He doesn't treat her like a typical patient. He let you practically move in with a dog and a baby. Didn't you ever think that was way above the duty of a nursing home?"

"She's gotta be fifteen years older than him and there's no way she remembers him back then or now."

"Phil is ten years older than I am. Besides, five years or fifteen years—it all evens out after fifty. I've been thinking about it. It probably started as a young man's crush on his brother's best friend's wife."

"It's beginning to feel very stalker-ish, don't you think?"

"It depends on whether you reference everything through the looking glass of Nora Ephron or the *National Enquirer*."

"Look what else is in that box."

Tig touched a smooth, round river stone, black and silky. She held it in her hand, smoothed her thumb against it. She placed the stone on top of the obituaries, and pulled out a small wooden heart fashioned from a light, porous wood. There was a green, gold, and blue enamel world globe the size of a marble, and a tiny red basket filled with the brown, dried petals of a hydrangea plant, resembling tiny paper hearts. Last, Tig pulled out a craft-store robin's egg, the color of her mother's eyes. "This is like a magpie's treasure chest."

There were two last things in the chest. One was a note that said, *I can't wait to say I told you so.* The other was a ticket from a theater in Chicago. *A Little Night Music*, 1972. Tig fingered the ticket, softened from years of remembering, examining, and stroking. Instead of replacing the small rectangle, Tig put it aside. "He must have meant a lot to Mom if she kept all this stuff. I'm going to talk to him about this tomorrow. Why didn't we know about him? Or why didn't he mention this to us?"

"I don't know. The more I learn about Mom, the more I learn about me. You're the expert, Tig. Is there such a thing as emotional genetics? Because none of us seem to be very good at relationships."

Tig started to protest, then said, "I'm really good at them when I'm alone. When I'm alone I know just what to do."

Chapter Twenty-Four
His Mistake

Tig woke slowly, stretching her legs. Before opening her eyes she listened to the quiet, white noise of the house. The hum of the refrigerator, the neighbor's wind chimes wandering around in the quiet breeze, and the total lack of requests from the world. She smiled, and as soon as she acknowledged that this solitary thing was good, the phone rang. She turned on her side, dropped her arm over the bed, and ran her fingers through Thatcher's silky fur. The phone rang again and Tig reached for it.

Jean Harmeyer spoke. "Tig, I've got you an appointment with Carolyn Hammer."

"Who?"

"Did I wake you? It's nine-thirty."

"Jet lag. Who is Carolyn Hammer?"

"The woman whose husband killed himself, remember? The one you want so badly to speak to, against all better judgment."

"Okay, when and where?"

"Get your game on, girl. Our lawyers aren't going to let you in the door unless you're in top form."

"I'm not going if the lawyers are going to be there. It's a conversation I want. Not a negotiation or argument. We can't be real if the lawyers are putting our conversation through a legal strainer and separating all the humanity out."

"Don't knock lawyers, Tig. My lawyer, Loraine, got Newman into a therapist and he's having a heyday examining his inner prickishness."

"Seriously?"

"Yeah. Loraine has a formula. Start with a conversation only the dog can hear. She hits the money octave, the reality-speak of a good old-fashioned Wisconsin divorce where it's all formula and percent of income. Country club membership loss follows a discussion of living accommodations. This usually scares the young girl-slash-love interest off. Then what you're left with is a lonely man who can't find the dry cleaner's bag and believes he is living in a third-world country—a.k.a., the duplex. That, my dear, is the scientific formula of how to get a man to therapy."

"Is he becoming a more sensitive male?"

"You know what they say. You can force a man into therapy, but you can't make him think. So, it's time for phase two."

"Do I dare ask?"

"Phase two is when he realizes that his fifty-percent custody in reality means what it's always meant: he sees the kids less than ten percent of the time. With work, golf, and beers after a hard day, he's only ever been there about ten percent of their lives, but since the math is being done by lawyers and not his wife, he finally sees it. That scenario has 'why me' written all over it. So, he pitches that tale of woe out to a counselor with a catcher's mitt especially designed to lasso dysfunction and voilà! Introspection."

"Okay, but Jean, a lawyer in this situation is only going to mess it up. I want to talk to Carolyn Hammer alone. Figure out how I could have done better by her. I need this for me." Tig paused, then added, "If you do this for me, I'll send you an e-mail with my proposal for a new show." It was quiet on the line. Jean breathed audibly. A spray of sunlight pointed out the dustiest corners in the bedroom like a spiteful mother-in-law.

"Her number is in the phone book. You didn't hear it from me. Carolyn Hammer—remember."

The phone went dead.

• • •

Carolyn Hammer agreed to meet at a downtown coffee bar. Tig, with the perfect posture of a first-chair flutist, sat at a corner table, an iced coffee sweating anxiously in her hand, the warm sun shining in on the lacquered table. For fifteen minutes, her head bobbed up every time the bell on the door signaled the entrance of a patron. She shook her head and talked herself out of looking again, making a very taxing game of it until another five minutes passed. She checked her watch again.

"Are you Dr. Monahan?" A woman stood above Tig, the sun dusting her blond hair.

"Carolyn?" Tig stood and sent her chair tipping backward, pulling the light coffee-shop table out of line.

"I don't have much time. My friend is watching Missy, my daughter." Carolyn Hammer wore jeans, a white peasant blouse, several large silver rings on her fingers, and casual elegance around her shoulders like a shawl. Tig hadn't expected this woman. She had expected someone more childlike, naive. Either much younger or much older; someone needing permission to say 'stop,' to hold someone accountable. Tig marveled at her prejudices, even after all those years of counseling. The elegant, educated, and brilliant had just as many relationship problems as the high school dropout and, if she were honest with herself, sometimes the dropouts had less.

"Thank you for coming." Tig tried a jittery smile.

Carolyn dropped a large, exotically colored fabric bag on the floor. "No. I wanted to. There isn't a soul I can talk to about this," Carolyn said, whispering, "Not a soul."

If Tig had seen this woman at the grocery store or in front of her in the line for a movie, she would have admired her style and obvious ability to have it all. Poise, genes, and a good hairdresser. She would have pictured the woman at her home filled with refined eco-friendly woods and hemp carpeting, muted sage paint in her foyer, global art on the walls. Her friends would hold their stemless wine glasses with nonchalance and breeding. Her child would have no chocolate smeared on the bridge of her nose, and would wear tastefully mismatched polka dots and stripes. The television version of the perfect modern life. Even after working as a therapist for years, Tig was still human and susceptible to the façades, the masks people wore to hide their true selves.

Carolyn inhaled sharply and placed her hands flat on the table. "Here's what you don't know. My husband didn't kill himself because he couldn't see prostitutes anymore; at least, not technically. He accidentally killed himself."

"Accidentally?"

"I'm sure that you, as a counselor, have heard of erotic asphyxiation. I found him in the garage. He had this leather slipknot thing around his neck and his pants around his ankles. He couldn't get it loose, and it killed him."

Tig's mouth dropped open. Was there anything more incongruous than sitting in a cookie-cutter coffee shop, listening to the antithesis of ordinary?

"They call it other things, too: Asphyxiophilia. Scarfing. My husband was a gasper." Carolyn scoffed in frustration—or disgust? "I had no idea."

"I don't think that's all that unusual—that you didn't know."

"Apparently, he used the prostitutes to keep it from me. So, when he couldn't get help with it—y'know, from the prostitutes— he tried to do it himself. That's when I found him."

A moment of vertigo washed over Tig. She closed her eyes and visualized walking into the garage. Seeing him hanging.

"The few people who know . . . my parents. The police. They hate him. Oh, they don't say it, but it's in their faces. Like he was a pervert. Like he did it without regard for anything." Carolyn looked in earnest at Tig. "He didn't, though. He did it with full regard. Can you imagine the shame he lived with? Keeping the secret, using the prostitutes. He wasn't that kind of man. He was a good man. A good father."

"You loved him."

"You're catching me on a good day. Yesterday, I wanted to dig him up in his grave. I have speeches in my head. Long tirades that leave me exhausted. What makes a person do that? Risk it all for something so fleeting. Why couldn't he tell me?"

"I'm sorry," said Tig. "I don't have any answers for you."

"God, I know it." Shaking her head, she said, "I have to tell you. If I wanted to sue someone, it wouldn't be you. It would be the makers of that ligature thing. You should be able to release it when you want. Christ." She put her head in her hands and sniffed.

The bell on the front door tinkled, and Tig glanced around the room. An older man with a newspaper and an empty coffee mug sat a few tables away, oblivious. Tig wondered if he had some sexual secret he kept from his wife. Maybe he was gay, or a woman, or a cross-dresser. People had secrets, proclivities, problems. As a counselor, Tig, of all people, knew that. Today she was just getting a refresher course.

"What will I say about how he died? To our daughter?"

"It will be several years before you have to find those words. You will be older, more experienced; you'll have a whole dictionary full of new words that will describe an entire world of new feelings that are coming your way. Be as gentle with yourself as you are being forgiving to your husband. You'll find the words when you need them."

"You think?"

Carolyn looked out the window and said, "I'll tell you one thing. I'm not going to keep it a secret from her. Secrets are the pin pulled from a grenade. It's just a matter of time until it all blows. The closer you stand, the more you have to lose."

"Why not start by thinking of your husband giving up something that made you unhappy, the prostitutes, as an effort of love that went wrong?"

"I want to both hold him and slap him."

Tig said, "That defines all of my relationships."

"That's why I listened to you on the radio. You make people see how ridiculous life can get and still be normal, okay. Speaking of ridiculous, I think I'm close to getting his family to drop the suit."

"I should have told you to get therapy. To talk. To explore what was happening."

"You would have if I hadn't hung up. I'd heard as much that day as I wanted to hear. Prostitutes are wrong. End of story. I wanted a bottom line. I got what I wanted. That's what I told my mother-in-law." Carolyn wiped her hands on her thighs. "I'm a different person now. I used to make these snap judgments. Divorce is wrong. Abortion is bad. McDonald's is the devil's food. I think God maybe did this to shut me the hell up." Nervously, she glanced at Tig and said, "But, y'know, in a good way. I was on my high horse, never letting anyone live. Really live. Make choices without my self-righteous, high-court decisions. I was careful not to talk about what I was thinking, but I was judging people, sending that poison into the universe."

"I'm no spiritual leader, that's for sure, but I'm pretty sure there are people out there sending more poison into the universe than you," Tig said. "I just don't think the Holy Spirit operates that way. I think it's too busy with Africa to spend time pointing fingers of terror at you." Tig held her hands up. "Just a thought, don't hold me to it."

This seemed to unlock Carolyn's tears. "My husband was a great guy, and now this terrible thing defines him."

Tig watched Carolyn, head down, beautiful hair falling forward and thought, *No one is immune. No one has enough antibodies to fight off life.* "I counseled a woman once. She was amazing, brilliant, loving, charitable. She was a surgeon who rebuilt breasts after mastectomies. She'd also had few friends, shoplifted, and got pregnant on a casual hookup. She came to me because she defined herself by the latter instead of the former characteristics. She couldn't forgive herself. The truth is, it's hard to be human, but the definition of 'human' is flawed."

Carolyn Hammer looked at her hands. "I feel very flawed. I feel like I betrayed him, and I miss him so much. He didn't need to protect me; I have my own secrets. Problems. We could have talked them out. Now what possible good can come of all of this?"

"It's a small thing, but I came to see how I could have done things differently by you."

Carolyn said, "Look. You'll be doing me a personal favor if you stop blaming yourself. He needed a myriad of counselors and sex therapists. If we decide there's no external blame, then we all have to understand it was his internal issue; and if that's the case, nobody has to do anything but miss him and remember loving him."

"That is very astute, Carolyn. You have no idea how astute."

"To be honest, I don't think I'd be feeling this way right now if I hadn't been listening to your approach on the radio. You listened and gave it straight up. That's what I'm trying to do now."

The overhead music transitioned from bluesy jazz to reggae, and the atmosphere in the room became all don't-worry-be-happy, a lift in the air that filled the coffee shop.

Tig's mind drifted to Pete and Hawaii, and then back to Carolyn. "What's next for you?"

"Raise my daughter. Calm my family down. Miss my husband. Maybe go back to school to do what you do." Carolyn took a sip of water. "What about you, Dr. Monahan? When will you go back on the air? People need you."

Chapter Twenty-Five
There Now

After Carolyn left the coffee shop, Tig continued sitting in her small wooden chair while considering secrets. She tossed her unfinished coffee into the trash and walked outside, the bell jingling a light goodbye.

She thought about taking a walk in the sunshine, letting the summer breeze crazy-comb her hair, and learn how to do what Carolyn Hammer was doing: let secret dogs lie. She turned, considering going to the park to think softly, realistically, and categorically about Pete and Alec. She flirted with the thought of greeting Dr. Jenson without giving him the third degree, allowing her mother's past to stay in the past.

Instead, Tig reached into the pocket of her jeans and pulled out the theater ticket from her mother's cedar box. She examined the softened paper and ran her fingers over the date of the show: September 9, 1972, the date of her father's death. She'd known her mother hadn't been home when her father died. Knew she had found him ostensibly resting on the sofa, forever in cardiac-arrest repose.

She reached for her phone, dialed her sister, and waited. Checking her watch, she saw it was afternoon naptime and was about to hang up. Out of the blue, a woman answered.

"Wendy?"

"Hi, Tig. No, this is Geri. Pete is running. He left his phone in the lab."

Tig closed her eyes. She'd called Pete, something she often caught herself doing, her awake mind picturing her sister while her subconscious was looking for Pete.

Tig felt a little sick, then another emotion she couldn't quite nail down. She started to hang up, but instead said, "Tell him Tig called." In her car, her levelheaded plans for a walk in the park hijacked, she thought about the musical chairs of relationships. Geri hadn't wasted any time slipping into Tig's chair; or had she? Maybe the phone answering was just helpfulness, and Tig was confused. With that thought, the answer to her mother's secret came to her.

She felt the throb of her heart in her throat, and when Hope House came into view, the feeling sped up. She slipped through the glass doors, past the birds, the front desk, and the supply closet; she was moments away from looking her mother in the eye. She silently prayed for a window of clarity from her today . . . a glimmer of memory . . . a slice of recognition.

Tig shoved open the heavy door to her mother's room. The bedside curtain swayed and Tig stopped, unable to move. Dr. Jenson and her mother stood, embracing. Her mother's arms were locked around Dr. Jenson's neck. One of his arms was around her torso, his hand fanned in the center of her back. The other arm hung self-consciously down at his side, a teen at the edge of a senior class party knowing a slow dance wasn't just a dance. They swayed lightly to a muted song on the radio. Tig recognized it as her mother's favorite, "Me and Mrs. Jones," the Billy Paul version from the seventies. Her mother said, "*Mon chèvre.*"

Alarmed, Tig cleared her throat. Dr. Jenson, startled, pulled away from Hallie.

Hallie beamed. "Hello! Is it time to go?" To Dr. Jenson, she said, "I'll get my wrap."

Tig's lips twitched. "No, Mom. You can take a seat. I need to talk to . . . ." She hesitated. "I need to talk to him for a minute."

Dr. Jenson eased Hallie into the chair nearest the picture window, handing her the baby doll. "I'll be right back."

Hallie called to him, "Don't be long. We don't want to be late."

Tig nearly jogged down the hall and into the conference room, a flustered Dr. Jenson trying to catch up. When he entered the room, Tig said, "Why is she calling you 'cheese'? For God's sake, what is going on?" Tig thrust the ticket stub at him. "I just figured it out."

Without thinking, he said, "It's not 'cheese.' It's 'goat.'" At the same moment that Tig heard the translation of the French word, Dr. Jenson touched the ticket stub. He looked at it first with question, then recognition, then disbelief. He touched it with reverence. "Where did you get this?"

Tig said, "You're the Goat?"

His face opened like a morning glory. "She saved this? She's kept it all this time? I . . . I don't know what to say." Then in a rush, like the words had been backed up, he reached for her. "Nothing is certain, Tig. Nothing has ever been confirmed. Hallie wanted it that way. When we discovered Dan that night, she pushed me out. After the funeral, when she discovered she was pregnant, she wouldn't talk to me about anything."

Tig's head snapped back as if struck. "What? What are you talking about?"

Dr. Jenson duplicated Tig's expression of confusion and terror. "What are *you* talking about? You said you figured it out. What did you figure out?"

"Just that you and my mom were together that night. At that musical." She took a step back, gesturing to the ticket. "That you had a thing for her all those years ago."

Dr. Jenson said, "It wasn't a long-ago thing. I still love your mother. I have always loved your mother, from the moment I met her to this very day."

Tig bent over, supporting herself on a chair. "Did your wife have something to say about that? Did my father?"

Dr. Jenson swept his hand through his hair. Tig moved away, pacing along the conference table. She trained her eyes on Dr.

Jenson. "You were having an affair with my mother while my father lay dying?"

"No, Tig. It wasn't like that."

"My mother cheated on my father. That's what you're telling me." She moved to the corner of the room and folded her arms across her chest. Then horror filled her face. She was born nearly nine months after her father's death.

Dr. Jenson moved closer to Tig. "If you could just stop talking and listen to me."

"You're lying."

"Lying?" Suddenly insulted, he said, "People do things for the people they love, Tig."

"You're stalking my mother. You're the ultimate stalker. How did I miss that?"

"No. God, you are your mother's daughter. Always so sure her reality was the only one that mattered." Sounding exhausted, he said, "She calls me 'Dan.' You think I get some kind of sick enjoyment out of that?" He gestured to the stock paintings of soothing landscapes and faux wood chair rails. "Before all this, Hallie and I meant something to each other. I'm not apologizing for the best night of my life, the best years." His voice shook. "Stop being your mother for five minutes so I can finish this. So I can tell you. Finally."

"No. I won't hear it." Tig turned away from Dr. Jenson and put her hand on the doorknob.

"I loved your mother. She loved your father, but none of us were perfect. She and I were together just once. Yes, there were a lot of questions about that one time, the timing, the pregnancy, the future, but there was never a question of love."

Tig raised her hand, trying to keep her composure. "Okay. That's enough. I need a minute." She left Dr. Jenson there, his story only partially told. A woman in a wheelchair sat at her breakfast chanting, "My, my, my my, mmmmmm." A call light buzzed, along with the repeated pinging of a WanderGuard, announcing a perimeter breach.

Then, at the front doors, Tig turned around and moved to her mother's room. She rounded the corner. She would bully her mother's dementia into giving up her secrets; this would end today, she thought.

"Tig! Dr. Monahan." Tig pulled up abruptly. Pam Gibson squirted antibacterial lotion on her hands, frowning. "Where are you going in such a hurry? If you had a gun, I'd call 911."

"To my mother's room; I gotta go."

"Whoa, girl. I've seen that expression before. You look ready to throttle someone."

Tig said, "I'll tell you later."

Pam put her hands on her hips. "Hark!" As if the word were a bridle, Tig jolted to a stop.

"Dr. Monahan, I am in charge of this nursing home today and you will calm down before you enter your mother's room. Do you hear me?" Pam's jaw and teeth were clenched tight. She crossed her arms in front of her slowly. Their eyes locked in a tug of war. One right, one righteous.

Narrowing her gaze, Tig spoke with sudden realization. "You knew."

Pam, with the slightest flicker of a tell, an almost blink, gave it away.

"You knew about Dr. Jenson and my mom. Of course you did. You had to have known about the finances." Tig slammed her palm into her forehead. "How could I have been so stupid?"

Without warning, she stomped the rest of the distance to her mother's room, rounding the final doorway. Hallie Monahan—mother, veterinarian, wife, lover—sat slumped in a high-backed chair in front of the picture window in her room. A nurse's call button, pinned to Hallie's off-white cardigan, pulled the neck open and exposed a flowered blouse, a sun-spotted collarbone, and a discolored bra strap. Her head lolled to the side, propped up by a pillow, shrugging itself free of the case. One of her tortoiseshell combs slid free and hung by a strand of hair. Yet Hallie clung to her baby doll, her plastic daughter, never once letting her drop from her lap.

Hurricane Tig lost her wind.

Pam hissed, "Tig." The torn expression on Tig's face brought out the calm in Pam's. She gently wrapped her soft, cool fingers around Tig's upper arm and led her into the hall, pulling the door to Hallie's room shut behind them.

Tig said, "I'm not the one behaving badly. I did not have an affair. I did not keep secrets."

Pam took a moment, then said, "I did know. But it wasn't my story to tell."

"My mother can't tell it; couldn't you have said something?"

"You of all people should understand confidentiality."

"Confidentiality and a secret affair are not the same thing."

Pete's face swam before hers, handsome, familiar, and completely unknown.

Pete's smile, Geri's voice. His anger at Tig's insistence that she needed to return home to her family. What had she returned to? Secrets and unanswerable questions.

"Tig, stop acting like a spoiled brat and start acting like the psychologist you are, for God's sake."

Tig touched her face.

"You're all about stopping the mollycoddling that goes on, so get a grip," Pam ordered. "What's so awful here? You found out today that your mother has been loved her whole life. The real question here is why she didn't accept that love. Why her daughter is outraged by the thought of it."

"I'm not outraged by the thought of it. It's the surprise, the uncertainty, the possibilities."

Pam said, "God forbid, the possibilities."

Pam walked over to the nurses' cart and plucked out a box of tissues. "You know what nurses are good at?" She proffered the box. "We're experts at calling 'em how we see 'em. You wanna know how I see 'em?"

"I think I have an idea."

"I think Dr. Jenson is a kind, thoughtful, gentle man who's had a lonely kind of life. Your mother was the charming, secretly guilty ball-buster in your house. Wendy rebelled by being an open door, and you, Tig, were the closed one. It's too late for your mother to change, but not for you."

"Dr. Jenson might be my father."

Pam blinked in surprise. Her mouth opened, then shut, then opened very slowly.

"Dear heart, if he is, you are one lucky little girl."

Pam took Tig by the shoulders, turned her around to face her mother's closed door, and gently pushed her inside. Tig dropped to the floor in front of her sleeping mother, resting her head on her mother's knee. Silent, she felt the warm tendrils of her mother's fingers gently touch her hair, heard her mother's voice finally reading a script from the past that worked:

"There now. There now."

Chapter Twenty-Six
Time Will Tell

"Tig?" Alec squatted, his hand a gentle pressure on Tig's shoulder.

There was an ache in her knee. Tig frowned and moved her hand through her hair.

"Are you all right? You're on the floor."

"Yeah, I'm fine. What time is it?" She looked into Alec's tired expression. His nose was red. "What's going on?" A pit opened in her stomach. She tried to recall why. "You look like I feel."

"My mom died this morning."

Tig stood, pulling Alec into a hug. "I'm so sorry."

After a long pause, he said, "I sent Erin off with a friend all day. I had a feeling. The funeral home just finished."

Tig examined the dry skin of his hastily shaved beard, the remnants of toothpaste in the corners of his mouth. She glanced at her own mother, still sleeping, the sun shining on the brown spots on the back of her hand. The yellowed nails, the tangled bluish veins still functioning, well enough to maintain her body if not her mind.

"One minute I could feel her. The next she was gone. It's as black-and-white as it can get. Even after going through losing my wife, and now my mother, I don't know anymore about how to prepare myself. How do you get ready for the nothingness where your love used to be?"

"No matter how ready you are, you're never ready enough."

"You must understand. You lost your father."

"I wasn't born yet." Unable to hide her bitterness, she said, "I don't know what I lost or didn't lose."

His eyes rimmed in red, he said, "What do you mean? What's wrong?"

She smoothed her hair and concentrated on Alec's face. "Nothing. Let's get out of here. Let's go someplace fresh. Can you do that? Do you want to?"

Alec closed his eyes. "I'm so tired."

"This nursing home must filter narcolepsy gas into its air ducts. Every time I come here, I regret not bringing pajamas. I fall asleep wherever I stop."

"Maybe you're still jet-lagged."

"And you're loss-lagged. What d'ya say we go to my place and take a nap. Everyone important has our numbers. Clementine's at my house sleeping all the time. She won't judge."

• • •

At Tig's house, the oddity of it all set in. Bringing a man home to nap after having discovered life-changing events in both of their lives was just strange.

"I feel weird now," smiled Tig. "Still tired, but weird."

Alec said, "I'm too tired to even consider the weirdness. Let's just say 'sleep is good' and give it a try." This was enough for Tig. Nonetheless, Alec added, "I need to sleep and I don't want to be alone when I wake up. It's as simple as that."

There were too many complex thoughts to process in Tig's head while awake. Maybe while sleeping, her subconscious would pitch some answers forward from her wiser brain stem, the prehistoric part of her brain that provided survival options. On the bed, she rested her head on Alec's outstretched arm.

Tig asked, "What was your dad like?"

"He was a good guy. Died seven years ago. Prostate cancer. It was a blessing."

"Did he go to all your athletic events and give you advice on women?"

"That was my mom. No, my dad was a product of his era. He worked all the time, and then died. He probably had no idea what he missed." He turned his head and added, "My childhood probably wasn't much different from yours. Strong mother, missing father."

"Were fathers of that time all like that, do you think? Present but missing, one way or another."

"I think about that a lot, considering I'm all Erin Ann has right now. You know, am I the father I need to be, or the father of our times? Back in the seventies, our moms were cutting their way out of a box that men wanted them to stay in." He smiled widely and laughed. "My mom used to say to my dad, 'I promise I'll never marry again.' My dad took that as a compliment; a profession of their soulmate status. That wasn't what she meant, though. I heard her ask her best friend, 'Why would I take on another full-grown infant, at my age?'"

Tig smiled at Fern's memory. "I've only ever had a fantasy father. He was made up of all the good things I saw in my friend's fathers. My imaginary father called me sweet pea, went to the father-daughter Girl Scout square dance, righted all wrongs. My dad was Atticus Finch from *To Kill a Mockingbird*, handsome and righteous." After a drawn-out pause, Tig asked, "Was your wife your soulmate?"

Hearing a raspy intake of breath followed by an exhale indicating sleep, not true love, she stared at him. Alec's rumpled white button-down shirt was frayed slightly at his chin, which made his dark coloring all the more striking. He had a freckle at the exact center of his closed eyelid, and a dark dusting of whiskers showing through his shaved jaw. She placed her lips on his jaw, breathed in his scent, considered staying in this position forever. Cutting the ties of her thoughts, she let them drift away like helium balloons.

• • •

In the margin between sleep and waking, Tig rolled to her side and snuggled into Alec's arm.

"Pete," she said, and just as she uttered the words she realized her mistake and froze, waiting. Her heart pounded. She checked for a change in his breathing. Nothing. She eased the breath out of her lungs and closed her eyes. Moving away from Alec's arm, she crept from her bed.

She remembered her mother hugging Dr. Jenson, calling him *mon chèvre*. Anxiety began creeping through her thoughts.

In the small cedar chest of her mother's, she searched for the photograph of the young Dr. Jenson. She examined his face and felt her anxiety pick up speed. It began to feel like a train was speeding down the track toward her. She said aloud, "Why am I feeling so anxious?" hoping the universe would give her an answer. She paced through her living room, reached to her throat, and rushed to the front door. She wrenched the handle, shoved the screen door forward, and nearly flattened her sister, who she hadn't seen moving up the porch steps.

Startled, Wendy said, "What? What's going on?"

"I'm just like Mom, aren't I? I can't be happy. I make myself miserable."

Wendy set Clementine's car seat down onto the sidewalk and grabbed her sister. "Tig. What is going on?"

"Dad's not my dad. I'm doing the same thing Mom did. I'm rejecting love. I've been doing it my whole life."

"What are you talking about?"

"I'm talking about my whole life being a repeat of Mom's." She pointed to her sister. "You had a father. You learned to love. I never did—and to think I could have. Mom took that from me. But I don't feel mad. I just feel really, really anxious."

Clementine awoke with a start and Wendy stooped to unhook her from her car seat and pull her into her arms. "Hush. Tig, what are you talking about?"

"I think my father, my *biological* father, is Dr. Jenson."

"That's ridiculous. How is that possible?"

"I don't know the timeline or how it actually happened, but Dr. Jenson all but confirmed it."

Wendy jiggled Clementine. "He did? Well, that is a real plot twist, isn't it? Can I come inside for this kind of earth-shattering news, or do I have to stand on the steps?" Wendy grabbed the car seat and said, "That kind of explains a lot doesn't it?"

"I think it explains why I'm such a mess. I push people away. I'm reliving Mom's life."

Wendy said, "Oh, shut up, Tig. Make a different choice, then."

The words blew Tig's fury away. She opened her mouth and said, "What?"

"You've been acting like you have some kind of deadline you have to meet to solve all your problems. Pete, your job, Alec . . . but if you have some kind of deadline, it's self-imposed." Handing Clementine to Tig, she said, "Here. Hold Clem. She's good at slowing things down for people." Before Tig could muster a rebuttal, Wendy said, walking into the house, "And don't even start with me by bringing up the time I left Clem with you. That was ages ago, and I was a different person."

Clem looked at her aunt and placed her hand on Tig's collarbone. A navy blue Impala drove into the driveway and before fully stopping, the car door opened. Dr. Jenson stepped out, an old man with white hair, not the young father of her imaginings.

"Tig," he said, "I know it seems complicated." The vibrations of his soft voice soothed her. He said, "Let's start making this a little easier. My name is Jeffrey Jenson. Your mother called me Goat. I may or may not be your father. Either way, we've got as much or as little time as we need."

Just then Alec stepped outside, rubbing his eyes and looking rumpled. "Is everything all right?"

Jeffrey Jenson said, "Right at this moment, we're not sure. But time will tell."

Chapter Twenty-Seven
Something to Know

The whir and sway of the electric baby swing—part pacifier, part hypnotist pendulum—seemed to focus and soothe the group. Hallie Monahan's memories, in the form of letters and photographs, lay scattered on the kitchen table between Wendy, Dr. Jenson, and Tig. Alec had returned to the nursing home to deal with his own mother's choices in her final days. Clementine dozed, emitting a fragile mewl on every exhale that seemed to put life into perspective for everyone.

Dr. Jenson examined the old photo of himself with his wife and Hallie. "Look at that head of hair. God, I was young." He smiled warmly and said, "I remember that afternoon. Hallie and Judy were so beautiful. It was the day I realized that your mother and Judy were the loves of my life, and the love of your mother's life was Dan Monahan." The summer sun from the photograph seemed to touch him, creating a golden halo of youth and remembrances . . . of unrequited loves and wistful glances.

"I loved my wife, Judy; I would never have left her. But you had to know your mother from an outside perspective to understand." Jeff Jenson looked up, examining the edges of his thoughts. "We spent a lot of time together, just the four of us."

Wendy stroked the box that held her mother's inner life and said, "Your brother, the one that was friends with Dad. Is he still alive?"

"He's not. But he wasn't the piece that kept the group together. It was the girls who made the effort. They organized everything. I think Judy felt almost the same way as I did about Hallie. I swear. You just couldn't not love her. She was light and laughter, your mother. You girls must remember that."

Wendy nodded. "Her clients at the clinic loved her. She was a tough parent. She had to be. She was both mother and father."

Dr. Jenson looked a long moment at Wendy and Tig and said, "Two years before Dan died, Judy and I discovered we couldn't have children. There was no fixing it. No working around it. We talked about adoption, but the life went out of Judy when she learned of our fertility difficulties. She went into a terrible, black depression. We tried all kinds of therapy, medication, even—God help me—electroconvulsive therapy. Nothing helped." Dr. Jenson licked his lips. "My wife loved Hallie, looked up to her. Hallie used to come, help out at our place, take Judy out. The night I brought home the tickets to see *A Little Night Music*, Hallie was there. Judy loved musicals. I thought, here's a chance to get her out of the house." Dr. Jenson's story sputtered and stopped.

Clementine started to fuss and Wendy said, "Go on."

"Judy gave me this blank look and quoted one of the songs in the show. 'Every Day a Little Death,' she said. 'I don't care. I don't care about going. Take Hallie. Just leave me be.' I'll never forget it. I got so angry with her. I wanted her to fight for us, even just a little." Sighing, he said, "I'm sure she suspected how I felt about Hallie, but she also knew how much I loved her."

Dr. Jenson placed both hands over his eye sockets and rubbed hard. "Maybe it's not right to say this, but your mother and Dan had a tumultuous relationship. Dan always wanted her to quit the clinic, stay home with Wendy. He thought Hallie's job reflected badly on him. He came home later and later at night. It crushed Hallie's spirit; she saw her own interest in working as a weakness, evidence of her lack of femininity." He dropped his hands and focused on Tig. "I'm not making excuses for our behavior. I want you to know how it was for us. We were young. We didn't understand consequences yet."

Tig said, "I really don't know if I want to hear this. I know I have to. I guess what I really wish is that there wasn't something to know."

"The night of the show, Dan was on a business trip, due to return home late. He never cared if Hallie and I did something together. He knew I wasn't a threat to their relationship. So, Hallie got a sitter and we drove into the city. We reasoned it would do us both good."

Wendy asked, "Did you make it to the show?"

"Yeah, the musical was terrific, a setup of misplaced desires and unrequited loves. It was like a mirror for me. After the show, we had dinner, drinks. More drinks and a long walk in the park."

Tig said, "I think I know what's coming."

Wendy touched Clementine's fat sponge of a foot and tucked it into her blanket. To Tig, she said, "Remember how cautious Mom used to be about us dating? Then when we were older, how she took us in for birth control? Mom wasn't taking any chances. I didn't lose my virginity for two years after getting those pills." Touching Clementine's hair, she added, "That's irony for you."

Tig said, "Mom used to say, 'Even the most immune can go astray. Best to plan for the unplanned.' I always thought it was a stray dog thing. Too many puppies and kittens. I never thought she was talking about me. That I was the unplanned thing in her life."

Dr. Jenson said, "No, Tig, you've got that wrong. Your mother was immediately regretful about our intimacy, but she never, even for a second, felt you were a mistake. She never acknowledged that possibility. She saw you as Dan's, through and through. There was no discussion. Since we didn't know for sure, you were Dan's daughter and there was no way to prove it otherwise."

Wendy said, "Go back to that night. What happened when you got home?"

"Hallie was determined to tell Dan about our encounter and to say goodbye to me. To tell Dan that she and I would never see each other again. We agreed to do it together, and then sever all ties. When we opened the door, the sitter was gone, Wendy was asleep in her bed, and Dan was on the couch. He had paid the sitter, and died suddenly and peacefully. Sudden cardiac death. The best and the worst way to die. No symptoms until there's death."

The details of the night so long ago washed over the two sisters. So much could happen while sleeping, or even before birth, that determined so much. Tig wanted to say something, anything, but just couldn't sort her emotions from her thoughts and get it together enough to make a sentence.

Dr. Jenson went on, "You're probably thinking I was glad about this. You know: an opening. But no door was ever open to me where your mother was concerned. Our infidelity clinched that. And, as it turned out, nine months later—" Dr. Jenson held the ticket up. "—give or take a few weeks, you showed up. Hallie never had the chance to confess, tell Dan she loved him, say she was sorry. That was the end of any kind of relationship we might have had."

Wendy said, "Did Mom ever say anything to anyone?"

Dr. Jenson's energy for the conversation seemed to leave him. "I think she talked to your Aunt Edith. It all seems so pointless, in a way. So much lost joy. Your mother was loyal and believed in black-and-white rules. No shades of gray. After that night, she shored herself up and took on the future. She devoted herself to helping my wife until she died from breast cancer in 1980. She expanded her veterinary practice, and gave every last piece of herself to you and Wendy. She said I reminded her of her weakness. Taking time for herself was always a limitation in her mind. After we were both single, she wanted to wait until you girls were grown, to try out being together. She wanted to be loyal to Dan."

Wendy said softly, "I don't want to be unkind, Dr. Jenson . . . Jeff . . . but maybe she didn't love you in the way you loved her. Maybe she knew Tig was the daughter of Dan Monahan, but couldn't bear to hurt you, knowing what a tough time you were having."

Dr. Jenson rolled up his sleeve. "I have the twin to that bracelet of hers you're wearing. The one she wore until it slipped off her wrist, along with her memory." He held out his arm. A silver ID bracelet, heavier, more masculine than the one Tig wore, slid down his wrist. He angled it to her so she could read the words: *I would let you know.* "Hallie had these made for us."

Tig said, "Oh my God. Why would she choose to be alone, all these years, if she could have had you?"

Dr. Jenson stroked the words engraved on the silver band. "She once told me she wasn't going to invest in anyone she didn't give birth to. She was afraid to love and lose, after Dan."

Tig didn't look up. She couldn't bear to see his face, to think he might be telling the truth. "My mother wouldn't do that . . . wouldn't have deprived me of a life without a father. She may have been guarded, determined, but never thoughtless and cruel."

"Your mother doesn't have a thoughtless or cruel bone in her body. You've got to understand the time. My wife was alive, her husband was dead. There was no insurance money. She had to make a livelihood. She was afraid a scandal would hurt her business, hurt her children. Leaving my wife would have killed Judy faster than the disease that ultimately took her life. I couldn't leave, and Hallie wouldn't have had me. That's the truth of it."

"What do you mean, no insurance money? We had trust funds from the insurance money. Both of us. It paid for our college. I invested that money."

Dr. Jenson said, "I was an MD without a family, without anything to bankroll but a widow with two little girls. I always felt it was an honor to invest my money that way. I still do. I promised to never voice my fantasies of having a daughter if she let me stay involved, even from a distance."

After another lengthy pause, while the fireworks that had seemed to be spitting and popping over their heads melted and dripped to their shoulders, Tig looked at her sister, who stared at Jeff Jenson.

"You made our lives so easy and we never knew," Wendy said. "How will we ever thank you?"

"What about after Wendy and I had lives of our own?" Tig asked. "When you were both single and there weren't children to consider?"

"By then, your mother had healed, moved on, had a back story and was sticking with it. She said there was no way of ever knowing the truth, so why open up a question that would never be answered? She wanted you girls to have strong identities, and she thought questioning who your father was would threaten that. She wouldn't even date me, saying that would be cruel to me, being around you, Tig, and never knowing. She didn't let other people vote."

"How do I think about this?" Tig asked desperately. "Should I be angry? Because I feel angry." She wiped her nose with her arm. "Who am I mad at? You? My mother? How can I be mad at a woman who can't recall if she's had lunch, let alone remember who my father is? Hell, most of the time she only remembers she had Wendy." Dr. Jenson handed his handkerchief to Tig, and she looked directly at him. "Maybe you're the one I'm angry at. If you wanted a child, why didn't you fight for me?"

He opened his mouth, closed it. Tried again. "I've been fighting for you by staying close, all this time. Respecting someone's wishes that are directly opposed to your own is the hardest thing to keep on fighting for. It's been a battle, Tig." Charging ahead, Dr. Jenson said, "For years there was no way of knowing, but times have changed. Science is accessible. There is DNA testing."

Tig put her hands out, dual stop signs. "Whoa, slow down. I need a break."

Dr. Jenson, looking all of his sixty-some odd years, said, "Of course you do. I'm sorry. This is a terrible shock. I never truly believed this conversation would happen."

Tig examined Dr. Jenson's face, the slope of his nose, the turn of his lips. Were those her ears? Did she have his hairline? "I don't know how I feel about any of this, if I even want to know you," she said. "I sure don't want evidence that says I have to know you." Tig stood and made a move for the front door.

Wendy yelled out, "Where're you going, little sister? Back to live with Mom? Off to Hawaii to mess with Pete, or maybe to Alec's to promise him half a life? It's time for the Monahan women to stay put and let some people in. Grow up. Live a real love."

Dr. Jenson looked from sister to sister.

"Oh, I know what you're thinking," Wendy said to Tig. "Who am I to talk? But I'm making progress. Clem and I, we're a match made in utero. Just like you and me. We're stuck with each other, and I'm sick of you. Let's bring in some new blood."

• • •

Tig did return to the nursing home that night. She walked slowly past the birds and the front desk, past a nursing assistant helping a man, all sinew and ghost-like skin, onto a commode chair. The privacy curtain rolled on oiled ball bearings and hissed into place as the nurse pulled it around their shoulders. On silent feet Tig nosed the familiar door open, stepped into the smell, part home part disinfectant, that she now associated with her mother. Tig saw that someone had braided her mother's hair, and a white rope of it curled at her neck in line with a blue vein that ran, bashful, beneath the neck of her light blue pajama top. With her mother asleep, the baby doll quiet in her arms, Tig could see her mother as others saw her. Old. Dry. Peaceful.

Tig unclasped the silver bracelet, warmed from her body, and slid it onto her mother's wrist. She latched the spring-loaded clasp and let the bracelet find its place nestled between condyle and joint.

Slowly, her mother opened her eyes. "Oh, you're here."

"Hi, Mom. I just left Jeff Jenson."

"Hmmm. Lovely man."

"Is he my dad?"

"Your dad will be home and then we can eat. I'm just going to close my eyes for a second."

"Do you think I should tell Pete I love him?"

An exhale from the back of her mother's throat sounded as disappointed as if her mother had remained awake and said, *Don't be silly. That ship has sailed.*

As Tig left the room, she ran into one of the night shift nurses she had come to know from her own midnights at Hope House. The nurse was old herself, a Norwegian woman through and through. No nonsense, few words, all business. As a greeting the woman said, "What d'ya know, Tig?"

"Well, for one thing," she said, "that Alzheimer's patients only give up their secrets in the movies."

The nurse nodded. "True story."

Chapter Twenty-Eight
Almost-Win, Almost-Lose

Since Pete had left and Thatcher had no one to run with, Tig had started walking Thatcher through the neighborhoods that bordered her home. She varied her routes and waved at the familiar faces peeking out windows: a jowly basset that lived with the equally jowly retired science teacher, the bouncing boxer with the talkative, gardening nurse. If she was walking the sidewalks, Tig could tell herself she was wasn't really hiding. People were everywhere.

When she called Alec and suggested they meet on a trail near Hope House, he'd said they were already there. Erin had picked out a dog at the Humane Society, and they were tiring him out. Once Tig arrived, it didn't take long for her to relay the entire saga of Dr. Jenson and her mother.

"That's quite a story."

Tig replied, "It is."

Alec shielded his eyes from the cinnamon-colored sun with his hand. He shouted to Erin Ann, who was struggling with a tiny mop of a dog, "Hang on to her, honey. Don't let go of the leash."

Thatcher zigzagged around the girl and the puppy like a mad herding animal with a broken internal compass.

"So, how are you feeling about it all?" Alec asked.

"Like the only place I'm comfortable is over at Hope House, or with other dogs. There's no subterfuge. No agenda. They smell your crotch, hump or don't hump, and move on. If there's a half-sister or -brother nearby with questionable parentage, nobody cares. All in a day's play."

"We could learn a lot from dogs."

"Yeah, but we don't. Why is that?"

"They lose a lot of credibility when they eat their own poop."

Tig nodded sagely. "Yeah, the poop-eating makes them appear far less wise."

Neither spoke as they walked along the mulch path. Tig looked over at Alec, the very image of a man in a dad catalog. His khaki pants were worn at the pockets, but not enough to look shabby; his denim jacket was about function, not fashion; and the rip in the neck of his navy sweatshirt seemed as if it might have happened rescuing a kitten from a flowering apple tree.

Tig said, "It was a good idea, getting Erin a dog. She needs a girl to whisper her secrets to. Everyone does. Turns out my mom did. All those years she was quiet about so much. No wonder her mind is mixed up like a blended beach drink."

"Hopefully Erin will tell me some of her secrets, even though I'm not a girl."

"There were plenty of times when I was growing up that I wished I had a dad to talk to. I knew enough that I didn't want any old dad, though. I certainly didn't want Sarah Wumka's dad. You could tell he was terrible just by the way he called his dogs. If I could have picked a father, he would have been like you."

Shaking his head, Alec said, "You're doing what everyone does, romanticizing the widowed dad. The sad sack who lost the love of his life. The perfect left-behind parent. Truth is, if my wife hadn't gotten sick, she probably would have left me."

Tig stopped walking. "Oh, I'm sure that isn't true."

"Oh, no. It's true all right. I meant well, but I was a terrible partner."

"But you're such a good dad."

"Whatever," Alec said. "Before Jennifer's diagnosis, I treated her like she would always be around. I missed dinners. Went to all the Badger football games, let her take care of all the details of Erin and our lives while I worked, thinking that since I made more money, that was okay." He coughed into his fist and swallowed. "I was always and without fail at least an hour late coming home from wherever I was."

"That doesn't sound too terrible, and believe me, I have counseled terrible."

He stopped walking abruptly. With a flash of anger, Alec reached out to stop Tig. "No? It's worse. It's neglect. You can divorce an abuser, a philanderer, but once you have a child, it's difficult to justify leaving someone who just blows you off, who treats you like an unvalued roommate, a servant who you want to have sex with occasionally, when you're home."

Alec yanked the leaves off a bush and pitched them to the ground. "I'm just lucky some man didn't swoop in, take her from me." He stopped walking and faced Tig. "God, actually, now I wish that would have happened. For her sake. I let her down, and no amount of holding her head while vomiting after chemo would fix that. I was a fucking idiot."

"I think that helping someone through a terminal illness is love. It may be the greatest of loves. Being present when people are at their worst." Tig felt an acute moment of sorrow for herself, realizing that this was why she could never nail her feelings down for Pete. He was there for her only during the good times, and bailed when she needed help. On some level, she had known this all along.

They walked silently for a while, contemplating the path.

"Since I'm confessing my failings," Alec continued, "I might as well get it all out. I've got one memory that haunts me. My wife was at the kitchen sink washing Erin's hair. I was sitting behind them, drinking coffee and reading the morning paper. Jennifer was telling me something she and Erin had done the day before. When I finally dragged myself away from the paper, Jen and Erin were gone. She'd stopped talking mid-story, and I didn't notice. I didn't notice she'd just walked away."

"I had a guy once who came in after his divorce. Just a regular guy. He'd go on and on about his marriage and how it had dissolved before his eyes. Kept saying he'd never seen it coming. Finally, one day I asked him what he had learned from the divorce, so he wouldn't make the same mistakes in a new relationship."

"Yeah? What'd he say?"

Tig smiled slightly. "He said that when your wife says turn off the TV, you should turn off the TV."

Alec laughed a loud painful bark of a laugh that stopped the dogs for a second before they went on to terrorize a vole. "Truer words were never spoken."

To Alec she said, "One of my professors, when I was getting a degree, was big into compromise. Y'know, win-win and all that. I said to him, 'Compromise means neither person gets what they want, so that's more like lose-lose—or almost-win, almost-lose. What's the word for that?'"

Alec smiled. "I don't know, but I bet Eskimos have, like, fifty words for it."

"I'm pretty sure I didn't get an A in that class. I remember him looking at me like I was in the wrong major and should reconsider being a counselor."

Tig looked at Alec's profile. Alec hugged Tig's shoulders with one extended brotherly arm. "You have to figure out how you feel about Pete."

"Sadly, I've got that nailed."

"Yeah? What's the verdict?"

"I'd give him a kidney and my old Dan Fogelberg tapes." Smiling, she added, "But he doesn't want them."

"The tapes?"

"None of it."

"You know that for sure?"

"As sure as I know who my father is."

On the way back to the car, Thatcher led the way with Erin and the puppy following behind, her step as light as popcorn popping, looking as freely happy as anything Tig had seen since a pod of dolphins in Hawaii. She did not notice a slight figure approaching her until a fawn-colored pug nosed her leg. Tig bent to pet the snorting animal.

"It's good to see you, Dr. Monahan."

Startled, Tig found herself staring at a new and improved version of the sad Mrs. Biddle, the woman who couldn't get past the loss of her adult daughter to cancer. She still had L'Oréal jet black hair and shocking red lips, but instead of the grayish pallor and the dried crêpe skin of a cornhusk doll, she had a blush to her cheeks Tig hadn't seen before. "What a nice surprise. This must be Mug."

In typical Mrs. Biddle fashion, she said, "I gave up smoking. I'm walking Mug instead."

"What a great idea."

"Julie said you might be back on the radio soon."

"She did?"

"She said everyone needs a change sometimes."

Tig nodded. "I needed a change. I just didn't know I needed it."

"I didn't know it, either." There was a self-conscious pause. She grimaced and Tig recognized her signature almost-smile.

Tig said, "It's good to see you looking so well."

Mrs. Biddle gave a tender pull on the leash and moved away, looking over her shoulder once to check if her message had been received.

Alec, watching the interchange with interest, said to Thatcher, "Your mommy's quite a gal, Thatcher. I'm glad we're friends." Thatcher, grateful for the adult conversation, showed her white teeth and tried to mount his knee.

Chapter Twenty-Nine
Hope House

Tig gazed out the window of her bedroom. The trees understood that the shorter fall days meant that the leaves need to drop, even though the weather maintained it was summer.

"I wondered where you wandered off to."

Tig turned to face Wendy. "I came in here to get Mom's memory box for her and I got distracted by the view. Check it out."

The two women watched while Erin, shouting encouragements, threw stick after stick for the puppy while Thatcher looked on in disdain.

Tig said, "Erin thinks she's in charge."

Alec stood nearby, trying to get Erin to come in for lunch, comically following the dog and girl around the yard.

Wendy said, "So does Alec."

Tig sighed and gestured to the small, muted, flat-screen television where athletes with black greased numbers on their arms and thighs grimaced in the Ironman's Hawaiian heat. "So did I."

Wendy picked up the remote and shut off the television. "This little party was meant to keep you away from the television, away from watching that race."

"I just wanted to see if I could catch a glimpse of Pete."

"I doubt when they have that many hot bodies on the highway they're going to pan to a professor holding a test tube and talking about muscle cells."

"God, I was stupid."

"Let's go. If you're admitting to stupidity on your own, I've got to have witnesses. Besides, Mom's getting funky and tired. She's calling Alec, and Jeff is looking a little lost. Clementine needs to take a nap, and you need to cut the cake."

"So this whole party was designed to keep me away from watching the Ironman on TV?"

"That, and to let you talk about your new radio show."

"Jean's been amazing. She loved the idea."

"It's a great concept. I can't believe you go live in a month."

Tig rested her head on the cool glass of the window. "You and Clem don't have to move out, y'know."

"Yes we do, little sister. You've got to figure out who you are without someone to take care of."

Unconvinced, Tig said, "I guess. But what if I know who I am, and who I am is someone who likes people around . . . and if they need help, all the better."

Wendy said, "You need counseling."

Tig glanced out the window at the crushed velvet–like leaves hanging from the old maple in her backyard.

Wendy said, "I'm not moving to the Galapagos Islands. Van Buren Street is three blocks away. Whenever you need to meddle, you can come over and give me a lecture on the evils of pacifiers or my passive-aggressive feng shui furniture arrangements. I'll listen, give you a cookie, then send you on your way."

"I might need a sleepover and a brownie occasionally. No nuts."

"I need to continue figuring out how to take care of Clem, and you need to figure out how to take care of you. After we do that, we can start auditioning men for the less significant roles of partner or father."

"I've got someone trying out for my own father role right now. I've got to make a decision about the DNA testing."

"Not today, you don't. Come on, there's another surprise, but I'm not saying a thing until you get out there and act like a person who is happy to welcome people into her home, and feed them chips and salsa without fixing all their problems."

"No surprises, Wen."

Wendy grabbed Tig by the elbow. "C'mon, Scrooge; it's a good, sane surprise. This isn't the movies. Nobody's waiting for you to come crashing in just as they're about to say their wedding vows. It's just the people you know, making life better."

Tig pulled Wendy into a hug. "It's nice having a big sister."

Wendy said, "Everyone has to grow up sometime. I figured I better do it before Clementine."

Jeff stood, helping Hallie get her sweater on in the living room. Hallie fretted anxiously over her doll's swaddling.

"Drive the car up, Dan. I don't want Clementine to get wet."

Jeff, Wendy, and Tig stopped moving and looked at Hallie Monahan.

Wendy bent down in front of her. "Who, Mom?"

Exasperated, pale, and annoyed, Hallie said, "I don't want this child to catch a cold."

Wendy pressed her mother's hands quietly and looked her in the eyes. "Who's this baby, Mom?"

"Hush, will you." Hallie untied and retied the baby doll's bonnet. "Shhh. There, *mon ami.*"

"What's her name, Mom?"

"I haven't any idea. I need Dan. Where's Dan?"

Wendy stood and hugged her mother around the shoulders, locking eyes with Tig. "I thought maybe she'd had a moment there."

Jeff nodded. He placed a large, soft hand on Hallie's shoulder, and that seemed to quiet her. Hallie turned and rested her cheek there, and closed her eyes. "Alzheimer's is the ultimate 'I told you so.' It even robs time to the finish."

Tig took them in. A tableau of love. Not the young, flawless skin of youth ever after. Not the hot passion of the soap opera, or the butterfly wings of the first kiss at prom. Amateurs, Tig thought. Turns out love looks like knowing when someone's had enough.

Just then, Erin scuttled through the door with Thatcher at her side. Alec followed them, saying, "You can have cake after you've eaten a piece of fruit." Erin rolled her eyes dramatically, and then the threesome stopped.

Jeff said, "Before I take Hallie back, I want to tell you a couple of things. First, Hallie's going to be a baby cuddler at the hospital. There was a long waiting list, but I pulled some strings and now several times a week, Hallie is going to hold sick babies."

On her way to the fruit bowl, Erin said, "Cool, Dr. J, Grandma Hallie loves babies."

"The other thing is that, because of the success of your efforts to stay close to your mothers, there are going to be some changes at Hope House. I've proposed to the board a way for families to room in with their loved ones, similar to the ways that you all did. Alec and I have been working together on this, and I think we have it sorted out that some of the larger corner rooms will be equipped with sleeping arrangements for family and accommodations for pets."

Jeff continued, "I think it's necessary that families bring in items from their past lives to their new homes, but it's not sufficient. Items don't make the difference. Loved ones make the difference. Once the board saw how Hallie benefited from her family, they were more open to the idea than they had been in the past."

"Well, that and the fact that you were financing the entire project and defraying costs," Alec added.

Jeff said to the others, "It's not as easy as it sounds. It's going to be a long time in coming. Alec and I are still fleshing out the details."

Looking from Jeff to her mother and seeing nothing but generosity, devotion, and kindness, Tig said, "I'd like to say something, too. But, after I say this, I want to turn on the TV and watch the Ironman, eat cake, and nap. Is that understood?" Thatcher wagged her tail. "I'd like to get our DNA tested, Jeff. I'd like to know if I've got some of that bigheartedness gene you seem to have so much of."

Wendy put her hand on her sister's shoulder.

Jeff flushed. "I'd like that. And Tiglet, it would be an honor."

Suddenly her throat filled with emotion, and she waited for it to pass before she said, "But if it turns out we don't have the same genes, and I'm filled with stingy, confused DNA, I hope you won't give up on me."

Jeff blinked and said, "I'd no sooner give up on either of you girls than give up on your mother. You'll see."

Chapter Thirty
Vampires, Lottery Winners, and Soulmates

Even after eight months of negotiations, interviews, and show restructuring, Tig looked about, delighted at the buzz around her. Tig lifted her headset and crossed the stage past the large banner with *It Ain't Business, It's Personal* painted in red, the new name for the show that was previously called *Is That Fair?* She waved to Macie, who said, "I'm leaving the bottled water on the console. Did you meet the new sound guy?"

Tig smiled at a tall man in olive-colored cargo pants and a *Doctor Who* T-shirt who held two orange extension cords in arms inscribed with the words "peace, love, bliss, share" woven throughout a vine of tattoos.

The decorated arms reached forward and grasped Macie's torso, folding her to him and the cords. "I'm not just the sound guy." He kissed the near white part in her hair and widened his eyes playfully.

Macie blushed, stepped closer to Tig, and whispered, "Julie's in the audience."

At the edge of the stage, Tig motioned for her old boss and current therapist, Julie Purves, to come forward. "Thanks for coming."

"I wouldn't have missed this for the world. Thanks for the ticket."

"I just can't do conservative counseling anymore. I need some time off from it."

"You don't have to apologize, Tig. There is no such thing as perfect therapy." Julie squeezed Tig's hand and said, "This is your time-on for good behavior. Knock 'em dead."

"Come here, Tig; I want you to meet the others," Jean Harmeyer called above the din of sound technicians doing their jobs testing microphones and acoustics. Tig moved through the bustle in the studio and touched Jean on the shoulder. Jean said, "You've worked with Diane Trevor, our sex therapist, and Jim Larson, our very own divorce lawyer, but I don't think you've met Sam McDonald, communications expert."

He looked just like a therapist should. Open, relaxed, and dressed in Dockers. Tig said, "As the resident speech-impaired couple's counselor, I can say with confidence that we really need you."

Sam McDonald shook Tig's hand. "I understand this new and improved show is your brain child. I have to tell you, it's a dream come true."

"For me, too. This is the way therapy should be done."

"A holistic approach. It's about time."

"Rumor has it no one person can be everything to everyone. Why should we try to do that in therapy?"

Diane Trevor, a middle-aged woman in a colorful pantsuit, said with a Long Island accent, "I've been saying that for years. I can teach y'all how to get off, but if you can't talk to each other after, my job is only half done."

Tig said, "This should be some program. Sam, I know you haven't been able to rehearse, but just jump right in. We like a natural feel."

Sam nodded and Macie said, "Take a seat, they want to do a sound check."

Tig collected her notepad, not noticing the man in the shadows off to the side of the velvet stage drapes. As she reached for a pencil, his voice startled her.

"Dr. Monahan?" Newman Harmeyer approached Tig, a docile, almost apologetic smile on his face.

"Newman Harmeyer." The last time she had seen Newman was during a mediation appointment where she, Newman, and Jean had met to discuss a future that might include all of them. "It's good to see you again. Did you come to wish your wife good luck on her maiden voyage?"

"Yes, I did." He nodded. "To watch her, and to say thank you to you. She wouldn't have talked to me if you hadn't insisted and refereed our conversation."

"I wanted to make up for my unprofessional behavior. I wasn't fair."

"But you were truthful."

"Everybody needs a come-to-Jesus moment. How's the progress these days?" Tig asked.

He weighed his hands up and down, and said, "Good and bad. I screwed up for a bunch of years. You don't fix that with a phone call and a few dinners."

"No. You don't. But it's a start."

"Why'd you do it? Why'd you meet with me?"

"When you called saying you wanted to talk, I was skeptical. But there was something missing in your voice."

"Pride?"

"Or arrogance. You'd given your swagger a rest. There's not much room for swagger in an apology."

"I was an idiot. Once Jean was gone and I had to listen to Tiffany's final exam schedule—man, a light went on. She wanted me to be her Facebook friend." He closed his eyes and shuddered at his own stupidity. "I was a world-class stereotype. Jean was right to leave me." Newman looked over her head to watch his wife finish with the last-minute details before the show went on the air.

"You look good, Newman."

Suddenly self-conscious, he touched his waist. "Thirty pounds. I'm running again."

"Well, make yourself comfortable and check out what your amazing wife has done here. She swept this together in just a few weeks." Tig squeezed Newman's arm and turned to join the others.

Macie rushed over and said, "Did you call Pete?"

Tig said, "I was too afraid to talk to him."

"Coward."

"I sent him a letter."

"You did? Good. What did it say?"

"I sent him the poem."

Macie furrowed her brow. "Nothing else?"

"The flier for this show. I sent that, too."

"Have you heard anything? An e-mail or a text?"

"No."

"How long?"

"Almost two weeks now."

Macie said, "You will. I'm sure of it!" Pulling a lint brush out of her tool belt, she quickly rolled it over Tig's shoulders and upper back. "You look great. Rested."

"Except for the Pete thing, I feel pretty good."

"You'd better, the show starts in minutes. Get out there and solve some problems."

Tig took her place, smiling warmly at the other counselors, who sat nearly motionless, looking expectant and a little fearful. Jim Larson clicked his pen until Tig gently removed it from his hand. Sam McDonald appeared paler and younger than he had just moments before. Only Diane Trevor had a hungry look on her face and seemed ready to discuss the sexual options of primates as far as their bandwidth could carry.

The audience was heavily weighted with women over men, but the auditorium was almost filled to capacity. After the cancellation of

Is That Fair? there had been raucous and impassioned commentary on the music radio channels, regional talk shows, and newspaper columns. People wanted a relationship referee. People wanted Tig.

The music in the theater surged and Macie's voice announced introductions, raffles, giveaways, and the cost of T-shirts and tickets. Once the calls started coming in, the first hour sped by. When a woman called complaining about a lack of spark in her marriage, the counselors jumped at the chance to discuss creative sexual toys, time management, and bargaining communication skills.

Sam McDonald began by saying, "Spark is overrated. Tender body parts can get singed. True intimacy happens after the spark quiets and you can begin to actually hear what the other person is saying—who they are, how to meet their needs."

Diane Trevor jumped into the conversation, saying, "And after you've discussed your hopes and dreams together, nothing says spark like a butt plug."

The surprised laughter and thunderous applause from the audience spurred Jim Larson, the legal eagle, to offer: "A butt plug is cheaper than a divorce, I hear, and with almost the exact same feeling."

Tig added, "But a divorce is probably less expensive than a perforated colon, so proceed with caution."

Diane finished the levity with the old joke, "Just remember, if you smoke after sex, you're probably doing it too fast."

After the initial laughter and banter, the caller discussed her disillusionment and boredom, her fears of watching her life pass by.

Tig shook her head. "Some of that is a problem of expectation. I blame Hollywood for that. The definition of life should be long periods of monotony and body maintenance punctuated by occasional moments of glory and despondency. At least we'd know what to anticipate."

Jim Larson burst out with a "Hear, hear!" and then looked around in embarrassment.

Tig continued, "Why do you think movies and fiction authors invent vampires, lottery winners, and soulmates? I'll tell you why: because watching someone brush their teeth, shop for sandwich meat, and change the toilet paper roll is as mind-numbing for the observer as it is for the observed. Problem is, we live the toilet paper life, not the vampire life."

Diane Trevor jumped in, "But we expect the vampires."

Sam McDonald nodded and then, realizing it was radio, said, "And sparks that last forever."

The caller spoke up. "You mean I should expect less?"

There was a resounding "no" from the panel. Tig said, "Not expect less. Look harder. Appreciate more from the less. Revel in contentment, acknowledge the sweetness in smallness of life."

Sam added, "The new love, the big bonus—recognizing the excitement in these things is for beginners. You have to be a connoisseur to see the glimmer in your husband's snoring."

Diane Trevor piped up. "Remind me what glimmers about my husband's snoring?"

Jim Larson laughed. "Well, at least he's home and not out snoring it up with someone from the office."

Sam McDonald said, "Be one with his deviated septum."

With that, the *Applause* sign lit up and the *On the Air* sign flashed off, signifying a commercial break.

The group of specialists looked at each other in wonder and laughed.

Jim Larson said, "Well, hell. That was fun."

Tig smiled and said, "I told you. The time just flies by. We probably only have time for a few more calls."

The audience sat quietly waiting while on stage waters were filled, people stretched their legs, and questions were answered about future shows. Macie drew the names for the raffle winners, and the music surged forward again while the *On the Air* sign flashed. The experts sat up, looking less fearful, more eager.

Macie signaled the presence of a caller and Tig said, "You're on the air."

"The love of my life loves me in theory, but not practice."

Tig froze. She stared at the speakers and answered as if in a dream. "No, that's not true."

The audience members put down their phones and iPads and waited, knowing that the show was nothing if not full of surprises.

"It is true. If I'm with her, she prioritizes just about everything and everyone over our relationship. But if I leave and try to carve out a life elsewhere, she wants back in."

Tig focused over the heads of the audience. "She's flawed."

Macie bit her lip and shushed Jean, who was vigorously tapping her on the shoulder.

The caller continued. "No. She's not."

"She's not?"

"I realized we ultimately want the same things. That we are actually fighting about wanting the same thing. Someone to count on. Someone to be there."

In front of all these people, on the air, in the studio, Tig flashed on the poem in her mother's things, the loneliness she'd felt reading the words and letting them wash over her. She recalled how she'd wanted to tell Pete about it, how sure she'd been that she had lost the kind of love in that poem, by not giving in, moving to Hawaii.

Now Pete continued, "I missed talking to you about my research. I found myself wanting to hear what you think. The students are fine, but I need you. You help me." The audience began to realize this was a personal conversation with their own Dr. Monahan.

Tig said, the previously unnamed irritation building in her chest, "Here's the thing. I've been without you for a while, and one of the things I realized was that you need me more than I can need you. I can't be weak with you. I can't fall apart. You need me too much. You expect too much. That's why I like you better when you're not around. You're work for me, not a partnership. It still may be love, but it's exhausting love."

"Tig, don't do this."

"There is no doubt in my mind I will always love you, Pete. But I also see it might be the kind of love I used to need. One for everyone else, but not for me."

"Can't we stop this old fight, just start new?"

"Don't you see? I don't want a new start. I have a lot of half-started starts right here in Wisconsin. I need to get to the ends of these. Look at what I've started here. How could you ask me to leave it?"

"For us. That's how."

"For you, Pete. I don't really think I'm in that equation. You pulled the plug when I really needed you." Then, in a moment of stellar airwaves magic, she said, "Geri's the one for you, Pete. You two will be beautifully needy together. And I mean that in the nicest of ways."

As the applause sounded, she noticed Alec stepping through the double doors at the end of the theater. He waved. Diane furrowed her brow, while Sam and Jim glanced between Tig and the man in the back of the theater.

Tig removed her headset and moved to the corner of the stage where the steps led to the audience. Macie fumbled and hit the button she prepared for a moment like this, and the lovely vowels of Judy Garland floated into the room.

"Somewhere, over the rainbow . . . ."

When Tig reached Alec, he took her hand. Tig escorted him to the front row and gestured for him to take a seat.

Diane threw up her hands. "So much for expecting less."

Sam spoke up. "For the listeners who don't have the benefit of seeing what's going on in this studio, our own Dr. Tig Monahan has reunited with someone who she appears to like very much. Not the someone on the phone."

• • •

After the show and the debrief with the other counselors, Tig found Alec backstage. Her heart thumped against her esophagus so enthusiastically, she had to press her palm to her chest and swallow twice before she found her voice.

"I won't give you my kidney, because I'm working hard to promise fewer organs to people, but I will hand over all my Fogelberg tapes if you take me out to dinner and rub my feet."

Alec lifted the corner of his mouth, weighing Tig's offer. "Got any George Strait? I'm partial to the country balladeers."

"I could throw in a greatest hits CD."

"Erin will be sure to get fingerprints all over them."

"I certainly hope so."

"Are you sure?"

"No."

"Good. I'm not, either." Alec pulled her to him gently, wrapping her in the white cotton of his work shirt. He smelled of grass and soap. Of nature and nurture. She tilted her head in time for him to catch her and hold her in a kiss. She swallowed, causing an awkward gurgle to emerge from her throat. She laughed and said, "Nothing magical about me. Give me a beautiful, poetic moment and I'll burp into it."

"That is the definition of magic—making something real out of something fantastic. Speaking of that, I hear there is going to be an unveiling of the DNA test."

"Yeah."

"So how did you decide?"

Tig looked up, confused. "About you?"

"No, I don't think you've decided about me." He laughed. "No, the DNA test."

"I had to get over my usual bullshit."

"Which bullshit?"

"If I find out he's my biological father, I'm stuck with him. I can't love the dream of my dead father from a distance anymore."

"You think you can handle that?"

With the earnest expression of a child who swears her homework is done, Tig said, "I've changed."

"Yeah?"

"Maybe."

"You're an odd little bird."

"You've always known that, yet here you are."

"Yet, here I am."

Chapter Thirty-One
The Moon in Love with the Sun

Growing up, the notion of a father had been a concept, not a reality, so visiting the grave of Dan Monahan as a child was a life-interruption rather than homage to the dead. Tig's father-images were not her own. They belonged to the mantle above the fireplace and her mother's bedside, where her parents stood smiling on their wedding day. Dan Monahan, young, handsome, gazing down lovingly at beautiful Hallie Monahan. The moon in love with the sun.

After the drama of the last few months, Tig could now see how she had worked for that look her entire life. What she didn't realize until now was what she needed—what everyone needed—was a chance to be on the receiving end of that look, instead of always being on the giving end.

Tig extracted the white business envelope from her purse and held it to her chest, shuffling leaves as she walked. Over the years she recalled listening carefully to father-lore. There was the tale of hiking a mountain trail and getting lost. Running low on water and sunlight, Dan had saved the day due to a miraculous compass inside his head. Or the glamorous stories of how he had paid his way through college by performing in a band fittingly named The Legends.

Tig strolled toward Dan Monahan's grave. It was marked with a nondescript headstone near a lilac bush that bloomed prettily in the spring and protected the site in the winter. This end-of-summer day, this fall-feeling morning, seemed to point to a season of clichés: things change. Time moves on.

Bits of life that felt solid and necessary, that caused panic if misplaced—keys, cell phones, relationships—would always be replaced by new phones, new panics, new fathers. She placed the envelope on the headstone, pressing the pristine paper onto the rough stone.

She smiled at Jeff Jenson as he made his way closer.

"Thanks for meeting me here. I know it seems overly dramatic." She started to add a "but" to the sentence, but couldn't think of an adequate justification for the feelings she couldn't name. "DNA probably shouldn't be revealed at a McDonald's."

"I've been here several times over the years. It's a peaceful place, and I've always had a lot of questions for Dan."

"Really?"

"The Monahan women are not easy women. I asked for a lot of advice."

"Did he have wise words from the grave for you?"

"Not from the grave, but sometimes when I was here I'd remember his life philosophies better."

Tig pushed a fallen leaf bundle with her toe, releasing a smell like musty nutmeg. "What did he say?"

"We'd be having a beer and waiting for the burgers to grill. Hallie would be entertaining us with an outrageous story about who knows what, and Dan would shake his head and say, 'Ya gotta love her.' And, you know, I always did."

The loss of it hit Tig. She felt full, engorged with the realization that she just didn't know what she didn't know. She didn't know Dan Monahan. She knew only a version of her mother, and here in front of her was a man whose DNA might fill in all kinds of gaps, but ultimately, what would it really provide? "Did you spend your life feeling robbed?"

Jeff shook his head. "I've been able to spend my life with your mother. Maybe not in the traditional sense—breakfast every day, decorating Christmas trees—but who's to say we would have been successful at that? Half of the people in the world bet on the absolute belief that they will be, and they're not."

"Dr. Jenson, you are a love."

Jeff took off his glasses and cleaned them with the tail of his shirt, a mannerism Tig had begun to recognize. "I'm not being generous, nor am I rationalizing the past. I'm just saying what's true."

"Didn't you want to shake her?"

"People are who they are, Tig. Danny was a good husband. He and Hallie fought about stupid things like all couples, like we would have if we had married. Instead, we never fought about the dandelions in the lawn. We never had to argue about money. Our time together was less fraught." He replaced his glasses and said, "It's true. I had to learn to live my life without ownership of what I loved best, but is that such a bad thing? I didn't own you, but I surely loved you." Forcing what Tig could clearly see was a stiff upper lip, he added, "As far as I was ever and always concerned, you were . . . ." He cleared his throat. "Excuse me, you *are* mine. Whatever that slip of paper says about us, it won't change a thing for me."

A puff of a breeze ruffled Tig's hair, and the envelope perched on the top of the headstone fluttered. Lifting her face to him, she saw that hitching her wagon to the past could only mean a journey in the wrong direction. She bent and picked up a handful of white stones and placed them on the envelope, securing it until sometime in the future, when she wasn't around to see it, the weather would pull her story apart.

Tig slipped her arm around Jeff Jenson's waist, and as naturally as if he had spent years and years fitting his arm around the groove in her shoulder, he pulled her in tight.

Turning away from the gravestone, Tig said simply, "C'mon, Dad, let's go visit Mom." Walking away from the markers of her past, she stopped, turned, and slipped away from Jeff Jenson's warm embrace. She jogged back to the gravestone and grabbed the envelope. "I know that would make a romantic end to this day, Goat, but I'm just not that kind of girl."

Jeff cleared his throat and said, "Good. I was hoping you were more your mother than your father, whoever that father may be."

Acknowledgments

This is my third book and yet there is still such a long list of people to thank.

My early readers who read drafts that were partially realized and filled with troubles. Thank you Christine Benedict, Wanda Dye, Amy Reichert, and Carolyn Bach; if not for you, I might have given this one up. For some reason, this book came harder; the characters were more difficult to pin down and I'm so grateful for your positive early enthusiasm. My later readers, Terri Osgood, Katie Moretti, and Holly Robinson gave such good feedback that I now feel like this book was no trouble at all. That kind of support is the kind that gets books written. That is the kind of support I needed.

My agent Jill Marr is, every day, full-on enthusiastic, and I always know she is in my corner. Additionally, I am so very thrilled to work with Tyrus Books and Ben Leroy on this publication. I went all over the world and there you were, right in my own backyard. Thank you, this means so much to me.

My girls Julie and Meghan never question my desire to continue to write, even though I miss a game or two and sometimes we eat nothing but noodles for dinner. I couldn't have written a word if I hadn't been your mother, and that is the truth. Finally, to my love Brian Osgood: oh, if I could tell you, I would let you know.